Russell Kavanagh

**Original Dramas, Dialogues, Declamations and Tableux Vivians**

for school exhibitions, May-day celebrations, and parlor amusement

Russell Kavanagh

**Original Dramas, Dialogues, Declamations and Tableux Vivians**
*for school exhibitions, May-day celebrations, and parlor amusement*

ISBN/EAN: 9783337343545

Printed in Europe, USA, Canada, Australia, Japan

Cover: Foto ©Andreas Hilbeck / pixelio.de

More available books at **www.hansebooks.com**

# ORIGINAL DRAMAS,

# DIALOGUES, DECLAMATIONS

AND

## TABLEAUX VIVANS,

FOR

SCHOOL EXHIBITIONS, MAY-DAY CELEBRATIONS,
AND PARLOR AMUSEMENT.

BY

## Mrs. RUSSELL KAVANAUGH.

LOUISVILLE, KY:
JOHN P. MORTON AND COMPANY.
1867.

# CONTENTS.

## ORIGINAL DRAMAS.

## DECLAMATIONS.

## MAY-QUEEN CELEBRATION.

## AMERICAN ORATORY.

## TABLEAUX VIVANS.

# PREFACE.

DURING the several years in which I have had charge of a school, a difficulty has always been experienced in procuring dialogues suitable for the annual exhibitions, and I have therefore been compelled, from time to time, to write out plays adapted to the tastes and capacities of my pupils. Reflecting upon the subject, I have concluded that a collection of these pieces in the form of a book will be an acceptable contribution to the literature of our schools. "The Wreath of Virtue" was at one time printed in a small pamphlet for the convenience of my pupils, and has been performed many times and with uniform success. The other pieces in the book have never before been in print. In presenting them to the public I am actuated by a hope that the dull routine of juvenile instruction will be occasionally enlivened with a charm not hitherto enjoyed.

As the dramas contained in this book are simple, they will be found suitable for home or parlor theatricals. A great deal depends upon the *expression* of the characters introduced. Those who perform what the school children call "funny parts" should, of course, assume a comical expression; and in the more serious characters a grave expression is necessary. The process required to obtain this is simple, but not original with the author of this volume, and is perhaps too well known to require an explanation. Possibly, however, some teacher, or the inmates of some home-circle, who have not had experience in getting up tableaux, etc., may like to know how to secure the different expressions required, and if so, the following hints may give them an idea that will be useful:

If you desire to appear comical, let your features assume a mirthful expression, and get some friend to mark the lines thus formed with a fine camel's-hair brush (such as is used by painters in water colors), dipped in light brown. This will cause the mirthful expression to remain after your face takes its natural form. In this way any expression you desire to assume can be retained—either a comical, angry, scowling, contemptuous, or silly look. If you wish to appear attenuated, draw a light tint of burnt cork under the eyes, about the sides of the face, and on the upper part of the chin.

I remember seeing, some years ago, a book published by Dick & Fitzgerald, New York, entitled "The Sociable." In it is contained accurate descriptions for planning the stage for parlor theatricals, and indeed every thing necessary to give inexperienced performers the proper ideas about arranging plays and tableaux for home amusements.

There is one point connected with performances of any kind upon the stage that ought to be impressed upon all who take part in such exercises, and that is *memorize your parts perfectly.* It is useless to try to interest an audience with a school-exhibition unless each actor is thoroughly versed in the part to be sustained, and it requires much more labor and practice than most persons are aware of to acquire the perfection needed. I recollect once being called upon to superintend a May-day celebration, gotten up by the young ladies of a small town in which I was sojourning. In the rehearsals I could not impress them with the necessity of learning their parts thoroughly, and although I "drilled" those concerned once a day for three weeks, when the day arrived the whole affair came very near being a failure.

I merely mention this to interest the girls and boys who are in the habit of engaging in such matters, hoping to induce them never to undertake a thing of the kind in public without being *certain* that they have *memorized their parts perfectly.*

THE AUTHOR.

Lebanon, Ky., June 1, 1867.

# ORIGINAL DRAMAS.

## THE WREATH OF VIRTUE.

### A DRAMA.

#### CHARACTERS.

MINERVA, *the Fairy Queen.*
CELESTIA, *the Genius of Virtue.*
VIRGINIA, *the Genius of Piety.*
URANIA, *the Genius of Beauty.*
AMORA,
EONA, } *Mortals.*
ELLA,

---

### SCENE I.

*Stage neatly arranged. Enter* AMORA, EONA, *and* ELLA.

AMORA.  Sweet is the breath of ruddy morn,
And bright the dew-drops on the lawn.
Come, let us to the woodland hie,
To catch Aurora's fervent sigh;
For surely nothing can impart
Such buoyant pleasure to the heart
As rural charms, in joyous Spring.
When Nature smiles, and warblers sing
Their notes of welcome to the day,
And blithely dart from spray to spray.
Retirement!  The happiest life,
Free from the care of noise and strife!
Let *solitude* and *prayer* be mine,
And Fashion's follies I'll resign.
EONA.  I must confess that Wisdom's voice

Would much applaud your peaceful choice.
To choose a safe and prudent part
Does honor to your head and heart.
By no such modest wish inspired,
*I* rather seek to be admired!
I would prefer the glittering crowd—
Among the gay and rich and proud,
Where etiquette and fashion dwell,
And grace and beauty still excel—
'Tis *there* I would my charms display,
Where noble knights their homage pay,
Whose highest pleasure is to seek
The smiles that warm a lady's cheek;
While *Beauty* lights my eyes with fire,
And connoisseurs the flame admire.
I would not seek the lonely glen,
Or leave the busy sphere of men.
*Nature* has beauties, I agree,
But *Pleasure* most entices me.
What say you, Ella, would you dare
Your real sentiments declare?
Since dearest friends must disagree,
Will you dissent from her [*to* Amora] or me?

ELLA.    My charming friend, I pledge my troth
Most frankly to agree with both;
And, strange to tell, my views retain,
While I your approbation gain.
I would not shun the flowery glade,
Nor spurn the sylvan forest shade,
Nor would I fly the courtly hall,
Nor leave the gay and splendid ball,
To seek for happiness and joy,
Without bereavement or alloy.
Naught can o'ercome the voice of strife,
Naught can allay the ills of life,
But a *contented, peaceful mind,*
To good or ill alike resigned.
O! let *contentment* be my lot,
In courtly dome or humble cot,
To me, dear girls, it matters not.
Should fate compel me to remain
In cities large or circles vain,

Had I *contentment*, all would be
A heaven or paradise to me:
Or should I be constrained to go
Where purling streams meandering flow
Thro' fertile vales, where lilies bloom,
And roses shed a sweet perfume,
A bright Elysium I would find
In a contented, quiet mind.
Amora, of the grove beware!
*Fairies, they say, inhabit there,
And sylph-like forms are often seen
Sporting within its shady green.

AMORA. Believe me, Ella, I would not fear
A being of another sphere;
I might among the fairy tribe
Some good impressions there imbibe.

EONA. The elfin race, I have been told,
Are ugly, and deformed, and old;
And must confess, without disguise,
Old, ugly people I despise.

ELLA. Eona, I must call you over nice;
*Age* is no crime—*deformity* no vice;
*External* forms, both ugly, dark, and old,
Oft cover spirits of the finest mold.
Sometimes within deformities we find
The traces of a good and pious mind;
Defects of *nature* we must learn to bear
If we would dwell in Charity's bright sphere.
Old age is honored, and commands respect,
Nor should with scorn be treated, or neglect.

EONA. We will not quarrel, my most charming friend;
Opinions all must have—there let it end.
I still maintain that *Beauty* has its worth,
And must be called the *prettiest* thing on earth.

AMORA. Come, let us hasten to the fragrant grove,
And there pour forth a grateful song of love;
And I will promise, should we meet a sprite,
To stand prepared for a retreat—or fight.
As I am told that sprites are but air,
Sure we can chase them or confront them there.

---

* The voice must be lowered.

Come! let *me* lead the way; I will be found
The *first* to enter the enchanted ground.     [*Exeunt.*]

(*Curtain falls.*)


## SCENE II.

*Stage decorated as a grove* (MINERVA *reclining on a hillock*).
*Enter* AMORA, EONA, *and* ELLA. AMORA *starts with surprise when she sees* MINERVA.

AMORA. O beauteous being! we are strangers here,
And have intruded in your path, I fear.
Lured by the sweetness of the morning fair,
We rambled forth to take the dewy air,
But little dreaming in this grove to find
A being so resplendent and refined.
We *heard* that spirits hovered in this vale,
Yet deemed it but a legendary tale
To frighten children, lest they heedless roam,
With steps unwary, far, too far, from home.
But had we known this sylvan, quiet spot
To *you* was sacred, we would surely not
Have thus encroached into its hallowed shade,
Nor this intrusion on your presence made.
We only wish your lovely charms t' admire,
To ask forgiveness, and in peace retire.
        [*They turn to leave the grove.* MINERVA *rises and
            approaches them.*]
MINERVA. Stay, daughters, stay! nor in such haste
            depart;
You have the interest of a loving heart;
Your youthful beauty my attention claims—
Your characters as different as your names.
        [AMORA, ELLA, *and* EONA *turn from* MINERVA *in a
            derisive manner.*]
Nay, do not start, nor in derision turn;
The spirit of your minds I can discern.
Gifted by Heaven with *interior* sight,
Your thoughts are open as the morning light
To my clear vision, and in truth I test
The ruling love which animates each breast.

To solitude *you* [*points to* AMORA] would for comfort fly,
And elevate your feelings to the sky;
The follies of mankind you would despise;
Both wise and prudent in your own bright eyes,
If friends entice, your spirit will not bow:
You say, "Stand back! I'm holier than thou."
A life of *use* you haughtily disdain.
And cloistered virtue makes you proud and vain.
Your mind, abstracted from the world below,
On wings of faith to *heaven's* clime would go.
The bliss of angels you would ever feel,
And deem *religion* dwells in pious zeal.
Now, dearest daughter, will you frankly own
The temper of your spirit I have shown?
If I have wronged you, or traduced your name,
An humble suppliant, I your pardon claim.
  AMORA.  I must confess, bright mistress of the grove.
Such solitude is what I dearly love;
But, sure, *devotion* can not lead to pride!
Prayer makes the spirit humble: and, beside,
A life untarnished by this world of sin
*Can not* contain the seeds of pride within.
They *must* be pure who only live for God;
Those who abjure the world, of course, are good.
  MINERVA.  The life of heaven can not dwell in hearts
Who in this world refuse to act their parts
In social intercourse, and never feel
The duties which devolve for public weal.
A selfish pleasure it must surely be
Which sets the mind from obligation free;
And *selfishness* must ever be allied
To all the feelings which engender pride.
Quite self-dependent man can never be.
Else he were GOD—from all assistance free.
And if from others a support we gain.
Useless to others we must not remain.
By pious thoughts and a secluded mind
You may some feelings of religion find.
Be not deceived.  Stern Reason's light will show
Such raptures from enthusiasm flow.
Though to the prayerful ecstacies are given,
The path of *duty* is the road to heaven!

To *you*, fair maiden [*points to* EONA], now I fain would
For *pleasure* and *preferment* you would seek;       [speak,
In courts, with princes, you delight to stay;
You love the beautiful, the grand, the gay.
You'd skim upon the surf of time, indeed,
Nor heed the rocks that might your course impede;
The deeper waters of reflection shun—
Too smooth, too calm, to suit the course you run.
Content to pass your life in splendid ease,
Or fetes or tournaments your taste would please,
Where *Beauty* charms and *Fashion* holds her sway,
Where gallant knights their flattering homage pay.
Now say, my sweet one, do you deem it wise
Your *brightest* moments thus to sacrifice?
In dissipation thus to spend your days,
Glued to the world, and fashioned by its ways?
Say, might you not some lasting comfort find
In being useful to the human kind?
In soothing sorrow and relieving pain,
Methinks you might the purest honors gain.
From active life the finest feelings flow,
And pleasures which the *idle* can not know.

EONA.   Transcendent being! native of the skies,
As fair as good, as beautiful as wise!
O, call me not ungrateful should I claim
The right to *act;* and think me not to blame
Should I object to such an arduous task
*As serving others.*   Also, let me ask,
How would I gain by such a listless course,
Which would, at best, be but a life of force?
For I could never, with a hearty will,
Such a humiliating work fulfill.
I know I love to dwell in halls of state;
I *own* I like the proud, and rich, and great.
Why should I not?   The human mind is free.
I choose my own delight; *this* pleases me;
And thus my happy moments I employ.
What pleases others, let them, too, enjoy.

MINERVA.   True freedom is the noblest pearl of heaven,
To every man and every angel given;
Yet happy they who live for some *good use*,
And dare not such a noble boon abuse.

The love of use does not your bosom warm;
Time and experience only can reform.
I only ask, when you the world have tried,
Again to meet me, and the point decide.
*[Points to* ELLA.]
To *you*, young lady with the blushing cheek,
Permit me now in kindest words to speak.
*You* seek *content*, and would not choose your lot—
Willing, you say, to dwell in town or cot.
Would you the pleasure of contentment feel,
Engage in *active* life with ardent zeal;
Perform good *use* to every child of man
Who comes within your sphere, far as you can;
And thus your days will pass with sweet delight,
And calm will be the slumbers of the night.

ELLA.   Thank you. dear lady! but I greatly fear
Your good advice will meet resistance here.
*[Lays her hand on her heart.]*
My soul's too selfish, and my mind too weak,
To reach the state of which you sweetly speak:
Yet I will try your maxims to retain,
And some small progress in such life to gain;
Some great misgivings in my heart I find,
Unless you aid me.   Will you be so kind?

MINERVA.   You may, dear daughter, my assistance claim,
While heaven's breath will fan the holy flame.
My dear young ladies, for your sake,
A strange proposal I will make:
I have *three* gifts, and each may choose
The one she likes, or *all* refuse.
If you will wear them one short year,
And promise then to meet me here,
In this retired, verdant grove,
The power of these gifts I'll prove.   *[Strikes her wand.]*
Genius of Beauty! I command,
Come forth, with girdle in your hand!

*Enter* URANIA, *girdle in hand.*

URANIA.   This brilliant girdle will bestow
Surpassing beauty on the wearer;
Though already young and fair,
The magic gift will make her fairer.

MINERVA (*striking her wand*).   Genius of Piety, appear,
With costly bracelet, rich and rare!

*Enter* VIRGINIA, *bracelet in hand.*

VIRGINIA.   This costly bracelet, on the arm,
Possesses a most glorious charm:
To her who wears it, it will give
Power the life of *faith* to live.

MINERVA (*striking her wand*).   Genius of Virtue! Child
of Heaven!
O, let your olive wreath be given!

*Enter* CELESTIA, *wreath in hand.*

CELESTIA.   This simple wreath contains a spell
Which suits the one who wants it well:
It has the power to impart
Virtue and goodness to the heart.

MINERVA.   Come, lovely maidens, now declare
Which of the presents you prefer.

EONA.   The pretty girdle must be mine;
O, see, it glistens quite divine!

[URANIA *approaches* EONA, *clasps the girdle
around her waist.*]

URANIA.   Lady, lady, you are fair
As the mountain lilies are;
Bright, O, bright your beaming eyes
As the stars that gild the skies;
On your cheek a tender flush
Which might make the wild rose blush;
Your graceful form and lovely face,
Both formed with symmetry and grace!
Wear the girdle, gentle maid,
And your beauty can not fade.

[EONA *embraces* URANIA.]

EONA.   Genius of Beauty, with me stay;
Illume my path from day to day.
You are 'twined around my heart;
We must never, never part.

AMORA.   The *bracelet* is the boon I crave,
The gift I would delight to have.

[VIRGINIA *clasps the bracelet on* AMORA's *arm.*]

VIRGINIA.   Lady, lady, you will be
The votary of *Piety;*

Your name be lauded to the skies,
While *Faith* will make you great and wise.
[AMORA *embraces* VIRGINIA.]
AMORA.   You shall be my guardian sprite,
And protect me day and night;
Never let *our* bosoms sever.
You must lead me ever, ever.
[CELESTIA *approaches* ELLA.]
CELESTIA.   The *Wreath of Virtue*, lady fair,
Alone is left for you to wear.
ELLA.   It hath fallen to my share;
I'm content the boon to wear.
[CELESTIA *crowns* ELLA.]
ELLA.   Of fadeless green, it speaks of peace—
Its beauty charms me none the less
Because from gaudy colors free,
And formed with great simplicity;
It suits me well—'t is bright and good.
[*Bows to* MINERVA.]
Lady, accept my gratitude.
CELESTIA.   The wreath of virtue now you wear;
How it becomes your glossy hair!
A talisman 'gainst evil love,
While you keep it, it will prove;
And sin your pleasure can not mar
While *Virtue* is your polar star.
[ELLA *embraces* CELESTIA.]
ELLA.   Genius of Virtue, you are mine;
Your wreath shall in my ringlets shine
While in this wicked world I stay.
When angels beckon me away,
O, the wreath will be divine,
For it will in glory shine.
MINERVA.   Fairest maidens, now adieu!
Go and wear the boons I've given;
We'll meet again, then each of you
Will prove the claim she bears to heaven.

*(Curtain falls.)*

2

## SCENE III.

*The grove.* *Enter* AMORA, EONA, ELLA, CELESTIA, URANIA, *and* VIRGINIA.

AMORA. How still and solemn is this hallowed place
Where first we saw Minerva's lovely face!
She is not here, dear girls, but we will wait
Until she comes, then we will learn our fate.

*Enter* MINERVA.

MINERVA. Fear not, my children, I am ever found
By those who seek me on this holy ground;
By me not governed is your fate, I own,
For that depends upon yourselves alone.
My good advice is all I can entail;
Your own volition, then, must turn the scale
To good or evil. Daughters, I would hear
How you have fared since last we parted here?
EONA. Your brilliant girdle I with triumph wore;
It gained me all I asked—nay, even *more*—
Of this world's praise than I had hoped to claim—
The palm of *Beauty* and the badge of *Fame!*
I proudly trod the crowded halls of state,
And reveled at the banquets of the great;
Princes and kings have called me quite divine,
And courtiers knelt at my all-conquering shrine—
And I was happy. But my spirit tired
When I discerned how Ella [*points to* E.] was admired,
Not for her *beauty*, but a *softer* grace—
Not for a perfect form or handsome face.
The *Wreath of Virtue* to my friend has given
Charms more divine, charms more allied to heaven.
What though her eyes were not as bright,
Yet they reflected purer light;
Although *her* face was not as fair,
Her modest and retiring air
Procured admirers of a caste
Whose talents very far surpassed
Coxcombs who fluttered in my wiles
And lived beneath my sunny smiles.

Though I attracted many more,
The quality made up for score;
With fewer friends, she seemed to glide
More smoothly down the swelling tide
Of life than I who could command
The sycophants who thronged the land.
Now *Beauty's* girdle I disdain—
The gift has proved both light and vain;
I beg to lay it quite aside,
And goodness then shall be my guide.
Have you another wreath to spare?
The badge of *Virtue* I would wear.
　　AMORA.　I wore the bracelet, and I liked it well,
For pious feelings did my bosom swell.
My thoughts on eagle's pinions mounted high—
I felt that kindred spirits, too, were nigh.
　　　　　　　　　　　　[*Points upward.*]
Up to the skies my towering spirit soared,
It reached to heaven, and that heaven adored;
The praise I gathered language can not paint—
Called by mankind a consecrated *saint;*
Thought to perfection I possessed a claim,
Till rumor published spotless Ella's fame,
While every one her active zeal could prove
In deeds of *charity* and works of *love.*
The simple path my virtuous friend pursued
Was *shunning evil* and *pursuing good;*
The best preferment she presumed to seek—
To aid the helpless and protect the weak,
To heal the sick, to set the captive free,
To scatter blessings; and, it seemed to me,
Compared with her I would no progress gain,
And *my* devotion had been all in vain.
Dear lady, pity, and my wishes grant—
The gift of *goodness* now is what I want.
The badge of *Piety* I would resign,
And pray a *Wreath of Virtue* may be mine.
　　ELLA.　Lady, the wreath you kindly gave
Imparted all the bliss I crave;
Peace and contentment I have found
Since that bright day when it was bound
Across my brow by that sweet girl; [*points to* CELESTIA]

Nor for a diamond or a pearl
Would I exchange the simple crest;
And often, often have I blessed
The hand which such a boon supplies
To one who merits not the prize.

[MINERVA *addresses* EONA *and* AMORA.]

MINERVA.   My dearest children, for *you* let me choose,
As you have taken both improper views.
The badge of *Beauty* [*to* EONA] you must not despise;
The badge of *Piety* you, too, [*to* AMORA] must prize.
The gifts of Nature by kind Heaven sent,
For recreation and good service meant,
We may enjoy or we may refuse—
Also have power those comforts to abuse.
Some we might worship with the mind and heart,
And thus perform a most ungrateful part;
A graven image we would fall before,
Forget the *giver* and the *gift* adore.
Such acts are sinful, and, than heathens worse,
We turn the blessing to a dreadful curse;
Such worship leaves us hopeless and forlorn—
To worship *God* the angel cautioned John.
What is true worship, you would like to know?
The life of *love* and *duty* here below.
We worship God when we the hungry feed,
Or clothe the neighbor if he stands in need;
As unto him the service we perform,
A righteous *act* is piety in form.
As you do it to the least, said He,
The deed must stand as surely done to me.
The blessing of retirement and prayer
We must not slight—the angels meet us there:
There is a time for that, but still we may
At other times be innocently gay;
Then social feelings make the heart expand,
Then man fulfills the great and wise command
Of loving others as he loves himself,
Nor barters friendship's gold for wordly pelf.

[*Looks at* EONA.]

And what is beauty?   Say, where doth it dwell?
Would you look for it in the shades of hell,
Or would you seek it in the heaven above,

Where every being is a form of love?
I ween there's beauty and perfection *there;*
Then should we scorn it while we linger *here?*
External beauty, like the vernal flower,
Must live, and droop, and fade, in one short hour.
Such beauties correspond to those within—
The beauties of a mind devoid of sin.
There's beauty in soft pity's melting eye;
There's beauty in a modest, sweet reply;
There's beauty in the voice of sympathy;
There's beauty in the hand of charity;
There's beauty in forbearance, temperance, truth,
And in the obedience of a docile youth;
There's beauty in an act of filial love.
Kindness to all the beautiful doth prove
In innocence there's beauty, and in peace;
In love there's beauty, and in holiness.
There's beauty in a patient, tranquil mind;
There's beauty in a spirit all resigned.
Bright cheerfulness is beauteous as the Spring;
And surely MERCY is a beauteous thing.
*Sincerity* is beautiful as fair;
In generous minds the beautiful is there;
*To do to others as you'd have them do,*
Is *perfect* beauty, and religion, too.
Thus VIRTUE, BEAUTY, PIETY, are ONE;
They can not live apart, nor each *alone.*

[URANIA *addresses* EONA.]

URANIA. Lady, lady, do not be
So very soon displeased with me;
If you the Wreath of Virtue wear,
Rest assured I will be here;
I can not now be driven away,
But ever with you will I stay.

[EONA *embraces* URANIA.]

EONA. Urania, sweet one, stay with me,
I may be good and cherish thee;
*Beauty* and *Goodness* now. I know,
Hand in hand will ever go!

[VIRGINIA *addresses* AMORA.]

VIRGINIA. Lady, lady, now you see
You must ever cherish me.

AMORA. Ever, dearest, thou shalt prove
The angel who protects my love.
       *[*CELESTIA *addresses* ELLA.*]*
 CELESTIA. Beauteous Ella, you and I
Together live—together die.
  ELLA. With thine image in my heart,
We never will consent to part.
       *[*MINERVA *points to* AMORA.*]*
 MINERVA. The badge of *Piety* you must retain;
        *[Points to* EONA.*]*
The badge of *Beauty* must with you remain;
A belt and bracelet, too, is Ella's share:
These useful presents each of you must wear.
    *[Presents* ELLA *with a belt and bracelet;* EONA
     *with a wreath and bracelet;* AMORA *with
     a wreath and girdle.* ]
Long as the garland your rich tresses twine
More lustrous will the belt and bracelet shine;
She who to *Virtue* still continues true
Possesses *Piety* and *Beauty* too.
O, Solitude! a solace for our hearts—
There piety its bracing grace imparts.
How sweet retirement after care and strife!
It fits us for the active scenes of life.
Society has many blessings, too;
'T is there our hearts are bound in friendship true;
'T is there we most resemble those above;
There we exchange the bliss of mutual love.
       *[Turns to audience.]*
*Virtue* and *Piety*, or faith and love,
Are *one*, this drama sure doth prove;
And beautiful the uses on them graven—
A glorious *Triune* and the type of heaven.

    (*Curtain falls.*)

## COSTUMES.

MINERVA. Dress of white, very light material, profusely spangled; a crown of brilliants; she bears a wand, wrapped with tinseled ribbon and flowers; the wand is finished at the top by a gilded spear, to which is suspended a girdle, a wreath, and a bracelet. (*Emblematic.*)

CELESTIA, VIRGINIA, and URANIA. These fairies should be represented by little girls; dresses of any light white material, spangled; wreaths of flowers on the head.

AMORA. Dress of blue silk, trimmed in blonde; pearl ornaments; wreath of flowers on the hair.

EONA. Dress of orange-colored tarlatan, trimmed in black; jet or brilliant ornaments; jeweled tiara.

ELLA. Dress of white tarlatan, the skirt trimmed in pyramids of pink satin ribbon; a berthe of blonde lace and pink ribbon; wide pink ribbon sash; hair plain.

# CINDERELLA, OR THE GLASS SLIPPER.

### SIMPLIFIED FROM THE ORIGINAL.

## CHARACTERS.

FELIX, *a Prince.*
ARABELLA POMPOLINO, ⎫
JOSEPHINE POMPOLINO, ⎬ *Sisters.*
CINDERELLA. ⎭
PEDRO, *a Servant.*
Fairy, *Godmother to Cinderella.*
Page.

## SCENE I.

*Home Scene.* ARABELLA *and* JOSEPHINE *standing before a mirror, arranging their toilets alternately.*

ARABELLA.　Josephine, how do I look?

JOSEPHINE.　(*They both come forward.*) Beautiful! Splendid! How do I look?

ARABELLA.　Enchanting! I wonder what has become of Pedro. I wish he would come; I am so impatient to see our things.

JOSEPHINE.　So am I.

ARABELLA (*walks about*).　O! how my heart beats! Just think, *we* are invited to the Prince's grand ball!

JOSEPHINE (*walks about*).　O! I'm all in a flutter.

ARABELLA.　Who knows but we may catch a duke for a husband?

JOSEPHINE.　And then we shall be called "My Lady!" (*Tosses her head.*)

ARABELLA.　Suppose the Prince himself were to fall in love with us!

JOSEPHINE.　Mercy! It is too grand to think about. But see (*looks out*), here comes Pedro at last!

*Enter* PEDRO, *loaded with paper boxes and bundles of various sizes; throws them down; gives a prolonged whistle.*

PEDRO. O, I have had such a time!

ARABELLA. Did you get all the things?

PEDRO. Yes; all that I didn't get. [*Takes up a box, reads.*] Kid slippers, number seven.

ARABELLA (*jerks the box*). They are mine!

PEDRO (*takes up another box*). Kid gloves. number eight.

JOSEPHINE (*takes box*). They are mine; that's my size.

PEDRO. Madame Nocquet says the dresses will be done in time.

ARABELLA (*touches one of the bundles with her foot*). What is this?

PEDRO. Stays.

JOSEPHINE (*touches another bundle*). What is here?

PEDRO. Ribbon and feathers.

ARABELLA (*touches another*). And this?

PEDRO. Powder and paint.

ARABELLA. You are so vulgar! You should say rouge.

JOSEPHINE (*points to another box*). What is in this?

PEDRO. Silk stockings.

ARABELLA. There it is again! Say hose.

PEDRO (*mimics her*). Well, *hose!*

ARABELLA. Now, Pedro, take all those boxes up-stairs—that is a good fellow—and then tell Cinderella to come to me.

PEDRO (*gathering up all the boxes and bundles*). I will.
[*Exit* PEDRO.]

JOSEPHINE (*walks to and fro*). O, I know my Spanish hat and feathers will be *so* becoming!

ARABELLA. If we can *only* catch a rich husband I will be satisfied. I do not believe that the lords and dukes can resist *my* charms! [*Tosses her head; walks about.*]

*Enter* CINDERELLA.

ARABELLA. Come here, you little ash-pat. Your sister Josephine and myself are invited to the Prince's grand ball to-night, and we wish you to get all your work done in time to assist us in dressing.

JOSEPHINE. And be sure you do it.

CINDERELLA. O, how I would like to go!

3

ARABELLA (*disdainfully*). *You* go! What would a little sneak like you look like in a palace?

JOSEPHINE. What impudence!

CINDERELLA. I do not care. I *would* like to go. I never was at a ball in my life.

ARABELLA. Humph! and you never will be—that's more. Go back to the kitchen, child, and do not trouble your silly head about balls.

JOSEPHINE. Yes, go along, for you are not fit to be in the parlor with ladies. [*Exit* CINDERELLA.]

ARABELLA. It would never do to let *her* go to that ball.

JOSEPHINE. No, indeed; she is too pretty.

ARABELLA. As long as we can keep her snuffing ashes in the kitchen corner she will not be in our way. But it is getting late, and we must begin to dress, and try to look our best; for if we do not secure a rich husband, father will never be done fussing about the bills.

JOSEPHINE. That is true.

(*Curtain falls.*)


## SCENE II.

*A dingy kitchen.* CINDERELLA *stands near a table, engaged in washing dishes.* Enter PEDRO.

CINDERELLA. O, Pedro! I am so glad to see you! Do, pray, come and help me. [PEDRO *assists her.*] Arabella and Josephine have given orders to me to finish my work so as to be ready to assist them in dressing for the Prince's grand ball to-night.

PEDRO (*wiping a plate*). I think the Prince must be at a loss for company when he invites them.

CINDERELLA. Don't you know the reason he invited them?

PEDRO (*wiping a saucer*). No. What?

CINDERELLA. Why, the Prince was hunting in the woods, and was separated from his companions and lost his way. Just then our father came along and helped him to find the right path; so, out of gratitude, the Prince invited the girls to his big ball.

PEDRO (*putting the plates together*). O-ho! that's the way of it? I think he ought to have invited you, for you have more beauty in your little finger than they have all put together!

CINDERELLA. I wish I could go to the ball! [*Arranges the dishes.*]

PEDRO. I wish you could, Cinderella; but, you know, "if wishes were horses, beggars could ride."

CINDERELLA. I wonder if I will *always* be stuck down in this old kitchen?

PEDRO. I hope not: but do you run along and help them jades to dress, for it will take a sight of pains to make them look pretty.

CINDERELLA (*takes the broom*). I have to sweep yet.

PEDRO. Go along! I will sweep. Here, give me that broom.

CINDERELLA (*hands* PEDRO *the broom*). Thank you, Pedro.
[*Exit* CINDERELLA.]

PEDRO (*sweeps a moment, comes forward, flourishes the broom*). Don't I wish I was a man? I would put Cinderella where she would never be imposed on! [*Sweeps; stops.*] It is a shame, the way they keep the poor girl hid in the kitchen! I hope Arabella and Josephine may take the cramp in their feet, so they will not be able to dance a step. Never mind! It's a long lane that has no turn! [*Puts the broom down.*]

### *Enter* CINDERELLA.

PEDRO. What! back already?

CINDERELLA. O, yes; they were so impatient they could not wait for me. Thank goodness! they are dressed and gone.

PEDRO (*places a chair near the front of stage for* CINDERELLA, *also one for himself*). I am glad too; but sit down, Cinderella, I want to talk to you. [CINDERELLA *takes a seat;* PEDRO *sits down by her.*] Cinderella, I have a sweetheart!

CINDERELLA. *You,* Pedro!

PEDRO. Yes, *me!*

CINDERELLA (*laughs*). I would like to see her.

PEDRO. O, she is a bird!

CINDERELLA. What is her name?

PEDRO. Her name is Mary; and when I get old enough we are going to marry.

CINDERELLA. Pedro, you are so funny!

PEDRO. There is no fun about that. We are going to be married; and I intend that you shall live with us, and then if any body imposes on you I'll— [*Knock heard outside.*]

CINDERELLA (*starts*). What is that?

PEDRO. O, it's nothing but the rats. You shall live with us, Cinderella, and— [*Another knock heard.*]

CINDERELLA (*rises*). O, Pedro, what is it?

PEDRO (*rises*). I tell you it is nothing.

CINDERELLA (*catches* PEDRO *by the arm*). O, I am so frightened! Maybe it's robbers!

PEDRO. Robbers, your granny's foot! Hold! Let me get the broom! [*Takes broom in his hand; assumes a defensive attitude. Knock heard again, louder.*] Come in; I'm ready for you!

*Enter* Fairy, *enveloped in a cloak.*

PEDRO (*starts*). It is a witch!

FAIRY (*drops cloak and appears in the dress of a fairy*). You are mistaken; I am no witch.

PEDRO. So I see now. [*Aside.*] She is a pretty little thing.

FAIRY (*to* CINDERELLA). I am a fairy, and presided at your birth. I am your godmother.

PEDRO (*aside*). A young-looking mother!

FAIRY. I promised to watch over you and guard you from evil.

PEDRO (*aside*). You've been a long time beginning!

FAIRY. I came to see you to-night. But, child, you look sad! What troubles you?

CINDERELLA. I am unhappy—I wish—I wish—

FAIRY. You wish to go to the Prince's grand ball. Have I guessed rightly, my goddaughter? Speak!

CINDERELLA. You have, dear godmother.

FAIRY. I will contrive that you go.

PEDRO (*aside*). I hope she is not going to play any tricks.

CINDERELLA. O, law! if you can do that, you are indeed a witch!

FAIRY. That is an ugly word, my child; I am more than a witch; I am a *fairy*, and fairies possess much power. But come, time is flying and the ball has begun. Pedro!

PEDRO. Well?

FAIRY. Run in the garden and bring me a pumpkin.

PEDRO. A what?

FAIRY (*stamps her foot and frowns*). Obey me!

PEDRO. I am gone. [*Exit* PEDRO.]

FAIRY. You will wonder at my power, Cinderella, but I never use it except on rare occasions; and it is for your good I now display my magic skill.

*Enter* PEDRO, *with a pumpkin.*

PEDRO. I wonder what this has to do with the ball?

FAIRY. Put it down. Now go and bring me four mice in a trap. and another pumpkin.

PEDRO. All right. [*Exit* PEDRO.]

FAIRY. Remember, Cinderella, you must obey all I say, to the letter.

CINDERELLA. I promise.

*Enter* PEDRO, *with trap, mice, and pumpkin.*

PEDRO. What are you going to do with these varmints?

FAIRY. Never mind. [*To* CINDERELLA.] In this [*points to first pumpkin*] you will find every thing necessary for your toilet.

PEDRO (*aside*). I'll believe that when I see it.

FAIRY (*to* PEDRO). You must go with Cinderella to the ball.

PEDRO (*looks down*). What! in these old clothes?

FAIRY. You will find a full suit in the pumpkin with Cinderella's clothes.

PEDRO (*aside*). That must be a wonderful pumpkin!

FAIRY (*to* PEDRO). Take these [*points to pumpkin and mice*], and after you are dressed break the pumpkin, and a fine carriage will appear. Then let the mice out of the trap: two of them will turn to splendid horses, and the other two will be changed to a footman and driver. You must go in the carriage to protect Cinderella.

CINDERELLA. I wonder if I am dreaming!

PEDRO. I wonder if I am, myself!

FAIRY (*to* CINDERELLA). Mark my words and obey me: You can remain at the ball *till the clock strikes twelve;* but if you stay one minute longer. your fine clothes will be turned to rags. and you will be betrayed.

PEDRO (*aside*). I begin to feel like a lord already. [ *To*

Fairy.] Do not fear; if Cinderella forgets, I will be on the watch.

FAIRY. Very well, then; I will trust you. [ *To* CINDER-ELLA, *raising her finger in a warning attitude.*] Remember! t-w-e-l-v-e o'c-l-o-c-k !*

(*Curtain falls.*)

## SCENE III.

Prince's *palace. Ball-room handsomely decorated. Several girls and boys, who have no other part in the play, can appear in this scene, as the ball-room must contain groups, so as to give the appearance of a real party. Ladies and gentlemen promenading, conversing in pantomime.* ARA-BELLA *and* JOSEPHINE *appear in extravagant costume. Prince* FELIX, *in front of stage, in full royal dress, walks to and fro. A band of music plays till the entrance of* Page. *The music should continue a few seconds after the curtain rises.*

*Enter* Page.

PAGE (*bows*). Gracious Prince, a beautiful princess, whose name we did not hear, has just arrived.

PRINCE. Conduct the stranger to our presence.
[*Exit* Page.]

ARABELLA (*advances near the front of stage, opposite the* Prince; *leans on* JOSEPHINE'S *arm*). A princess without a name! Who can she be?

JOSEPHINE (*aside*). I hope she is ugly.

*Enter* CINDERELLA *and* PEDRO.

PEDRO (*to* Prince). O, most magnificent Prince! [*Bows.*] O, most contemptible Prince! [*Bows.*] O, most diabolical Prince! [*Bows.*] Allow me [*takes* CINDERELLA *by her hand*] to present to you this lovely lady. [*Bows.*]

PRINCE (*comes forward*). Welcome, most beautiful Prin-cess; and grant me the honor of your hand for the dance.
[*Exit* PEDRO.]

---

* Care must be taken by the teacher to place the performers in the best attitudes at the end of each scene, so that, when the curtain falls, the group will form a grand tableau.

[CINDERELLA *courtesies;* Prince *takes her hand, leads her to the dance; a cotillion or quadrille is formed; all dance. When the dance is ended,* Prince, CINDERELLA, *and company promenade, and converse in pantomime.* ARABELLA *and* JOSEPHINE, *near front of stage, looking enviously at* CINDERELLA, *but do not recognize her.* Enter PEDRO, *with a large piece of cake in each hand; bites each piece alternately; approaches* ARABELLA.]

PEDRO. While you were all dancing I got my supper. Do you love cake? [ARABELLA *looks contemptuously at* PEDRO. *Aside.*] By the piper, she does not know me! I'll ask her to dance! [*Runs to side of stage; puts the cake close against the wall; covers it carefully with his handkerchief; returns to* ARABELLA; *bows profoundly.*] Most beautiful lady! will you dance with your humble-come-tumble? [ARABELLA *accepts; another cotillion is formed; all dance. When the set closes, the* Prince *claims the hand of* CINDERELLA *for a fancy dance; they schottische, waltz, or polka. While they dance the clock begins slowly to strike twelve;* PEDRO *runs to* CINDERELLA; *pulls her without ceremony from the arms of the* Prince; *he resists;* PEDRO *succeeds in pulling* CINDERELLA *off the stage; in the confusion she drops one of her tiny slippers. Music ceases. The* Prince *picks up the slipper, walks to front of stage, holds the slipper in full view of the company.*]

PRINCE. Half my kingdom would I give to know the owner of this slipper.

*Enter* Page, *hastily.*

PAGE (*approaches* Prince). Your gracious highness, there must be witches about! I thought you would like to know the whereabouts of the strange Princess, and so I followed her and that queer servant of hers: and, would your Majesty believe it? as quick as that [*snaps his fingers*] they had vanished, and there was nobody at the gates but a little dirty-looking girl and boy, who had been skulking round the palace, no doubt to steal something; and I drove *them* off.

PRINCE (*frowns*). Away with your prating, and break up the dance; for I will henceforth have no peace till I find the owner of this slipper!

(*Curtain falls.*)

## SCENE IV.

*Stage as in first scene* (ARABELLA *and* JOSEPHINE *seated at breakfast.*)

ARABELLA. This is abominable tea.

JOSEPHINE. And this bread is not fit to eat. [*Throws it down passionately.*]

ARABELLA. I do not know what has come over Cinderella lately. She is positively good for nothing.

*Enter* CINDERELLA *in home dress.*

ARABELLA. Look at her! She looks as if she had been dissipating.

JOSEPHINE. O Cinderella! you ought to have been at the ball.

CINDERELLA. Did you enjoy it?

ARABELLA. O, yes, it was magnificent! There was a young *princess* there, the most angelic creature you ever saw!

JOSEPHINE. Yes; dressed so elegantly!

CINDERELLA. Who was she?

ARABELLA. Aye, that's it! Nobody knew where she came from. She disappeared as suddenly as she came. The Prince fell desperately in love with her.

JOSEPHINE. Do you know, Arabella, I thought the fellow who was with her looked like our *Pedro!*

ARABELLA (*curls her lip*). Why, Josephine! I am astonished. He danced one set with me, and I was enchanted. He was so graceful!

CINDERELLA (*aside, laughs*). I'll tell Pedro.

*Enter* PEDRO; *flourishes a printed paper.*

PEDRO. Run here, every body! Rise, Jupiter, and snuff the moon! Hurrah for hurra! [*Flourishes paper.*]

CINDERELLA. What is the matter?

PEDRO. O, here is a proclamation by the Prince!

ARABELLA. By the Prince? [*Rises.*] Let *me* read it. [*Tries to take it from* PEDRO.]

PEDRO. No! let *me* read it.

JOSEPHINE (*approaches* PEDRO). Let *me* read it! [*All scuffle for the paper.*]

PEDRO (*takes paper; comes forward*). No, no! Let me read it, I say! [*Reads in a loud voice.*]

"PROCLAMATION BY SUPREME COMMAND.

"We, Felix the Second, ruler of this domain, do hereby make known that we will take to wife and share our heart and throne with her whose foot shall fit the little glass slipper found at the ball last night."

PEDRO (*looks at* CINDERELLA). Aye!

ARABELLA. O, mercy! I must go and prepare to make a trial; for, if *squeezing* will do any good, I will get that slipper on! [*Exit* ARABELLA.

JOSEPHINE. And I will chop off my heels and toes but *I* will get it on! [*Exit* JOSEPHINE.

PEDRO (*looks after them and puts his thumb on the end of his nose; turns to* CINDERELLA).

> They may pare their heels
> And cut their toes,
> But on *your* foot
> That slipper goes!

CINDERELLA. Ah, Pedro! it will never go on my foot. I have no clothes fit to appear in, and the fairy will not come again.

PEDRO. Fairy or no fairy, you shall go to the palace and try on that slipper.

CINDERELLA. But look at this shabby dress!

PEDRO. It doesn't matter about the *dress;* your *foot* is all that is wanted.

CINDERELLA. Pedro, they will refuse me a trial.

PEDRO. Not when they see that foot. Small as it is, it will kick down all objections.

CINDERELLA. If they refuse, I can but die!

PEDRO. Die, indeed! If I know you to do such a foolish thing, I'll never forgive you! Come along; we must go. I'll saddle the blind mare in a minute, and we can trot to the palace in less than no time. So, come along! [*Takes* CINDERELLA *by the arm.*]

(*Curtain falls.*)

## SCENE V.

Prince's *Palace.* *Ladies in attendance.* Prince *walks to and fro in front of stage.*

PRINCE (*stops*). My project thus far has failed. The slipper does not fit a lady present; and yet, I know not why, my heart seems lightened since I have taken this method to discover the owner of this toy. [*Twirls the slipper in his fingers.*] If it fails, my hopes are all destroyed.

*Enter* Page.

PAGE. The Ladies Pompolino are in the ante-chamber. They have come to try the slipper.

PRINCE (*aside*). Those silly, simpering maidens! [*To Page.*] Admit them. [*Exit Page.*] All eager to claim my hand. But I know this [*holds the slipper in view of audience*) will never fit the Ladies Pompolino. The idea is too absurd.

*Enter* ARABELLA *and* JOSEPHINE.

PRINCE (*bows*). Ladies, you are welcome! Permit the Page to superintend your trial.

ARABELLA. Gracious Prince, this is flattering.

[Page *leads* JOSEPHINE *to center of stage, near the front, where a seat is arranged for those who try the slipper.* JOSEPHINE *sits down; takes the slipper from the hand of* Prince; *examines it.*]

JOSEPHINE. Sweet Prince, if, fated by fortune, this should fit my foot—

ARABELLA (*sneeringly*). Your foot! Why, Josephine, your foot is like a mill-stone! [*Turns to* Prince.] It is for me, no doubt, dear Prince, the honor is reserved.

PRINCE (*coldly*). The result will show, madam.

JOSEPHINE (*to* Page). I am ready.

PAGE (*takes slipper and kneels at* JOSEPHINE'S *feet*). Now, make your foot as small as possible. [*Tries on the slipper.*]

JOSEPHINE (*shrinking*). O, dear me!

PAGE. What the deuce is in your stocking?

JOSEPHINE (*wincing*). My foot! O, dear! I can not stand the pain!

PAGE (*forces the slipper*). Where the plague is your heel? [JOSEPHINE *screams with pain, takes her own shoe in her hand and hobbles to the side of the stage.*]

ARABELLA (*advances*). I knew it! I knew it! Your foot always was enormous! [*Takes seat.*] Now, sir! [Page *kneels and tries the slipper on* ARABELLA'S *foot.*]

ARABELLA. Gently! You are so awkward!

PAGE. Indeed, I am not awkward.

ARABELLA (*with grimace*). Do you want to cripple me?

PAGE. It is worth a lame foot to be the wife of a prince. There, it is on!

PRINCE (*starts forward in surprise*). How?

PAGE. I mean—all but the heel!

ARABELLA. I can not bear it. The slipper is too short.

PAGE. It is your foot that is too long. [ARABELLA *rises and hobbles to back of stage.*]

VOICE (*without*). You can't come in here.

PEDRO. I will go in.

VOICE. Back, I say!

PEDRO. I won't go back!

PRINCE. What noise is that?

PEDRO (*without*). I'll have my say, or I'll die!

*Enter* PEDRO.

PEDRO. O, most wise, extravagant, and dreadful Prince, hear me first, and then—drive me out!

ARABELLA. It is Pedro, as I live!

PAGE. Shall I take the fellow out?

PRINCE. No; attention to inferiors is becoming in all ranks. What do you seek, good fellow?

PEDRO. My business here is to try the slipper. [*All laugh.*] Not me; but I ask the trial for a lady. She is without, and all she wants is to show her foot.

PRINCE. Conduct the lady before us. [*Exit* PEDRO. *A soft strain of music.*] O, those sounds!

*Enter* PEDRO *and* CINDERELLA. *Music ceases.*

PEDRO (*to* CINDERELLA). Keep your little heart up, and show your foot.

ARABELLA. What assurance! She shall starve a month for this.

JOSEPHINE (*aside*). I'll tear her eyes out, the upstart!

CINDERELLA (*looks down*). Mighty Prince, I have ventured into your presence to try—to try—

PEDRO. O, to try on the slipper! Speak it out, and show your foot—show your foot!

PRINCE (*in surprise*). You!

PEDRO. It's no use to stand on trifles. Sit down here, Cinderella. [*Leads her to the seat.*] Show your foot, I tell you—the sooner the better. [CINDERELLA *takes the seat.* PEDRO *jerks the slipper from the hand of* Page; *stoops and puts it on* CINDERELLA's *foot; puts the heel in the palm of his hand; raises it in view of the audience; looks triumphantly at* Prince.] See, your highness, it is a perfect fit!

[Prince *covers his face with his hands. All the company press forward and form a semi-circle around* CINDERELLA, *between her and the audience, thus affording* PEDRO *and* CINDERELLA *time to slip off the outer dress which hides their ball dresses, without being seen by the audience. When this is accomplished, all fall back. The* Prince *discovers* CINDERELLA; *runs to her; takes her hand and leads her to front of stage.*]

PRINCE. My fondest hopes are realized; and now, fair one, tell me your name.

CINDERELLA. My name is Cinderella, and I am the sister of the Ladies Pompolino. [ARABELLA *and* JOSEPHINE *turn their faces away.*]

PRINCE. Can this be true?

PEDRO (*swaggering proudly*). Yes, sir, it is true. They have abused and trampled on Cinderella, and now they are being paid for it. Chickens will come home to roost. [*Looks mischievously at* ARABELLA *and* JOSEPHINE.]

CINDERELLA. Silence, Pedro! (*To* Prince). The cruel treatment of my sisters is forgotten in the happiness of this hour. I freely forgive them, and beg you to treat them kindly.

PRINCE. I will take them into favor upon one condition only, and that is that you will make me master of this hand. [*Takes her hand.*]

PEDRO (*aside*). And foot! For that did the work!

CINDERELLA. And I will grant your request upon one condition.

PRINCE. Name it.

CINDERELLA. That Pedro shall become one of our household. He has been my friend in *adversity*, and must remain my friend in prosperity.

*Enter* Fairy Godmother; *approaches* Prince *and* CINDERELLA; *stands between them, in full view of the audience.*

FAIRY. Mortals, behold the example of this good and beautiful child, and know that *Virtue* and *Humility* are Heaven's peculiar care. Sweet Cinderella, thou hast been *humble* in thy *poverty:* be *modest* in thy *greatness.* [*Joins the hands of* Prince *and* CINDERELLA.] My pleasing task is done!

(*Curtain falls slowly. A strain of soft music accompanies it. The closing scene of this play forms a beautiful tableau.*)

---

## COSTUMES.

ARABELLA and JOSEPHINE, in the scenes at home, should have on tawdry morning dresses.

CINDERELLA is dressed (until her appearance at the ball) in a loose home dress, of dingy colors; this dress should be made to tie up in front, the sleeves tied in the same way with short tape strings, As this dress is slipped over the ball dress (in the last scene), and when the company form a half circle around her at the trial of the slipper, it can be untied and slipped off so quickly that, to the audience, the change is like magic. CINDERELLA's ball dress is light illusion or tarlatan, spangled profusely; the slippers made of white satin, and covered with spangles or mica to represent glass.

PEDRO, in home scenes, must have a loose suit, as the transition in the last scene must be the same as that of CINDERELLA. PEDRO's ball dress ought to be ludicrous in the extreme: tight knee-breeches; silk stockings; slippers with enormous buckles; a swallow-tail coat; big brass buttons; fancy vest; particolored neck-tie; high shirt-collar; a "stove-pipe" hat.

FAIRY. Dress of white, spangled; gauzy wings would be an addition.

PRINCE. A handsome Highland dress would look well; white satin trousers; satin doublet, both embroidered with gold; a cardinal or slashed coat of velvet or satin; velvet cap and plumes. (This, or any of the dresses in the play, can be varied to suit the taste of each performer.) This is a capital play for parlor theatricals. The ladies and gentlemen in attendance should be dressed in party style.

ARABELLA and JOSEPHINE. Ball dress in the extreme of fashion; lace, flowers, feathers, flounces, furbelows, fans. They ought to be highly rouged, and hair powdered.

The play of "CINDERELLA" (or rather the story) is an old one, and the characters, to make it more life-like, ought to be dressed as lords and ladies of the "olden time."

# BEAUTY AND THE BEAST.

## CHARACTERS.

RUDOLPH.
MUNDANE,
ELVIRA,    } *Daughters of* RUDOLPH.
BEAUTY,
Queen of the Fairies.
First Fairy.              Fourth Fairy.
Second Fairy.             Fifth Fairy.
Prince CARLOS.
DAMON, *a Servant.*

## SCENE I.

*A Cottage furnished poorly. Enter* RUDOLPH, *holding in his hand an open letter.*

RUDOLPH. A letter from India! This is unexpected—imperative in its nature. There is no alternative. I must go. [*Calls.*] Elvira! Mundane! Beauty! Where are you?

*Enter* ELVIRA, MUNDANE, *and* BEAUTY.

ELVIRA. O, papa! what has happened?
MUNDANE. You frightened us out of our wits.
BEAUTY. What is the matter, dear father? Has any calamity befallen you? Tell us.
RUDOLPH. Do not be alarmed, my children; nothing has occurred, except that I hold in my hand a letter from India, requiring my immediate attendance.
ELVIRA (*aside*). I am glad of it; we can then be at liberty.
MUNDANE (*aside*). What a God-send!
BEAUTY. O, my father, we can not bear your long absence. We will so miss your society. How long will you be absent?

RUDOLPH.   Three months at least.

BEAUTY.   So long, dear father?

RUDOLPH.   My daughter, you must not grieve.   Our fortunes depend on this trip.   If I am successful, we will be independent.   The poverty that now haunts our door will be driven away forever.

ELVIRA.   If this be true, the sooner you start, dear father, the better.

MUNDANE.   Yes—for I long to be rich.

BEAUTY.   I prefer your company, dear father, to all the wealth of the Indies.

*Enter* DAMON.

RUDOLPH.   How now, good Damon?

BEAUTY.   O, Damon, such dreadful news.   [*Covers her face with a handkerchief.*]

DAMON.   What 's in the wind?

MUNDANE.   O, nothing but what will bring good fortune to us.   Our papa has been called to leave home on a long journey.

ELVIRA.   And when he returns we shall be rich.

DAMON.   But where, dear master?

RUDOLPH.   Across the high seas; and perhaps I may never return.

BEAUTY.   Do not say that, dear father.

DAMON.   Kind Heaven forbid, my master.

RUDOLPH.   Cheer up, my children.   If I succeed, I will bring to each of you a handsome present.   Come, name what it shall be.

MUNDANE.   For *me* diamonds, and the richest velvet that can be bought.

ELVIRA.   And for me oriental pearls, and the rarest silks that the East affords.

RUDOLPH.   Has little Beauty nothing to ask?

BEAUTY.   I want your blessing before you go.

MUNDANE (*aside*).   The little hypocrite!

ELVIRA (*aside*).   I could choke her!

RUDOLPH.   Beauty, you must choose a gift from your father.

DAMON.   O, yes, little Beauty, choose something.

BEAUTY.   Well, then, father, bring me a rose, the fairest that blooms on Eastern soil.

MUNDANE (*disdainfully*). A rose!

ELVIRA. The simpleton!

RUDOLPH. Your wish shall be granted, my child, if it costs me a world of danger. But the vessel is ready to sail, and I must go. [*To* BEAUTY.] Go bring my cloak. [*Exit* BEAUTY. *To* DAMON.] To your care, Damon, I leave my children. Guard them as you would a casket of jewels.

DAMON (*bows*). With my life, kind master.

*Enter* BEAUTY; *places the cloak about* RUDOLPH's *shoulders.*

RUDOLPH (*embraces his children*). Farewell! May Providence protect you! [*Starts.*] Damon, remember your pledge. [DAMON *bows.*]

MUNDANE. Do not forget the diamonds, papa.

ELVIRA. And my pearls and silk, papa. [BEAUTY *falls upon a chair; weeps.*]

DAMON. Alas, my good master. [*Exit* RUDOLPH.

(*Curtain falls.*)


SCENE II.

Prince CARLOS's *Palace. The stage in this scene ought to be tastefully decorated. In one vase a single rose blooming, placed in full sight of the audience.* RUDOLPH *reclines asleep upon a couch. Enter* Fairies.

FIRST FAIRY (*approaches couch and looks at* RUDOLPH). What means this? A mortal!

SECOND FAIRY. How came he here?

FIRST FAIRY. I know not. He has a clear conscience, else he would not sleep so soundly.

SECOND FAIRY. Does the Prince know that he has such a visitor?

FIRST FAIRY. I can not tell. It is a strange circumstance. No mortal has crossed the threshold of these doors for years.

SECOND FAIRY. Here comes our Queen; she will explain.

*Enter* Queen.

FIRST FAIRY. Dear mother [*points to* RUDOLPH], tell us the meaning of this.

4

QUEEN. It means much that is good to our Prince. It is the harbinger of his release.

ALL. Indeed!

QUEEN. The stranger you behold has been upon a long, perilous journey, and is now returning to his family. Last night, when the storm raged so furiously, I led him by my power to seek shelter in the palace. Prince Carlos knows not that he is here, and will not, unless the stranger takes some unwonted liberty. Poor man, he was shipwrecked, and was cast by the waves upon the shore; he became bewildered in the forest, and when the storm arose would have perished but for my timely aid. I can divulge no more. Time will unfold all. The night is waning, children. The release of Prince Carlos is near at hand; come let us have our nightly song, for morn will soon break upon mortals, and we must away to our elfin home. [*Sings.*]

> Come! come! come!
> Off with care,
> Pleasure share;
> Here we meet by pale moonlight.
> We belong
> To elfin throng,
> Where life is always bright.

FAIRIES (*join in chorus*).

> It is the witching midnight hour,
> When fairies love to wield their power.
> O, 't is sweet,
> When fairies meet,
> Singing merrily,
> Tra, la, la, la, tra, la, la; Tra, la, la, la, tra, la, la.
> O, 't is sweet,
> When fairies meet,
> Singing merrily.

QUEEN (*sings*).

> Come! come! come!
> Merrily,
> Full of glee,
> Now we meet to dance and play.
> Faces bright,
> Bosoms light,
> We gladly pass each day.

FAIRIES (*join in chorus*).

It is the witching midnight hour,
When fairies love to wield their power.
O, 't is sweet,
When fairies meet,
Singing merrily.
Tra, la, la, la, tra, la, la: Tra, la, la, la, tra, la, la.
O. 'tis sweet,
When fairies meet,
Singing merrily. [*Exeunt* Fairies.]

[RUDOLPH *wakes; rises to a sitting posture; rubs his eyes; looks around.*]

RUDOLPH. Did I not hear music? Where am I? O, yes, now I remember. Last night, when the storm was at its height, I saw a glimmering light that led me to this enchanted spot, for enchanted it must be. The doors opened to receive me, but not a living thing did I see. [*Rises; walks to and fro.*] One day more and I will be again with my children. The vessel was wrecked almost in sight of my cottage. I dread to meet my children, as my journey has been one of toil and failure. I will search this house and discover, if possible, to whom it belongs.
[*Exit* RUDOLPH.]

[*The band should play until* RUDOLPH *returns. At the close of the air, enter* RUDOLPH.]

RUDOLPH. I have searched in vain. 'Tis strange, amid such luxury, there is no human creature to be seen. [*Approaches the vase containing the rose; breaks off the rose.*] Beauty, at least, will be gratified. It was well her wish was one so humble. [*A terrible noise heard outside.* RUDOLPH *looks around alarmed.*]

*Enter* BEAST.

BEAST. Vile man! had you the audacity to break my rose, my favorite flower!

RUDOLPH (*bows low*). Pardon me if I have transgressed. It was the parting request of my youngest daughter that I should bring her a rose. I could find no one to ask, and thought it no harm to pluck a single flower.

BEAST (*loudly*). Silence, base man; your life shall pay the forfeit!

RUDOLPH. I am a poor man. Think of my helpless, destitute children [*kneels*], and spare my life!

BEAST. Speak truly—are you *very* poor?

RUDOLPH. Alas! I am, and without my care my children would starve. Ah, Beauty! Beauty! little did you know the trouble your simple request would bring upon your father! [*Covers his face with his hands.*]

BEAST. Rise, and we will come to terms. I will spare your life, wretched man, upon one condition.

RUDOLPH (*rises*). Name it.

BEAST. Do you see this palace? Notwithstanding I have the form of a beast, all this wealth is mine. It is in my power to summon a band of soldiers and behead you instantly; but, hark! [*takes* RUDOLPH *by the arm,*] I will release you upon condition that you return to my palace and bring with you the favorite daughter you spoke of— AND HERE LET HER REMAIN.

RUDOLPH (*clasps his hands*). O, Beauty, my child!

BEAST. Decide. If you refuse, you must die instantly!

RUDOLPH. I will return to my cottage and inform my daughter of what has occurred. If she consents to your terms, I will return and bring her.

BEAST. If she refuse, then return yourself, or else a worse fate than death awaits you. Remember, you are in my power completely.

RUDOLPH. I obey. [*Bows.*]

BEAST. Take the rose; it is a gift from BEAST to BEAUTY.

RUDOLPH. Your word is my law. [*Bows.*]

(*Curtain falls.*)


## SCENE III.

RUDOLPH's *cottage.* ELVIRA *and* MUNDANE *seated listlessly.* BEAUTY *near a table reading.*

MUNDANE. It is time papa was returning.

BEAUTY (*looking up*). He has been gone so long, and not one word have we heard from him.

ELVIRA. I wish he would hasten and bring the riches he spoke of. It is so inconvenient to be *poor.*

MUNDANE. It would be so charming to have our own carriage and servants; we would then have suitors. Men all like rich girls.

BEAUTY. I would not marry a man who sought me because of my wealth.

ELVIRA. Of course not, Miss Perfection. I'll tell you one thing, we will never get husbands while we remain poor.

BEAUTY. I would want my husband to love me for myself alone.

MUNDANE. You are rather young, miss, to be thinking of marriage. It would be more becoming in you to wait until Elvira and myself are settled in life. But you have been told you are pretty until it has turned your head.

ELVIRA. Yes; but only wait until papa brings home the fortune, and we will *make* you remain in the background.

BEAUTY. Our father said there was some doubt as to the result of his voyage.

ELVIRA. I'll be bound, you would croak if this cottage were changed to *gold*.

BEAUTY. Not so, sister. I wished to warn you not to be too sanguine.

ELVIRA. Reserve your sermons for those who can appreciate them. [*Looks toward entrance.*] But, look! Here comes Damon with a box upon his shoulder that seems to be filled with something heavy. What can it mean?

MUNDANE (*rises; looks out*). He fairly bends under the weight.

*Enter* DAMON *with a box upon his shoulders; deposits it on the floor.*

DAMON (*fans his face with his hat*). Good news! good news! fair dames! This box is laden with gold!

ELVIRA and MUNDANE (*excitedly*). Gold, Damon? *Gold!*

DAMON. Yes; my master has returned, and bid me carry the treasure. But see, he comes; let the good man speak for himself.

BEAUTY (*springs forward*). My father here?

*Enter* RUDOLPH.

BEAUTY (*embraces* RUDOLPH). My dear, dear father!

MUNDANE (*approaches* RUDOLPH). Did you bring my diamonds, papa?

ELVIRA. And the pearls and silk, papa?

RUDOLPH (*to* BEAUTY). Bring me a seat, dear Beauty, and I will tell you all. [BEAUTY *hands a chair;* RUDOLPH *sits down; they all gather about him.*] You know, my children, that I have been absent a long time. I made the voyage to India, but failed to procure the fortune we so much needed.

MUNDANE. But the box, papa. Damon said the box was filled with gold.

RUDOLPH. Patience, child, and I will explain.

ELVIRA (*aside*). I want no explanation, so we get the gold.

RUDOLPH. Last night, when the vessel in which I returned hove in sight of land, a tremendous storm arose— such a storm as I never want to witness again. Notwithstanding the united efforts of crew and passengers, our ship became a wreck. I seized a plank, and, after struggling manfully for some time, a friendly wave lifted me and landed me upon the beach. It was very dark when I came to my senses, and I found myself, as soon as I was able to stand, upon the borders of a dense forest. By the aid of the frequent flashes of lightning I discovered a footpath; this I followed for some time, and finally saw in the distance a glimmering light. As I approached nearer, I discovered the outline of a large building, which, after a difficult walk, I reached. It was a magnificent palace. The doors were open, and I entered, glad to find shelter from the storm. Every comfort that wealth can procure was before me. A tempting repast was spread upon a table in dishes of solid silver. But, amid all this luxury, not a living soul was visible. I satisfied the cravings of hunger, and, worn down by fatigue, fell asleep upon one of the couches in the apartment. This morning I was awakened by strains of delicious music. I looked around, but was alone. An inviting breakfast stood before me, and I ate as before. After the meal was concluded I determined to make a search for the inmates of this princely domain. I went from room to room, and the same elegance met me at every turn; but no living thing met my view. Bewildered and disappointed, I returned to the apartment in which I had passed the previous night, to secure my cloak. As I turned to leave the room I cast my eyes around, and they rested upon this single rose [*holds the rose in view*]. blooming in a vase. I thought of Beauty's request, and plucked the fatal flower. No sooner had I done so than the most awful sounds penetrated the apartment. and in another instant a hideous beast appeared before me; and with a loud voice exclaimed: "Vile man! had you the audacity to break my rose, my favorite flower!" I fell upon my knees and begged for pardon; also explained to the monster why I had transgressed. But I could not appease his wrath. He declared my life should pay the forfeit.

BEAUTY. My poor father!

MUNDANE. Who was this beast?

RUDOLPH. I know not; except that he informed me that the palace belonged to him. and that I was entirely in his power. I told him of my helpless children, and he then relented enough to say that he would spare my life on *one* condition!

ALL. What was that?

RUDOLPH. That I would return immediately to the palace, bringing with me my darling daughter, Beauty, *and there let her remain!*

MUNDANE. But the gold.

ELVIRA. O, yes, tell us of the gold.

RUDOLPH. After I left the palace I was followed by a carrier, bearing this box of gold, with an imperative command from the Beast to accept it, and if I refused to return and die.

BEAUTY. And will my going to the palace save your life. dear father?

RUDOLPH. It will: but I ask no such sacrifice. I only returned to bid you farewell, and then return and meet my doom!

BEAUTY. Never! You shall not die; for I will go immediately.

RUDOLPH. I can not permit such a sacrifice.

MUNDANE. Why not? Let her go.

ELVIRA. Yes, allow her to go.

MUNDANE (*aside*). She is so pretty I want to be well rid of her. [*To* RUDOLPH.] Papa, Beauty would rather die than that *you* should be killed.

ELVIRA. And her life is not worth much.

RUDOLPH.   Unfeeling children—no! Beauty shall not go!

BEAUTY.   It is useless to remonstrate.   If you will not go with me, dear father, I will go alone.   Let us go together and see this Beast; he may listen to my pleadings and spare you.

RUDOLPH.   By heaven, this is a bright thought!   We will go, and perchance all may yet be well.   [*To* DAMON.] Damon, remove this box to my apartment and keep it securely.   [*To* BEAUTY.]   Go! prepare for your journey. [*Exit* BEAUTY.   *To* MUNDANE *and* ELVIRA.]   Come to my room, for I have much to speak of before I go.

[Exit RUDOLPH.]

MUNDANE.   Go, Damon, and carry the box to papa's room, and when he is gone we will examine its contents.

ELVIRA.   And help ourselves to a good share.

DAMON (*shoulders box*).   You'll never help yourselves while this is under my charge.

ELVIRA (*mimics* DAMON).   Yaw! yaw! yaw! we will see, Mr. Impudence!

DAMON.   I will never see you open this box while it is in my possession.   If I do my name is not DAMON.

[Exit DAMON.]

MUNDANE.   We can drug him!

ELVIRA.   Yes; and we will.

(*Curtain falls.*)


## SCENE IV.

*The Palace.   Enter* RUDOLPH *and* BEAUTY.

BEAUTY.   What a delightful place!   There is nothing terrible in coming here, dear father.

RUDOLPH.   There is nothing in it to charm me.   I would not give *you*, Beauty, for all the palaces on earth.   [*Noise heard outside.*]

*Enter* BEAST.   BEAUTY *starts; draws near* RUDOLPH.

BEAST.   You have redeemed your pledge, I see.

RUDOLPH.   Yes; this is my daughter, Beauty.   [*Presents* BEAUTY.]

BEAST.   Welcome, sweet lady; my palace is at your command.

BEAUTY. Thank you, kind sir. I came to beg you to spare the life of my father.

BEAST. He knows the conditions. Are you willing, Beauty, to remain with me?

BEAUTY. If it will save my father's life.

BEAST. Was it your wish to come?

BEAUTY. Yes, as I said, if it will save *his* life.

BEAST (*to* RUDOLPH). You have heard her decision.

RUDOLPH. Will nothing less satisfy you?

BEAST. Nothing.

RUDOLPH. Then I will die!

BEAUTY. No, my father; you shall not die! I will remain.

BEAST. You are a noble girl. Beauty. [*To* RUDOLPH.] Come, take your last farewell. Your daughter is willing to die for you. I will return when you are gone.

[*Exit* BEAST.]

RUDOLPH. O, Beauty, why did you come? I can not leave you with this horrid monster.

BEAUTY. I do not fear him. Come, cheer up, and tell your little Beauty good-by.

RUDOLPH. Go home, my child, and let me die. I can not leave you thus!

BEAUTY. Do not grieve, my father. I will treat the Beast so kindly that he can not find it in his heart to kill me. [*Noise heard without.*] It is the monster returning! Go, dear father, go! Do not make him angry, lest he slay us both. Farewell! Think often of me, will you, father? [*Embraces* RUDOLPH.] There, go. I hear his footsteps! [*Exit* RUDOLPH *weeping.* BEAUTY *falls upon a couch; covers her face with her hands.*] My father! O, my father!

(*Curtain falls.*)


## SCENE V.

*The Palace. The stage in this scene should be beautifully decorated.* BEAUTY *seated; near her a guitar, books, sheets of music, flowers, etc., etc.*

BEAUTY Two months since I came to this palace. and it seems only a few days. Instead of being murdered, as I expected, I have been basking in luxury. Strange, too, my heart yearns to the Beast as it never did to mortal before. For all he is so hideous in form, there is a charm about him that draws me nearer to him every day. How can a mind so cultivated and refined be encased in such a shape! I do not love him; O, no! I could not love a beast. And yet when he is absent I am sad. Heigho! I am not in love. [*Noise heard without.*] He is coming.

### *Enter* BEAST.

BEAST (*sits beside* BEAUTY). Alone, my little Beauty?

BEAUTY. And wishing for your presence, Beast.

BEAST. Ah! this is flattery. Could I *dare* to hope that you cared for me?

BEAUTY. You know, Beast, I *do* care for you.

BEAST. Not enough, Beauty! not enough!

BEAUTY. What more can you wish?

BEAST. Do not be angry, Beauty; I wish for much more. I want you to be my wife.

BEAUTY (*starts*). *Your* wife? the wife of a *beast?*

BEAST. Yes. For though I am a beast, I have a heart filled with devotion for you. O, say, Beauty, that you will pity me and be my wife.

BEAUTY. It can not be. How could I wed a beast?

BEAST. I was a fool, mad, to ask it. But, O, my little Beauty, if you knew how much I love you! how your presence is my life! I could not exist if it were not for you. [BEAUTY *sighs.*] Do not spurn me. If you were to leave me I should perish.

BEAUTY. You could spare me a little while.

BEAST. No, no! not an hour!

BEAUTY. But, Beast, I *must* see my father. I have been separated from him two months, and if I do not see him *I* will die, and then you will *have* to do without me.

BEAST. I can not let you leave me.

BEAUTY. Just for one week! I will return. [*Kneels; looks imploringly at* BEAST.] Just one short week!

BEAST. Rise, Beauty; I can not resist such pleading. But, O, promise me that you will return! Do not deceive me!

BEAUTY. I could not deceive one who has been so kind to me. But you hold the power to keep me here. I can never find my old home unless you guide me.

BEAST (*hands* BEAUTY *a ring*). Place this ring upon your finger when you retire to-night, and you wake on the morrow in the cottage. When you wish to return, place it under your pillow when you go to bed at night, and you will return to me.

BEAUTY. O, what a dear, delightful Beast! [*Rises; puts her hand on* BEAST's *shoulder.*] If you were not so ugly I would be your wife. How can I repay such kindness?

BEAST. Ah, Beauty, how your words tear my heart!

BEAUTY. May angels guard you in my absence. [BEAST *weeps.*]

BEAUTY (*aside*). Strange that a *beast* can weep! [*To* BEAST.] I can not bear to see you grieve. Take my hand, and let us walk. The fresh air will revive you.

BEAST (*takes* BEAUTY's *hand; rises*). Do as you will. I am your slave. [*They start to go.*]

(*Curtain falls.*)


SCENE VI.

*The Palace.* BEAST *asleep upon a couch. Enter Fairies and surround him, with faces to audience.*

FIRST FAIRY. Our Prince is sleeping, dear mother.

QUEEN. He sleeps, 'tis true, but he suffers. Alas! I thought his deliverance was near. But if Beauty returns not soon, he will expire.

SECOND FAIRY. What ails him?

QUEEN. His heart is well-nigh broken. He is grieving for the absent one. I have waited for the last two nights for Beauty to place the ring under her pillow, but she has failed to do so.

FIRST FAIRY. What can be the cause?

QUEEN. Her malicious sisters. When Beauty returned to her old home they envied her happiness, and coveted her rich clothing and jewels, and they are using wicked arts to prevent her return.

SECOND FAIRY. But why is it their wish to detain her?

QUEEN. They know Beauty pledged her word to our Prince to return in one week, and by a foul device they have detained her now ten days. It is jealousy and envy that prompts them. They can not bear to see Beauty living in splendor, and wish to incense the Prince, and thereby cause him to destroy her. I have sent two vigilant fairies to watch by Beauty's bedside to-night. Their influence may warn her of the danger of our Prince. But, see! he is growing restless. [BEAST *groans*.] Soothe him by your nightly song. [Fairies *sing*. *As the song closes they retire*.]

*Enter* BEAUTY. *Advances to front of stage.*

BEAUTY (*puts her hand to her forehead*). Last night I had such a frightful dream! I thought I saw Beast in the agonies of death. I did not know till then how much I loved him. Why did I stay away? Why did I allow Mundane and Elvira to persuade me to remain? Where can Beast be? I have looked in his apartment, and the bed is untouched. O, my benefactor! my friend! I can never forgive myself!

BEAST. Beauty, my little Beauty!

BEAUTY (*turns, discovers* BEAST, *approaches the couch, falls on her knees beside him*). My noble Beast, are you indeed alive?

BEAST. Ah, Beauty, you have forsaken your poor Beast! You no longer love me.

BEAUTY. Do not say so. I am here to lay my life at your feet.

BEAST. You promised to return in one week.

BEAUTY. I know I did; but my sisters induced me to remain. Do not drive me from you, dear Beast. Do not spurn your little Beauty. [ *Weeps.* ]

BEAST. But you will not be my wife.

BEAUTY. I will! I will! You shall be my noble husband, and I your happy wife.

BEAST. You forget I am a *beast*.

BEAUTY. I care not for your form. Your heart is right. You are all the world to me, and I will be your wife. Will you, *can* you refuse your little Beauty? [BEAST *rises, drops the covering of the* BEAST, *appears as a* Prince.]

BEAUTY (*rises, starts with amazement*). How is this, my lord? Where is the Beast?

PRINCE. Beauty, you are my guardian angel. [ *Takes her hand, leads her to front of stage.*] You see in me a wretch, who was doomed, years ago, by a wicked fairy, to keep the form of a beast until some lady would consent to marry me. You have promised to be my wife, and this breaks the charm. You love me for myself. I can never reward you sufficiently, as you have made me the happiest prince alive.

*Enter* Fairies.

QUEEN (*joins the hands of* Prince *and* BEAUTY). Beauty. you have acted wisely. A good heart is of more value than external beauty. You love this man for his noble qualities, and not because he is rich in worldly goods. He loves you for your sincerity, purity, and devotion. May the blessings of heaven smile upon your union!

(*Curtain falls.*)

---

## COSTUMES.

RUDOLPH. Cottager's dress.

DAMON. Servant's dress (of olden time).

ELVIRA and MUNDANE. Home dresses, of faded, tawdry material.

BEAUTY. Neat home dress in first and second scenes. In all the scenes at the palace BEAUTY should be attired as a princess.

PRINCE CARLOS. In the first scenes he appears in a beast's skin. This dress is more easily procured than one would suppose, as in these modern times there are so many varieties of shaggy looking cloth that a beast's head can be easily formed. And this kind of cloth is not so oppressive as the real skin of an animal. (Astrakhan cloth is a good substitute.) In the last scene the Prince should be dressed in royal style: a velvet or satin suit, slashed with gold lace; a cap with plumes.

FAIRIES. Dresses of light tulle or tarlatan, spangled profusely; crowns of brilliants. The Queen ought to have a richer crown than the lesser Fairies, and also bear a wand in her hand.

# THE TATTLER.

### DRAMATIZED FROM A STORY THAT APPEARED IN T. S. ARTHUR'S POPULAR MAGAZINE IN 1868.

## CHARACTERS.

Mr. PENDERGRASS.
Mrs. PENDERGRASS.
Mrs. JOHNSON.
Miss PERKINS, *the Tattler.*

## SCENE I.

*Room.* Mrs. PENDERGRASS *and* Miss PERKINS *seated near the front of the stage.*

Mrs. PENDERGRASS. If Ruthy Ann Johnson said that, she is no lady.

Miss PERKINS. Well, she *did* say it, and more too.

Mrs. PENDERGRASS. Did she say that my Hester was ugly as sin?

Miss PERKINS. Yes, she did; and a great deal more.

Mrs. PENDERGRASS. What else did she say, Miss Perkins?

Miss PERKINS. She said Hester was as ugly as sin, and she could make a better face out of dough.

Mrs. PENDERGRASS (*rises and walks to and fro excitedly*). Very well, Mrs. Ruthy Ann Johnson! very well, madam! very kind talk for a neighbor.

Miss PERKINS. I would n't get excited. She said a great deal more about me, but I just let it pass. [*Looks indifferent.*]

Mrs. PENDERGRASS. Pass, indeed! You are not spunky, like I am. A better face out of dough! Give me patience! But, never mind, I'll have it out of her; see if I do n't.

Miss PERKINS. Ruthy Ann likes to talk. She is a little glib with the tongue, and is always talking about somebody. She thinks it is smart. You know she said Phebe Jenkins's face had no more expression than a turnip. I guess she did not mean any harm about what she said of Hester.

Mrs. PENDERGRASS. I don't care what she meant. I'll tell her this much: she has got to keep her glib tongue off of me and mine. Hester is as good-looking as any of her brats. [*Enter* Mr. PENDERGRASS.] Law! Mr. Pendergrass, what do you think? Ruthy Ann Johnson has been slandering our Hester!

Mr. PENDERGRASS. Indeed! what has she said?

Mrs. PENDERGRASS. Why, she told Miss Perkins, there, that Hester is as ugly as sin!

Mr. PENDERGRASS. Well, that is no slander. I never thought Hester much of a beauty; but she is a good girl, which is better than all. As to her being ugly as sin, that is a mere extravagance of expression sometimes indulged in by thoughtless people like Mrs. Johnson. It amounts to nothing. Let it pass as an idle wind.

Mrs. PENDERGRASS. Indeed, I won't let it pass. Nobody has a right to talk so about my Hester, and I intend to give Ruthy Ann Johnson a piece of my mind!

Mr. PENDERGRASS. You had better not, Maria: no good will come of it. You will only make an enemy of her.

Mrs. PENDERGRASS. I don't care; I would rather have such a woman for my enemy than my friend.

Mr. PENDERGRASS. Never make an enemy, Maria. Enemies are always dangerous.

Mrs. PENDERGRASS. It is no use talking to *me*, Pendergrass: you never did have any spunk.

Mr. PENDERGRASS. I always had spunk enough to maintain my dignity; and, if I were you, I would not condescend to notice any thing Mrs. Johnson has said.

Mrs. PENDERGRASS. Well, Pendergrass, you needn't think I am going to let such a woman as Ruthy Ann Johnson talk about me with impunity. "Dough face," indeed!

[*Exit* Mrs. PENDERGRASS *and* Miss PERKINS.]

Mr. PENDERGRASS. I see it is useless for me to say any thing more. Where a woman sets her head, all creation can not turn her.

(*Curtain falls.*)

## SCENE II.

*A different room.* Mrs. Johnson *seated at work.* *Enter* Mrs. Pendergrass.

Mrs. Johnson (*rises from her seat*). Good morning, Maria; I am glad to see you.

Mrs. Pendergrass. No you ain't!

Mrs. Johnson. What is the matter? what do you mean?

Mrs. Pendergrass. Just what I say. You are *not* glad to see me; you are a mean hypocrite!

Mrs. Johnson. Let me be what I am, no lady would use such language in the house of a neighbor.

Mrs. Pendergrass. *You* are no lady; you are a mean hypocrite.

Mrs. Johnson. Maria Pendergrass, I do not understand your conduct, and I will not listen to any such insulting language in my own house.

Mrs. Pendergrass. Yes, you will; for I told Pendergrass this very morning that I intended to give you a piece of my mind.

Mrs. Johnson. You had better not give me too large a piece, or you will not have any left. [*Smiles.*]

Mrs. Pendergrass. Ruthy Ann Johnson! you shall not stand there poking fun at me. You are a low-flung hypocrite, and I despise you!

Mrs. Johnson. Maria! your passion has gotten the better of your judgment, and I advise you to go home, and stay there till you can talk like a reasonable woman.

Mrs. Pendergrass. O, yes! this is mighty fine talk; but I'll show you, you mean hypocrite. I'll throw rocks and break your windows! and I'll kill your pet lamb! and I'll trample down your flower-beds! I'll—I'll have my revenge!

Mrs. Johnson (*approaches* Mrs. Pendergrass). Maria Pendergrass, you've got to leave my house, and I never want you to come in it again till you can act like a decent woman. There is the door! [*points,*] and the sooner you leave the better!

Mrs. Pendergrass. O, yes! I understand! You are a mean, cowardly hypocrite, and can't look me straight in the face. To be sure I can go home, and I can stay there; but

I'll have my revenge—see if I don't! [*Recedes as she talks.*]
[*Exit* Mrs. PENDERGRASS. Mrs. JOHNSON *looks after her in surprise.*]

Mrs. JOHNSON. What in the name of wonder has come over Maria? I believe she is going crazy! What can it all mean? But I see Miss Perkins coming, and maybe she can throw some light on the matter. She always knows every thing about every body. I'll pump her.

*Enter* Miss PERKINS.

Miss PERKINS. Good morning, Mrs. Johnson.

Mrs. JOHNSON. Good morning—you are the very person I want to see! Have a seat. [*Hands chair. They both sit down.*]

Miss PERKINS. Indeed!

Mrs. JOHNSON. Yes; I want to ask you when you saw Maria Pendergrass?

Miss PERKINS. Well, let me think. [*Studies.*] It has been three or four days since I was there. O, yes—now I remember—it was last Tuesday.

Mrs. JOHNSON. You haven't seen her since?

Miss PERKINS. Not since. It is a little curious I haven't heard of her being out; and that is strange, for you know she is always on the pad.

Mrs. JOHNSON. Maybe she is sick.

Miss PERKINS. Shouldn't wonder, for I don't know what else would keep her in; you know she is such a gad-about. By the way, do you remember the funny speech you made about her Hester once?

Mrs. JOHNSON. No! What was it?

Miss PERKINS. O, I've laughed about it a hundred times. It was so funny and still so true! [*Laughs.*] For you know Hester is as ugly as mud.

Mrs. JOHNSON. She is not handsome, but you know she is good. and that is better than beauty.

Miss PERKINS. Just what you said afterward to take the edge off your funny speech!

Mrs. JOHNSON. What did I say? I have forgotten.

Miss PERKINS. You said you could make a better face out of dough!

Mrs. JOHNSON. It was thoughtless and unkind in me to say it, and by no means expressed my true feelings to the

child, for I really love Hester. But ludicrous ideas often
present themselves to my mind, and I have a bad habit of
speaking from impulse, when it were better to be silent.

Miss PERKINS. Somebody who heard you say this was
kind enough to tell Mrs. Pendergrass.

Mrs. JOHNSON. O, no—surely no!

Miss PERKINS. It is true, and she is as mad as she can be
about it.

Mrs. JOHNSON. I do not wonder. It was thoughtless in
me to make such a speech, but it was more wicked in the
one who repeated it.

Miss PERKINS. Yes, there are always mischief-makers
enough to repeat these little things. It was not only wicked,
but very malicious. [*Nods her head with energy.*]

Mrs. JOHNSON. I wonder who could have been so unprin-
cipled!

Miss PERKINS. Really, I can't tell.

Mrs. JOHNSON. Well, I'll go and see Maria and tell her
exactly how it was. She shall know the truth.

Miss PERKINS. O, *don't*—indeed I would n't.

Mrs. JOHNSON. I will go, and you must go with me.

Miss PERKINS (*surprised*). What! *me?*

Mrs. JOHNSON. Yes, you shall go with me; for Maria
will want to know who told me.

Miss PERKINS. Indeed you must excuse me.

Mrs. JOHNSON. I shall not excuse you. Come, I'll get
my bonnet.                              [*Exit* Mrs. JOHNSON.]

Miss PERKINS. Now, have n't I got myself in a mess!
Such a rippet as these two women will have; for Maria
Pendergrass is just like a match, ready to blaze at the first
touch, and Ruthy Ann has a temper of her own. But my
wits never forsook me yet. I can lie out of it.

(*Curtain falls.*)


SCENE III.

Mrs. PENDERGRASS *alone.*

Mrs. PENDERGRASS. What a fool I have made of myself!
What must Ruthy Ann Johnson think of me? She will
tell her husband, of course, and he is a fiery, hot-headed

little whiffet, and will be after Mr. Pendergrass for expla-
nations! I am so mad with myself. Why did n't I talk to
her right. I had it all laid off, every word in its place.
I am a fool! I wish Miss Perkins had staid home and
minded her own business. But, law! [*Looks toward the
door.*] Who is that coming this way? Ruthy Ann Johnson and Miss Perkins, as I live!

*Enter* Mrs. JOHNSON *and* Miss PERKINS.

Mrs. JOHNSON. How d' ye do. Maria?
Mrs. PENDERGRASS. Very well, thank you. Have seats.
[*Hands chairs.*]
Mrs. JOHNSON. No, Maria; I came to ask you a candid
question. Will you give me a candid answer?
Mrs. PENDERGRASS. I will.
Mrs. JOHNSON. Who told you that I spoke unkindly of
your daughter?
Mrs. PENDERGRASS. Why, Miss Perkins. [*Points to* Miss
PERKINS.]
Miss PERKINS. O, no! you are mistaken; it was not me.
You 've forgotten, Mrs. Pendergrass.
Mrs. PENDERGRASS. Not at all. My memory is very clear
on the subject. You are my informant. and no one else.
Mrs. JOHNSON. What did she say, Maria?
Mrs. PENDERGRASS. That you said my Hester was ugly
as sin.
Miss PERKINS. I never used such language, nor any
thing like it. [*Indignantly.*]
Mrs. PENDERGRASS. You did. And more than that, you
said you could make a better face than Hester's out of
dough.
Mrs. JOHNSON. Maria, I did utter this thoughtless speech,
and was sorry for it as soon as I said it, and I said directly
afterward that Hester was good, and that was better than
beauty. Did you tell this? [*Turns to* Miss PERKINS.]
Mrs. PENDERGRASS. No, Ruthy Ann, she did not, evil-
minded mischief-maker that she is.
Mrs. JOHNSON. Maria, forgive my foolish speech; there
was no real meaning in it, and would have done no real
harm if there had been no evil tongue to bear it to your
ears.
Mrs. PENDERGRASS. And pray, Ruthy Ann, forgive my

hasty words, uttered in blind passion. I have been sufficiently punished.

Mrs. Johnson. And so have I. As to your Hester, I have always liked her. Miss Perkins has heard me say many a time that I wished my daughter was as thoughtful of me as Hester is of you; and, as to *beauty*, I do not think there is any thing to brag about on either side of the house. My daughter is plain as a pipe-stem, and if you could n't make as good a face out of putty, I would not give much for your skill.

Mrs. Pendergrass (*turns to* Miss Perkins). And now, my lady, I have a rod in pickle for you. You low, mean, tattling—

Mrs. Johnson (*takes* Mrs. Pendergrass *by the arm*). Maria! Maria! do not waste words upon her; she is not worth a decent woman's indignation.

Mrs. Pendergrass. Thank you, Ruthy, for the timely words. You are right; but I must say this. [*Looks at* Miss Perkins.] You have darkened my door *once* too often.

Miss Perkins (*tosses her head defiantly*). Humph! there are plenty of people in the world besides you and Ruthy Ann Johnson. [*Exit hurriedly.*]

Mrs. Pendergrass (*looks after her*). The sneaking hypocrite!

Mrs. Johnson. I would have liked her more if she had shown fire and fight; but *tattlers* are always cowards. And now, Maria, if you hear any more of my foolish speeches, come to me in frankness, and not as you did.

Mrs. Pendergrass. You need not fear. I will never make a fool of myself again. By the memory of this we will be better friends.

*Enter* Mr. Pendergrass.

Mr. Pendergrass. Good morning, ladies! I see by your countenances that you have made up your little difficulty, and I am glad of it, for I despise women's quarrels.

Mrs. Pendergrass. O, yes; we are good friends once more.

Mrs. Johnson. And never would have been enemies but for that tattling Miss Perkins.

Mr. Pendergrass. Many friends have been made enemies before you by careless words innocently spoken.

[*Turns to the audience.*] It is the tattler who is the social criminal. Her offense is capital, and she ought to be hung without judge or jury.

*Curtain falls.*)

[*The characters in the above play should speak slowly and distinctly.*]

---

## COSTUMES.

The dresses in this play are plain home dresses, suitable for the age of the character personated.

# THE AUNT'S LEGACY.

## A PLAY FOR LITTLE GIRLS.

### CHARACTERS.

LOUISE, ⎫
ANNIE,  ⎬ *Sisters.*
LULY,   ⎭

KATE, *an Orphan and Cousin to the three sisters.*

Old Woman, *Fortune-teller.*

SUSAN, ⎫
MARY,  ⎬ *Servants.*

### SCENE I.

*A room neatly furnished.* ANNIE *seated near a small table sewing.* LOUISE *standing before a mirror arranging her hair.*

LOUISE (*throwing down the hair brush impatiently, approaches* ANNIE). O, Annie! put down that everlasting sewing and join me in some amusement.

ANNIE. No, no, Louise. Pa says he wants to see us work in the morning and play in the evening.

LOUISE. Pshaw! That is one of pa's odd notions; he is so curious.

ANNIE. I do not think so.

LOUISE. I do. This thing of work in the morning and play in the evening is all nonsense.

ANNIE. If you do not want to work, there is the piano. Why don't you practice?

LOUISE. I despise the piano.

ANNIE. Well, there is the library; you can read.

LOUISE (*contemptuously*). Read! There is nothing in the library but rusty old law books and dry histories, and who wants to read such stuff?

ANNIE. O, Louise, I am afraid you will always make yourself miserable.

LOUISE. Indeed, Miss Propriety!

ANNIE. No one can be happy unless they are useful.

LOUISE. You are such a little pharisee. Do n't you know that our aunt, who lives in New York, is going to leave me a fortune.

ANNIE. I have heard of it. But money will not make you happy, unless you are good.

LOUISE. I know money will make me happy. Just wait till I get that fortune! I 'll ride in a fine carriage, and I 'll go to dancing school, and I 'll have a set of diamonds, and I 'll—

*Enter* KATE *and* LULY.

KATE. O, girls, there is a beggar at the gate!

LULY. And she is dressed so funny!

KATE. And she wants to come in.

LOUISE. She shall not come in here.

ANNIE (*rises from her chair*). Yes, she shall come in, for pa says we must always be kind to the poor.

LOUISE. Never mind; when I get my fortune I 'll let you see if beggars come in *my* house.

KATE. Your fortune!

LOUISE. Yes; *my* fortune! My aunt is going to make me rich because I am her namesake.

LULY. O, mercy!

KATE. I think I see you with a fortune now!

LOUISE. Silence, miss! You are nothing but a poor, dependent orphan, and have no right to express your opinion.

ANNIE. Shame, Louise! [*Turns to* KATE *and* LULY.] Go bring the old beggar in. [*Exit* KATE *and* LULY.]

LOUISE. Ridiculous! The idea of bringing in our house every rag-tag that comes along.

ANNIE. You are unfeeling!

LOUISE. No, I am not; but I despise *poor* people.

ANNIE. How can you talk so? [*Turns to the door.*] But here they come; pray, Louise, do not hurt the old woman's feelings.

*Enter* Old Woman, KATE, *and* LULY.

ANNIE. Have a seat, good woman. [*Hands chair.*] Are you tired?

OLD WOMAN.   Yes, lady; I have traveled a long way.

ANNIE.   Are you hungry?

OLD WOMAN.   No, lady; but I would like a drink of water.

ANNIE (*to* LULY).   Go bring some water.   [*Exit* LULY.
*To* Old Woman.]   You look feeble.   How old are you?

OLD WOMAN.   I can not tell.

LOUISE.   No wonder; you look like you come out of
Noah's ark.

*Enter* LULY.   *Hands* Old Woman *water.*

LOUISE.   Why did n't you make one of the servants do
that?

LULY.   Because I 'm not like you; too lazy to wait on
other people.

LOUISE.   You are a jewel!

OLD WOMAN.   Are you all sisters, young ladies?

ANNIE.   All but Kate; she is our cousin.

LOUISE.   It is none of *your* business.

OLD WOMAN.   Are you rich, young lady?

LOUISE.   No—but I will be.

OLD WOMAN.   Do you know I am a fortune-teller?

ALL.   Indeed!

LOUISE.   Do you tell fortunes with coffee-grounds or
with cards?

OLD WOMAN.   Neither.   I tell by looking in the palm of
the hand.

ANNIE (*reaches out her hand*).   Do tell mine.

OLD WOMAN (*takes* ANNIE'S *hand; looks in it*).   Yours is
a bright fortune, lady.   You will be very rich, and very
happy, too, because you love to make others happy.   [*Lets
fall the hand.*]

KATE.   I thought it was Louise that is to be rich.

LOUISE.   Who made you so wise?   [*Gives her hand to
the* Old Woman.]   Now tell mine!

[Old Woman *holds Louise's hand and shakes her head sor-
rowfully.*]

LOUISE.   What now?   Do you see any thing so dreadful
in my hand?

OLD WOMAN.   I see sorrow and disappointment!   You
will be covered with grief before another week!

LOUISE.   I will be covered with money, you mean; for I
am to get a great fortune.

OLD WOMAN. It is no such thing!

LOUISE. You are wonderful wise: but I'll see if you are not put out of this house. Madame Impudence!

ANNIE. Come, my good woman, and I will show you where you may lie down and rest.

OLD WOMAN. Thank you, lady. [*Turns to* LOUISE *as she rises.*] I pray you be less selfish and conquer that dreadful temper.

LOUISE (*approaches* Old Woman). The sooner you get out of this room the better. [*Pushes* Old Woman *by the shoulder.*]

(*Curtain falls.*)


## SCENE II.

KATE *and* LULY *seated.* Old Woman *reclining on a sofa.*

LULY. I would like to see that rich aunt of ours; wonder what she looks like?

KATE. Goodness knows. I never saw any body as rich as she is.

LULY. I don't believe she would give the fortune to Louise if she knew how ill-natured she is.

KATE. I hope you will not tell her.

LULY. Of course not.

KATE. I wonder what Louise will do with the money?

LULY. She will hold on to it like wax; for she is too stingy to give a cent away.

KATE. I must ring the bell for the servants. It is time for us to dress. [*Rings bell.*]

*Enter* SUSAN *and* MARY.

LULY (*rises*). We want you to stay here and take care of this old woman while we dress to receive our rich aunt.

SUSAN and MARY. Yes ma'm.

KATE. And take good care of her, for we must not let the poor suffer if the rich are in the house.

OLD WOMAN. Who taught you to be so thoughtful about poor people?

LULY. Sister Annie. Ever since our mother died she makes us say our prayers and behave properly.

6

OLD WOMAN. Does not your sister Louise teach you, too?

KATE. Louise!

LULY. It would look funny to see Louise teach any body to be good.

SUSAN. Miss Louise had better learn to be good herself before she teaches other people!

KATE. Well, don't express your opinion till it is asked.

MARY. If she kicked and cuffed you about like she does us, I'll be bound you'd speak.

LULY. Well, she is going to be rich soon, and then she will always be in a good humor.

SUSAN. All the money in the world won't make people good, if they are not so naturally.

MARY. That's a fact! You can't pull silk out of a sow's ear, nor squeeze blood out of a turnip.

(*Curtain falls.*)

## SCENE III.

*Room in confusion. Enter* SUSAN *and* MARY, *with brooms in hand.*

MARY. I never saw such a house as this is in all my life; every thing is turned up-side down.

SUSAN. It's all the fault of that sloven, Miss Louise. She never puts any thing to rights.

MARY. I don't know what that aunt of hers is going to leave her a fortune for.

SUSAN. She had a sight better give it to Miss Annie, for Miss Louise has got the big-head so bad now that if she gets a fortune I'm afraid her head will burst.

MARY. I do despise Miss Louise.

SUSAN. I do, too; but maybe, when she grows older, she'll grow better.

MARY. Yes, in a horn; when she gets to be good, ducks will fly with their backs down.

SUSAN Hush, for goodness' sake! She is coming—I see her. [SUSAN *and* MARY *busy themselves cleaning the room.*]

*Enter* LOUISE.

LOUISE. Mercy on me—you two lazy things! haven't cleaned this room yet!

MARY. We are cleaning it fast as we can.

LOUISE. My aunt will be here this very night.

SUSAN. How do you know?

LOUISE. Pa got a dispatch, and she will be here in an hour.

MARY (*to* SUSAN). Gal! we had better hurry.

LOUISE. You had that—get out of my way! [*Pushes them aside.*] I must fix up and look as pretty as I can. [*Goes to the mirror.*] I am determined to make a *scene* when my aunt comes. I am going to cry, and laugh, and hug her, and kiss her, and make her think I love her better than sugar!

MARY (*aside*). You'll never look pretty.

SUSAN. O, look! here come the other girls. [*Looks toward the door.*]

MARY. And the old woman, as I live!

*Enter all.*

LOUISE (*turns to* Old Woman). What are you doing here, you old trap? Nobody wants you to be prying into family affairs!

ANNIE. O, Louise, let the old woman alone. We came to tell you that our aunt will be here in a few minutes.

LOUISE. Well, Miss Wisdom, I knew that before. Don't you see I am fixing to meet her. I'll make her think I'm an angel till I get her money, and then she may go to Guinea for all I care!

ANNIE. Don't you love her for any thing but her money?

LOUISE. O, you are so green!

ANNIE. I love her, although I have never seen her, because she is our dear dead mother's sister.

LOUISE. You are so sanctified. I don't care a button for old aunty, if she will just give me her money. I intend to honey her up and make her think I love her, and *she* will never know the difference. [Old Woman *throws off her cloak and hood, and comes forward.*]

OLD WOMAN. Poor, mistaken girl! *I* am your aunt. I am sorry for your terrible disappointment. I took the garb

of a beggar to test the disposition of my nieces, and I find
that you are selfish and vain and wicked, while Annie is all
that is good, gentle, and kind.  Therefore, instead of giving *you* the fortune, I will give it to Annie, except one
thousand dollars I reserve for Kate, who is a poor, dependent orphan.  [MARY *and* SUSAN *clap their hands and jump
with glee.*]

BOTH.   O, I am so glad! I am so glad!  [LOUISE *comes
forward and kneels before* Old Woman.]

LOUISE.   O, aunt, forgive me for being so wicked.

ANNIE.   Give the fortune to Louise.   She will be so unhappy.

KATE (*comes forward*).   My dear madam, I wish you to
give the money you intend for me to Louise.   I am sure she
will never be selfish and ill-natured again.

OLD WOMAN.   No, my children, I shall not give Louise
one cent!  Her punishment is just, and I hope it may be
the means of making her a better woman.   You will all
learn from her example that, as Solomon says, [*turns to
audience,*] "A good name is rather to be chosen than great
riches, and loving favor better than silver and gold."

(*Curtain falls.*)


[*The attitudes in this last scene should be well studied, so as
to form an interesting tableau as the curtain falls.*]


## COSTUMES.

### SCENE I.

ANNIE.   Dress of checked gingham, white collar and cuffs.
Hair plain.

LOUISE.   Dress of gay-colored de laine, white collar and
cuffs.  Hair plain.

KATE and LULY.   Plain home dresses.

OLD WOMAN.   A black dress, over which is thrown a short
cloak, in gypsy style; an old bonnet; a staff in her hand.

### SCENE II.

The same as the first scene.

### SCENE III.

LOUISE. Dress of white tarlatan, suitably trimmed for a girl of fourteen.

ANNIE. A light silk or poplin, with the proper embellishments for a girl of sixteen.

OLD WOMAN. Throws off her cloak, and appears in a neat black silk; a becoming dress-cap upon her head.

SUSAN and MARY. Dressed as house-maids

# PREPOSITION *vs.* PROPOSITION.

## CHARACTERS.

ANABEL SHELBY, *Cousin to Mary.*
MARY OBANNON, } *Sisters.*
AGNES OBANNON, }
JAMES COMPTON.
Servant.

## SCENE I.

*Room in home style.* ANABEL *and* MARY *seated, dressed neatly.*

MARY. What is the reason, cousin, that you will not marry James Compton? He is rich and handsome, and I know he loves you.

ANABEL. Mary, we have always been friends, and you are entitled to my confidence; yet you will laugh when I tell you, in truth, why I can not marry Mr. Compton.

MARY (*eagerly*). Well, *do* tell me, for I am dying to know.

ANABEL. You speak extravagantly.

MARY (*impatiently*). Tell me if you intend to, Anabel; for we have already been so long away from the parlor that mother will wonder where we are *at.*

ANABEL. There! you have saved me a long explanation. I will not be the wife of Mr. Compton simply because he is constantly committing, in conversation, the little blunder you just this moment made.

MARY. And, pray, to what blunder do you allude? I was not conscious of making a blunder.

ANABEL. Why, sticking the little word "at" to the end of almost every question or sentence you utter.

MARY. I stand corrected, cousin. I have often thought

of the careless habit you mention, and as often determined to break myself.

ANABEL. It is not strange, Mary, that you should fall into the common error; for I assure you that every third person I have met since my stay in Kentucky indulges in the same careless habit. You do not know how it grated on my ear at first, and, in fact, still does.

MARY. And is this the *only* fault you find in James Compton?

ANABEL (*decidedly*). It is.

MARY. And would you cast aside the love of a faithful heart for so slight a cause?

ANABEL. I consider, Mary, that "*little* things make up the sum of human bliss or misery." When I left Virginia to make my present visit, many of my friends prophesied that I would find a husband in Kentucky, and since my acquaintance with Mr. Compton I have thought their prophecy might be fulfilled. I have marked his graceful form, and looked at his fine features, lighted as they are with frankness and intelligence, and the thought of presenting him to my circle of relatives and friends at home would for the time thrill my bosom with pride; but ah! this "fairy vision" would crumble and fall beneath the weight of that little word *at*.

MARY. I am ready to cry. I was just thinking of James Compton and his wealth, position, and handsome person. He has been in the State Senate, and has been actually spoken of for Congress. Half the girls in Frankfort are head and ears in love with him, and *you* could bear off the prize so easily but for that miserable little *at*.

*Enter* AGNES.

AGNES. Sister Mary, what are you and cousin Anabel thinking about? Mother sent me to look for you. She says Mr. Compton has been waiting to see you for at least fifteen minutes.

MARY. Where is he *at?* [*Looks mischievously at* ANABEL.]

AGNES (*mimics* MARY.) He is *at* the parlor. Our teacher says we ought not to ask where is any thing *at*.

MARY. Really, your teacher must be a Virginian. Didn't she come from Richmond?

AGNES. Sister Mary, you know Miss Martin came from

New York, and she says the New Yorkers don't say "at," like the Kentucky people.

MARY. And I suppose she has come here to revolutionize Kentucky.

AGNES. No, she didn't say *that;* all she said was that it surprised her when she asked Judge Sanders to patronize her school, he asked where she taught *at;* and told all the scholars not to say "at" that way.

MARY. I hope Miss Martin and you, together, will bring things straight. Ask her if she wants any new scholars? Tell her that old Mr. Compton has a son who wants to learn to talk so that he can visit in the first families of Virginia without making his friends ashamed of him.

ANABEL (*severely*). Mary Obanon! if I did not know you so well I would be very angry; but you may be as sarcastic as you like, I will not recall what I have said.

MARY (*coaxingly*). Do not get mad with your best friend, Anabel. I was fretted to think you would allow such a little thing to have so much weight; besides, you know that Virginians, as a general thing, are so arrogant.

ANABEL. You have forgotten what one of your great lawyers, Mr. Thompson, said in a speech in my hearing, that "Frankfort was the biggest little place in the world."

MARY. Well, well! we will lay aside sparring, for a while at least, and join our hero in the parlor.

(*Curtain falls.*)


SCENE II.

*Same room, occupied by* MARY, *seated near a table, sewing.*
*Enter* JAMES COMPTON.

COMPTON. Is it possible I find you alone, Mary? Where is your fair cousin, Miss Shelby?

MARY. She went to Lexington on the train to-day to visit her relations there, and will not return for several days.

COMPTON. I am glad of it.

MARY. I scarcely credit this assertion, James, for you must know that we have all noticed your growing partiality for cousin Anabel.

COMPTON. I do not deny my admiration. But I am glad Miss Shelby is absent; for I was anxious to question you concerning her. I am certain, Mary, that you are aware of my love for your cousin, and I believe, too, that you know why she rejects that love. I have thought sometimes that she favored my suit, but at other times there is such a marked coldness in her manner that I can not comprehend her real sentiments. Ah, Mary, from your tell-tale face I fear there is something more serious than I expected.

MARY. It is a great pity that you and Anabel can not be married. You love each other so much.

COMPTON (*eagerly*). Then you think she loves me?

MARY. I *know* she loves you, but she would be very angry if she knew I had told you.

COMPTON. Then why does she refuse to accept me?

MARY. The reason is so simple that really I fear to tell.

COMPTON (*rises and walks to and fro*). For mercy's sake, Mary, end this suspense.

MARY. Well, James, if nothing else will do, and you *must* know, the truth is this: you have, in the presence of my high-born, aristocratic cousin, committed the unpardonable sin of misapplying the little preposition *at*.

COMPTON (*in surprise*). Mary!

MARY. Do not interrupt me; I will tell the whole story. You have at various times been guilty of this gross blunder. For instance, the last visit you made here, as you were about leaving, you very innocently asked Agnes, "Where is my hat at?" Now this is too much for the refined taste of Miss Shelby, and grates upon her aristocratic ear!

COMPTON (*draws himself up proudly*). The nation it does!

MARY. It is useless to grind your teeth, or bite your nails, or to indulge in theatricals generally. The only thing for you to do is to correct this abominable habit, and Anabel is yours. [*Rises to leave the room.*] So, Mr. James Compton, put that in your pipe and smoke it. [*Exit MARY.*]

COMPTON (*advances; twirls his hat on his hand*). And this is the woman I have loved with such fond devotion! To throw away a love like mine for such a cause! I will banish her, together with her airs and graces, forever from my heart! [*Walks to and fro; curls his lip.*] Humph! a great story indeed, that because a fellow is guilty of using

7

a provincialism he is to be hissed at and spit upon by a contemptible Virginia aristocrat. [*Puts his hand to his forehead and pauses.*] What a fool love makes of a man! I wish I could forget this girl! I wish I had never seen her! [*Twirls his hat.*] ' Where is my hat at—eh? Ha! ha!

(*Curtain falls.*)


## SCENE III.

*Room as in Scene I.* ANABEL *dressed in traveling costume, standing near a table looking over a newspaper. Enter* MARY.

MARY (*approaches* ANABEL; *kisses her*). O, cousin! I am so glad you have returned. We are to have a grand masquerade and fancy ball at the Capitol this evening, and I was afraid you would not get here in time.

ANABEL. I heard of the ball. Indeed I received an invitation while I was in Lexington, and came expressly to attend it. But I must get you to decide my costume; you have so much taste.

MARY. Away with your flattery, cousin. The very name of masquerade carries with it, to me, romance. I begin to think directly of gallant knights, gay cavaliers, and fine ladies of the olden time, grim castles, old ruins, and a host of other things. Come, rouse yourself, Anabel, and let us put our wits to work a d decide the characters we will assume.

ANABEL. Indeed, Mary, you must choose for me.

MARY. If you are in earnest, and insist upon it, my decision is soon made. I always wanted to see you arrayed as a *bride.* The wreath of orange blossoms will contrast so beautifully with your dark hair; and, then, the rich, flowing veil! O, my! I can scarcely wait until to-night.

ANABEL. You little impulsive witch! And, pray, what character do you intend to personate? Something mischievous, no doubt?

*Enter* AGNES.

AGNES. There are some ladies in the parlor, sister, who have called to see you about the ball.

MARY (*to* ANABEL). We will decide upon my character after these ladies are gone. Till then, fair cousin Anabel, adieu. [*Courtesies and kisses her hand playfully.*]

(*Curtain falls.*)

## SCENE IV.

*A room.* ANABEL *is in full bridal attire before a mirror; her servant (a negro girl) is giving the "finishing touch" to* ANABEL'S *dress.*

DEBBY (*walks round* ANABEL; *looks proudly at her*). Dar now, chile; de ball is wound, and you looks good enough to eat.

ANABEL. Ah, aunt Debby, you are an old flatterer; you always say I look well.

DEBBY (*places the wreath on* ANABEL'S *head*). To be sure! and you always does look *purty*, chile. Now, if you don't caper round and git your *skeerts* all mussed up. dar ain't no dress in dat ball-room gwine to look like yourn; but if Miss Mary 'Bannon 's comin' in here fust, dar ain't no tellin'. She so wild and skittish like.

ANABEL. You should not speak so of Mary, aunt Debby; she is so kind.

DEBBY. Well, honey, I know she 's kine; but, law! she wild as a deer. [*Knock heard at the door.*] I 'spec dat her now. [*Opens the door ; a decrepit old woman appears ; advances toward* ANABEL.]

OLD WOMAN (*in a trembling voice*). I saw a light in this room, lady, and your beautiful face, through the window, and I made bold to come in and ask your charity. I 've traveled a lonely road to-day, and I am tired and hungry.

ANABEL. Have you no home?

OLD WOMAN. Yes, lady; but it 's a long way off.

DEBBY (*aside*). I 'll bet she 's possumin'.

ANABEL. How did you gain access to this room?

OLD WOMAN. Where there is so much show and glitter a poor body like me can slip along without notice. There 's few that care for a poor, starving old woman. [*Sobs audibly.*]

ANABEL (*takes her purse from the table, opens it, hands Old Woman a coin*). Here, my good woman, if this will be of any use, take it. [*Old Woman drops her cloak and mask, and discovers* MARY OBANON.]

MARY (*laughing*). Keep your gold, cousin, and I will say after this, that if Virginians are arrogant, they are also charitable and generous.

ANABEL. O, you wild creature! And is this the garb you have chosen for the ball?

MARY. And why not? If I can so easily deceive you, I will be safe with strangers. Won't I have sport, testing the liberality of the beaux? But, Anabel [*takes her hand, draws toward front of stage*], come nearer the light! How becoming your dress is! Poor Jim Compton, how I pity him.

ANABEL. O, Mary, how can you rattle so! [*Sighs.*]

MARY. Why do you sigh, cousin? I am sure Mr. Compton is devoted to you, and you are a great simpleton not to marry him, especially as he seems to have overcome the abominable little at. I have been watching him closely, and he has positively not used it, or misused it, since you went to Lexington. But I must be off; and Compton is waiting for you below. This, till we meet again. [*Kisses her hand.*]                                   [*Exit* MARY.]

(*Curtain falls.*)


## SCENE V.

*Stage decorated as a grove or arbor.* JAMES COMPTON *and* ANABEL *promenading.* ANABEL *dressed in bridal costume as before.*

COMPTON. Anabel, why is it that you persist in rejecting my suit? Do you doubt me?

ANABEL. I do not doubt you, Mr. Compton, but—

COMPTON (*eagerly*). Speak! tell me, are my attentions indeed distasteful? Say!

*Enter a mask in the dress of a Gypsy girl, with a guitar swung carelessly across her shoulders by a gay ribbon.*

GYPSY (*approaches* ANABEL). Truly, this is a night for lovers. Come! let me read your destiny by the moon's pale light. [*Catches* ANABEL'S *hand; looks in the palm.*] Ah!

lady, yours is a bright future. The luxury of wealth, the idol of a happy home, and, above all, the homage of one faithful heart. [*Drops* ANABEL'S *hand.*]

COMPTON. This is flattering. [*Holds forth his hand.*] Now, my damsel, what can you say for me? [*Gypsy takes his hand; looks in it; shakes her head ominously.*]

COMPTON (*impatiently*). What do you see?

GYPSY (*drops his hand*). I would rather not read your fate. Crosses and disappointments often fill up the web of life.

COMPTON (*contemptuously*). You are, perhaps, no adept in your art.

GYPSY (*sighs*). Perhaps so. Every heart knows its own sorrow.

ANABEL. You are becoming too serious for the things around us. Come, let us have a song. [*Points to the guitar.*]

GYPSY (*arranges the instrument and sings. Tune,* " Rosin the Beau.")

> A gentleman, noble and great,
>   Loved a lady bewitchingly fair;
> He wanted his warm love returned,
>   And his feelings he wished to declare.
> He sought the dear girl of his heart—
>   In a sweet shaded bower she sat—
> But his offer she treated with scorn
>   Just because the poor lover said *at*—
>   Just because the poor lover said *at*.

COMPTON. O, you witch! [*Releasing* ANABEL'S *arm, springs forward, tears the mask from the face of the singer; it is* MARY OBANON.]

MARY (*coming forward*). I hope you will pardon me; but it was a pity this little matter should remain unexplained when it presented so small a barrier to so much happiness. [*Turns to* ANABEL.] I am sure my cousin will thank me for correcting a trivial fault in the man of her choice. [*Turns to* COMPTON.] Of *your* forgiveness I am certain.

COMPTON. *My* forgiveness, Mary! Yes; from my heart. But ANABEL has not said yet that I am the man of her choice.

MARY. O! but she *will!* Will you not, cousin?

ANABEL (*places her hand in that of* COMPTON). This is no time for false modesty. I have but one word to say— Yes!

MARY. As this is settled, and Miss Anabel Shelby has consented to become the wife of Mr. James Compton, I would like to make one inquiry.

ANABEL and COMPTON. Name it.

MARY. Well! I would like to know when the wedding will take place, and where it will be celebrated *at?*

COMPTON. All this you shall know in due time.

(*Curtain falls.*)

In the Fourth Scene, MARY OBANON is dressed as an old beggar woman. In the Fifth Scene, she is dressed as a Gypsy dancing girl; a red petticoat (short) and a fancy bodice; a jaunty hat upon her head.

# THE MECHANIC'S DAUGHTER.

FOR MIXED SCHOOLS.

---

## CHARACTERS.

Mrs. NELSON, *Daughter to* Mrs. MURRAY.
Mrs. MURRAY, *Mother to* HORACE.
Aunt AILSIE, *Sister to* Mrs. MURRAY.
HORACE.
SUSAN, }
MARY. } *Sisters to* HORACE.
ELIZA, *a Servant.*

---

## SCENE.

*A room neatly furnished. Aunt AILSIE seated with a hank of yarn on her lap.*

AUNT AILSIE (*in a loud, shrill voice*). Mary! Mary! [*Enter* MARY.] Come here and hold this yarn for me to wind. [MARY *approaches;* Aunt AILSIE *puts the hank across* MARY's *hands.*] Where have you been all day?

MARY. At sister Lucy Jane's; and, law! Aunt Ailsie, what do you think?

AUNT AILSIE. That would be hard to tell; I think so many things.

MARY. Sister Lucy Jane's Jennie told me that our 'Liza told her that brother Horace was courting Miss Louisa Lorraine!

AUNT AILSIE. You are a pretty chap to be talking about courting. But children now-a-days are ahead of me. Who is Miss Louisa Lorraine?

MARY. Law! don't you know? Why, she is the tinner's daughter.

AUNT AILSIE (*excitedly*). *What?* A *tinner's* daughter! [*Jumps up; throws the yarn one way and the chair the other.*]

Mercy on me! Go call your mother. I must see into this matter. [*Exit* MARY. *Walks to and fro; fans herself.*] The idea of one of the Murrays courting the daughter of a mechanic! O, we are all *ruined!*

*Enter* Mrs. MURRAY, MARY, *and* SUSAN.

Mrs. MURRAY. What do you want with me, Ailsie?

AUNT AILSIE. We are all about to be disgraced! That little wretch, Eliza, is raising a report that will *ruin* us!

Mrs. MURRAY. Indeed! what is it?

AUNT AILSIE. Ask Mary.

Mrs. MURRAY (*turns to* MARY). What news is this you have been tattling?

MARY. I wasn't tattling. Our 'Liza told sister Lucy Jane's Jennie that brother Horace was courting the tinner's daughter.

Mrs. MURRAY (*agitated*). What tinner's daughter? Who is she? Where does she live?

SUSAN. I will tell you, ma. You know that big still over the door of that big shop on Main Street? That is the place.

Mrs. MURRAY. Goodness gracious! What does all this mean? [*To* MARY.] Go call Eliza. [*Exit* MARY.] Sister Ailsie, did you ever hear of any thing so ridiculous?

AUNT AILSIE (*fanning furiously*). Never in my life! There must be some mistake! some mistake! some mistake!

*Enter* MARY *and* ELIZA.

Mrs. MURRAY. You little vixen, come here! What tale is this you have been telling about your master Horace courting this Miss ——! What do you call her? [*Turns to* MARY.]

MARY. Miss Louisa Lorraine.

Mrs. MURRAY. Yes, Louisa Lorraine. You minx! I'll twist your neck off! Who put you up to this wickedness?

ELIZA. Nobody didn't put me up to it. 'Kase Mr. Moore's Sam told our Jim that Miss Smith's Patsy said that Randall's *Ben* told *her* that marse Horace writ Miss Louisa Lorraine a love-letter.

Mrs. MURRAY. A high story, indeed! And how came Randall's Ben to know so much? Did Miss Lorraine tell him?

ELIZA. No, marm; but he say he knowed it was a love-letter, 'kase she turned red as a beet in de face when he gin it to her.

AUNT AILSIE. You ought to whip Eliza severely for raising this report, for I know she made it.

ELIZA. No I did n't make it, bekase Miss Smith's Patsy said Randall's Ben told—

MRS. MURRAY. Do n't you say Randall's Ben again; if you do I 'll shake the life out of you. Where did your master Horace get acquainted with this tinner's daughter?

ELIZA. At Miss Lucy Nelson's, marm. Dey lives next door to Miss Lucy.

MRS. MURRAY. It is just as I expected. Lucy Jane always had a hankering after low people. [*To* ELIZA.] Go this instant and tell your Miss Lucy Jane to come to me.

ELIZA (*starts toward the door*). Yes, marm.

MRS. MURRAY. Come back here. Now listen! If you tell your Miss Lucy Jane what I want I 'll murder you!

ELIZA (*starts again*). Yes, marm.

MRS. MURRAY (*stamps her foot*). Come back here, you imp! Tell your Miss Lucy Jane to come quick. Now fly!

ELIZA. Yes, marm. [*Exit* ELIZA.]

SUSAN (*coming forward*). O, Mary, if brother Horace marries Miss Louisa Lorraine, we can get as many tin-cups and corn-poppers as we want for nothing.

MARY. And pa can have a tin roof and new gutters put on the house, because—

AUNT AILSIE. Silence, children; you make me nervous.

MRS. MURRAY. I wonder if you think a *Murray* would disgrace the name by marrying the daughter of a tinner?

AUNT AILSIE. You forget, children, that you belong to one of the *first families of Virginia!*

*Enter* Mrs. NELSON *in haste; falls on a chair.* *Enter* ELIZA.

MRS. NELSON. O, ma! what is the matter? I was lying on the divan in the parlor, asleep, and that little wretch [*shakes her fist at* ELIZA] came in and woke me, saying that you said I must come here directly, and that if she told me what you wanted you would skin her alive; and that it was something dreadful!

MRS. MURRAY. And it *is* something dreadful. It will be a blow from which the *Murray* family can never recover!

Mrs. NELSON. Well! I have made up my mind to bear it all. What is it? Is any body dead?

Mrs. MURRAY. There is no necessity for being so frightened. Nobody is dead; but we are all about being disgraced, and all owing to *your* imprudence.

Mrs. NELSON (*in surprise*). *My* imprudence! [*Rises from her seat.*] What do you mean?

Mrs. MURRAY. Why, I mean that you have struck up an intimacy with old Lorraine's family, and now it is reported all over this town that *your* brother Horace is courting the *tinner's* daughter!

Mrs. NELSON. I am not intimate with old Lorraine, as you call him.

AUNT AILSIE. You do n't deny going to their house?

Mrs. NELSON. No. But Miss Louisa was kind enough to come and stay with me while Mr. Nelson was gone, and I only went out of gratitude to see them.

Mrs. MURRAY (*raising her hands in horror*). You do n't tell me, Lucy Jane, that you have really been in old Lorraine's house!

Mrs. NELSON. Yes, I went there once; but it was nearly dark, and I did not think any body would see me; and, besides, whose business is it where I go?

Mrs. MURRAY. Well! you see what your imprudence has done! Your brother Horace met this girl at your house, and now his name is bandied all around town with hers.

Mrs. NELSON. I can not help it. Miss Lorraine is beautiful, and brother Horace might do worse than marry her, if she *is* a tinner's daughter.

AUNT AILSIE. Why, Lucy Jane, I am astonished to hear you talk so.

Mrs. NELSON. Well, you need not be; for, besides being pretty, Miss Lorraine is accomplished. She plays, and sings, and understands French, and—

Mrs. MURRAY. One thing is certain: she shall never marry *my* son!

Mrs. NELSON. What are you going to do about it?

Mrs. MURRAY. Why, I will see Horace and sift this thing to the bottom.

Mrs. NELSON. That will not do any good; for when a young man falls in love he won't listen to reason.

Mrs. MURRAY. Reason, indeed! I will never give my

consent for Horace to marry this low-born daughter of a mechanic!

Mrs. NELSON. O, ma! you are so imprudent. Miss Lorraine might hear of something you have said, and I would not hurt the poor girl's feelings.

AUNT AILSIE. Mechanic's daughters have no business having feelings.

Mrs. NELSON. O, Aunt Ailsie!

AUNT AILSIE. You need n't "Aunt Ailsie" me. I have no regard for people who want to step out of their place. There never was a *mechanic* in *my* father's parlor.

MARY. I do n't know how he got his parlor built unless there was a mechanic in it.

AUNT AILSIE. You are too pert, miss! No doubt, when you get old enough, you will be running off to be married to some trifling mechanic.

MARY. I would rather do that than be a dried-up old maid like you.

Mrs. MURRAY. Mary! Mary! leave the room this instant, you sauce-box. [*Exit* MARY.]

Mrs. NELSON. I wonder where brother Horace is? I would like to have this matter settled before I go home.

SUSAN. O, ma, I hear him whistling in the hall now. [*Whistle outside.*]

Mrs. MURRAY. Call him in. I will make the youngster give an account of himself. [*Exit* SUSAN.]

Mrs. NELSON. Ma, you are too impulsive. Do not be too hard on poor Horace.

Mrs. MURRAY (*stamps her foot*). Silence, Lucy Jane!

*Enter* HORACE *and* SUSAN.

HORACE. What can be the matter? Susan came running after me, and says the whole house is topsy-turvy, and I can make no sense out of any thing she says.

Mrs. MURRAY. O, yes, master Horace, you just do n't want to understand!

HORACE. I do not understand *you*, certainly.

AUNT AILSIE. You are a nice young man!

Mrs. NELSON. O, Horace! you are going to catch it!

HORACE (*looks bewildered*). What does all this mean? I would as soon be in a yellow-jacket's nest as have so many women's tongues lashing me.

AUNT AILSIE (*exultingly*). Maybe you would rather be in old Lorraine's tin-shop.

HORACE. What do you know of old Lorraine's tin-shop?

MRS. MURRAY. Not as much as Mr. Horace Murray knows of old Lorraine's *daughter*, if all reports are true.

HORACE. To what reports do you allude?

MRS. MURRAY. Do you know that it is the common talk of the town that you are courting the tinner's daughter? [*Sneers.*]

HORACE. Where did you get your information?

MRS. MURRAY (*points to* ELIZA). From Eliza, there.

HORACE. O, ho! I see the news comes through an "intelligent contraband." Well, my ma, since it is fashionable to receive information through such sources, I suppose I must pardon you for listening to negro news.

MRS. MURRAY. You do not deny an acquaintance with this dainty Miss Lorraine?

HORACE (*bowing*). Indeed, I do not.

AUNT AILSIE. You do not deny going to her house?

HORACE. I do not deny that either.

MRS. NELSON. You do not deny being in love with her?

HORACE. I do not, assuredly.

ELIZA (*grinning*). You don't deny sending her dat love-letter, does you, marse Horace?

HORACE. No, indeed—I do not.

MRS. MURRAY (*raises her hands despairingly*). O, Horace!

HORACE. With due deference to you, my aristocratic mother, I acknowledge that I did make Miss Lorraine an offer of my hand and fortune.

MRS. MURRAY. Well, sir, I will undo all you have done.

HORACE. It is unnecessary.

MRS. MURRAY. It is not unnecessary! I will write a note to this plebeian girl and decline the alliance!

HORACE. I tell you it is needless. Here, sister, [*to* MRS. NELSON, *takes a letter from his pocket,*] this is Miss Lorraine's answer to my proposal. Read it for the benefit of the house.

MRS. NELSON (*takes the letter, approaches front of stage, reads*): "Mr. Horace Murray: I received your courteous note containing an offer of your hand and fortune; but, under existing circumstances, must decline the honor you wish to confer upon me. Respectfully, LOUISA LORRAINE."

AUNT AILSIE (*approaches* Mrs. NELSON, *places her hand to her ear, assumes a listening attitude*). Read that again; I am a little hard of hearing.

Mrs. NELSON (*reads in a much louder tone*). "Mr. Horace Murray: I received your courteous note containing an offer of your hand and fortune; but, under existing circumstances, must decline the honor you wish to confer upon me. Respectfully,                                    LOUISA LORRAINE."

AUNT AILSIE. Well! well! well!

Mrs. MURRAY. The up-start! to reject my son.

Mrs. NELSON. Horace, what does she mean by "existing circumstances?"

HORACE. That, sister, is easily explained; for Miss Lorraine was married this very morning to Brigadier-general John A. B. C. Smith!

AUNT AILSIE. Well! well! The idea of a brigadier-general marrying the daughter of a tinner! It is my opinion that aristocracy is played out in this part of the country. [*All retire to back of stage, but* ELIZA, *who comes forward.*]

ELIZA. I knowed it! I knowed it!—counting chickens before dey is hatched! Dis is what white folks git by listening to nigger news. [*Sings* "O, I wish I was in Dixie!"]

(*Curtain falls.*)

------

## COSTUMES.

Mrs. MURRAY. Dark silk dress, modern style; handsome cap; gold-rimmed spectacles.

AUNT AILSIE. A true type of a Virginia aristocrat of the olden time. Black satin dress; cap elaborately trimmed; spectacles; a large fan.

Mrs. NELSON. Plain home dress, fashionably made.

MARY and SUSAN. Home dresses, of modern style.

HORACE. Plain citizen's dress.

ELIZA. Cotton (striped) dress, waist-apron, gaudy-colored head-handkerchief.

# THE MECHANIC'S DAUGHTER.

ARRANGED IN A MANNER TO BE ACTED BY GIRLS
ALONE.

---

## CHARACTERS.

Mrs. MURRAY, *Mother to* HORACE.
Aunt AILSIE, *Sister to* Mrs. MURRAY.
Mrs. NELSON,
SUSAN,     } *Daughters to* Mrs. MURRAY.
MARY,
ELIZA, *a Servant.*

---

## SCENE.

*Room.* AUNT AILSIE *seated, holding a hank of yarn across
her lap.*

AUNT AILSIE (*in a shrill voice*). Mary! Mary! [*Enter*
MARY.] Come here and hold this yarn for me to wind.
[MARY *approaches and takes the yarn.*] Where have you
been all day?
MARY. I've been to sister Lucy Jane's; and, *law!* Aunt
Ailsie, what do you think?
AUNT AILSIE. That would be hard to say; I think so
many things.
MARY. Well, sister Lucy Jane's Jennie told *me* that our
'Liza told her that brother Horace was courting Miss Louisa
Lorraine!
AUNT AILSIE. You are a pretty person to be talking about
courting. [*Turns to audience.*] But children now-a-days
are ahead of me. [*To* MARY.] Who is Miss Louisa Lor-
raine?
MARY. She is the tinner's daughter.
AUNT AILSIE. *What!* a tinner's daughter! [*Jerks the
yarn from* MARY, *rises and pushes back her chair.*] Mercy

on me! Go call your mother, I must see into this matter. [*Exit* MARY. Aunt AILSIE *walks to and fro, rubbing her hands and fanning herself violently.*] The idea of one of the *Murrays* courting a mechanic's daughter! O, we are all ruined!

*Enter* Mrs. MURRAY *and* MARY.

Mrs. MURRAY. What do you want with me, Ailsie?

AUNT AILSIE. We are all about to be disgraced! That little wretch, 'Liza, is raising a report-that will ruin us!

Mrs. MURRAY. Indeed! What is it?

AUNT AILSIE (*fanning herself*). Ask Mary.

Mrs. MURRAY (*to* MARY). What news is this you are tattling?

MARY. I wasn't tattling. 'Liza just told sister Lucy Jane's Jennie that brother Horace was courting the tinner's daughter.

Mrs. MURRAY (*excitedly*). What tinner's daughter? Where does she live? Who is she?

MARY. You know that big still over the door of that high shop on Main Street? That is the place.

Mrs. MURRAY. Goodness gracious! what does all this mean? Go call Eliza. [*Exit* MARY.] Did you [*to* AUNT AILSIE] ever hear of any thing so preposterous?

AUNT AILSIE. Never in my life. [ *Walks about.*]

*Enter* ELIZA, MARY, *and* SUSAN.

Mrs. MURRAY (*to* ELIZA.) You little vixen, come here! What tale is this you have been telling about your master Horace courting this Miss ——— what do you call her? [*To* MARY.]

MARY. Louisa Lorraine.

Mrs. MURRAY. Yes, Louisa Lorraine. You minx! I'll twist your neck off! Who put you up to all this wickedness?

ELIZA. Nobody didn't put me up to no wick'ness. [*Raises her arm and gesticulates.*] Mr. Moore's *Sam* told *our* Jim dat Miss Smith's *Patsy* said dat Miss Brown's Milly 'clared dat Randall's Ben told *her* dat marse Horace writ Miss Lorraine a love-letter!

Mrs. MURRAY. A high story, indeed! And how did Randall's Ben come to know so much? Did Miss Lorraine tell him?

ELIZA. No, marm. But Randall's Ben say he knowed 't was a love-letter, 'kase when he give it to her her face turn red as a beet.

AUNT AILSIE. You ought to whip Eliza *severely* for raising this report, for I know she made it.

ELIZA (*quickly*). No, marm, I didn't make it, 'kase Randall's Ben told ——

Mrs. MURRAY (*angrily*). Don't you say Randall's Ben again! If you do, I'll shake the life out of you! Where did your master Horace get acquainted with this tinner's daughter?

ELIZA. At Miss Lucy Jane Nelson's, ma'm. Dey lives next door to Miss Lucy Jane.

Mrs. MURRAY. It is just as I thought. Lucy Jane always had a hankering after low people. [*To* ELIZA.] Go this instant, and tell your Miss Lucy Jane to come to me!

ELIZA (*starts toward the door*). Yes, marm.

Mrs. MURRAY (*stamps her foot*). Come back here! Now listen! If you tell your Miss Lucy Jane what I want, I'll skin you alive!

ELIZA. Yes, marm. [*Starts again.*]

Mrs. MURRAY. Come back, you imp! Tell your Miss Lucy Jane to come quick. Now fly!

ELIZA. Yes, marm. [*Exit* ELIZA.]

SUSAN. Law, ma, if brother Horace marries the tinner's daughter, we can get as many little patty-pans and tin-cups as we want—for nothing!

MARY. Yes, and pa can have new gutters put to the house, because—

AUNT AILSIE (*impatiently*). Mercy on me! Children, you make me nervous!

Mrs. MURRAY. I wonder if you think a MURRAY would disgrace the name by marrying the daughter of a mechanic?

AUNT AILSIE (*walks about proudly*). You forget, children, that you belong to one of the *first families of Virginia!*

[*Enter* Mrs. NELSON, *falls into a chair and throws off her bonnet.*]

Mrs. NELSON. O, ma! what *is* the matter? I was asleep on the divan, in the parlor, and that little wretched 'Liza [*shakes her fist at* ELIZA] came running in and said you wanted me directly, and that if she told me what you wanted you would skin her alive; but it was something dreadful!

Mrs. MURRAY. It is something dreadful!

Mrs. NELSON. Tell me the worst. I have made up my mind to bear it. Is any body dead!

Mrs. MURRAY. You need n't look so frightened. Nobody is dead, but we are about to be disgraced, and all owing to your imprudence!

Mrs. NELSON (in amazement). My imprudence! What do you mean?

Mrs. MURRAY. Why you have struck up an intimacy with old Lorraine's family, and now it is reported all over town that your brother Horace is courting the *tinner's* daughter!

Mrs. NELSON. It is a mistake, I can assure you, for I am *not* intimate with "old Lorraine," as you call him.

AUNT AILSIE. You do n't deny going to their house?

Mrs. NELSON. No; but Miss Louisa was kind enough to come and stay with me while Mr. Nelson was gone, and I only went there out of gratitude.

Mrs. MURRAY (clasps her hands). O, Lucy Jane! You do n't tell me that you have been in old Lorraine's house?

Mrs. NELSON. Yes, I went there once; but it was dusk, and I did not think any of our set would see me.

Mrs. MURRAY. Well! see what your imprudence has done. Your brother Horace met this girl at your house, and now his name is bandied about with hers.

Mrs. NELSON. I can't help it. She is as good as brother Horace.

AUNT AILSIE. Why, Lucy Jane! I am astonished at you!

Mrs. NELSON. You needn't be; for, besides being pretty, Miss Lorraine is accomplished. She sings and plays, and understands French and—

Mrs. MURRAY. One thing is certain: she shall never marry *my* son!

Mrs. NELSON. You can't help it. When a young man falls in love, he won't listen to reason!

Mrs. MURRAY (excitedly). I'll let you see whether I can help it or not. [*To* MARY.] Go bring me the pen, ink, and paper. [*Exit* MARY.]

Mrs. Nelson. What will you do?

Mrs. Murray. I am going to write to this dainty and accomplished miss, and tell her what I think.

*Enter* Mary *with writing materials.* Mrs. Murray *seats herself and writes.*

Mrs. Nelson. O, ma! do not hurt the poor girl's feelings.

Aunt Ailsie. Mechanics' daughters have no business having feelings.

Mrs. Nelson. O, *Aunt* Ailsie!

Aunt Ailsie. You need n't "O, Aunt Ailsie" me! I have no patience with people who want to step out of their place. There never was a mechanic in *my* father's parlor!

Mary. I do n't know how he got his parlor built if there never was a mechanic in it.

Aunt Ailsie. You are too pert, miss! No doubt, some of these days you will be running off to be married to some trifling mechanic!

Mary. I had rather do that than to be a dried-up old maid like you.

Mrs. Murray (*rises from her seat*). Mary! Mary! Go out of this room instantly. [*Exit* Mary. *Hands* Mrs. Nelson *a letter.*] Now, read that. I think when Miss Lorraine gets this she will feel humbled.

Mrs. Nelson (*reads aloud*). "Miss Lorraine: I understand, from a reliable source, that you have received a love-letter from my son Horace, and I write this to let you know that if you imagine that he intends to marry you, it is useless to indulge in any such dream of grandeur, as his father and myself will never countenance a marriage between our son and the daughter of a tinner. E. Murray." O, ma! do not send such a note as this.

Mrs. Murray. Lucy Jane, I am not to be interfered with; so, silence! [*To* Eliza.] Take this note and give it to Miss Lorraine.

Eliza. Yes, marm. [*Exit* Eliza.]

Aunt Ailsie. It serves her right. She has no business having such high notions.

Mrs. Nelson. Yes, but I would not hurt an innocent girl's feelings; and, then, what will Horace say?

Mrs. Murray. Horace is not to be consulted. He must not disgrace the family.

Mrs. NELSON. You have done more to disgrace the family, ma, than Horace would by marrying Miss Lorraine, for she would be an ornament to society anywhere.

Mrs. MURRAY. Do you imagine that all Miss Lorraine's accomplishments, as you term it, will ever raise her from obscurity. No man of position would link his fortunes with a mechanic's daughter.

Mrs. NELSON. I am not so sure. But here comes Eliza, out of breath.

*Enter* ELIZA, *panting.*

Mrs. MURRAY. Did you give Miss Lorraine the note?

ELIZA. No, marm, She want thar. But old Miss Lorraine sent dis. [*Hands* Mrs. MURRAY *a note.*]

Mrs. MURRAY. Lucy Jane, read it, and let us hear what the old thing says.

Mrs. NELSON (*comes forward; reads*). "Mrs. Murray: Your very polite and elegant note was received, but it came too late for my daughter Louisa to have the exquisite pleasure of reading it, as she was married this morning to the Hon. George Keith, member of Congress from the Sixth District. They started immediately to Washington City, as Congress is now in session.

"Very respectfully, M. LORRAINE."

AUNT AILSIE (*leans toward* Mrs. NELSON *with her hand against her ear*). Read that again. I am a little hard of hearing. [Mrs. NELSON *reads the note again in a much louder tone.*]

Mrs. MURRAY. The up-start! to refuse *my* son.

AUNT AILSIE. Well! well! The idea of a member of Congress marrying the daughter of a tinner. My opinion is that *aristocracy* is played out in this part of the country.
[*Exeunt all but* ELIZA.]

ELIZA (*comes forward*). I knowed it! I knowed it! Dat's what white folks git listening to nigger news. [*Sings and dances off the stage.*] "O, I wish I was in Dixie!"

(*Curtain falls.*)

# THE SPELLING LESSON.

### CHARACTERS.

KATE PRESTON.
NANNIE FOSTER.
FRANK FOSTER, *Brother* to NANNIE.
DAVID WELLINGTON.

### SCENE I.

*Home scene.* FRANK *and* DAVID *seated near a table, on which is a backgammon-board.*

DAVID. Who was that beautiful young lady we saw, Frank, at the seminary last evening?

FRANK. Who was she, indeed? Be more explicit; how was she dressed?

DAVID. Pshaw! how do I know any thing about a woman's dress. I mean the one who was crowned the Queen of Flowers.

FRANK. Ah! that was Kate Preston, the daughter of our professor. 'T is said she inherits her father's fine intellect. She is to make her *debut* into society on her next birthday, when she will be just seventeen. She and my sister Nannie, the young lady who represented the Violet, are very intimate, but as different as day and night; but the Queen of Flowers bends to give the humble Violet her friendship.

DAVID. Her part was well selected, for she looks a queen.

FRANK. I will do myself the pleasure of introducing you to Miss Preston, as I see she has made a decided impression upon the fastidious Doctor Wellington.

DAVID. I shall be very grateful, Frank; for I do assure you I am decidedly in love.

FRANK. Love at first sight. But I am not surprised, for Kate is very lovely.

DAVID. *You* are not in love with her, I hope?

FRANK. I in love with her! *No, sir!* I would as soon think of winning the morning star for a breastpin as the peerless Kate for a wife. And, notwithstanding, my friend, you are the son of a *millionaire*, I doubt if you can succeed in making an impression on her.

DAVID. And why not? I flatter myself that I am good-looking enough, and I know—

FRANK (*interrupting* DAVID). Your good looks will have but little effect upon Kate. Nothing short of a Napoleon will satisfy her ambition. I believe she would demand all the qualities and genius of Virgil, Shakespeare, Moore, and a host of others combined, in the man she chooses for a husband.

DAVID. And why may *I* not aspire to her hand? I have wealth; my family is aristocratic enough to satisfy the most sensitive disposition.

FRANK. True enough. I know you are worthy, but you know, too, that although you have naturally a fine mind, you have never "paled your cheek" by "burning the midnight lamp." You can converse brilliantly, and I have heard ladies exclaim, "What a charming fellow Dr. Wellington is! Such a genius! So intellectual!" But these were the every-day girls we meet. Kate Preston is of a different order; and there is one weak point (pardon my frankness) in your character that would condemn you forever in the eyes of Kate Preston.

DAVID. And, pray, what is it?

FRANK. Do not get angry, Doctor, if I speak plainly. Whether it results from carelessness, or an actual want of knowledge, I know not, but you are a miserable *speller!*

DAVID. I acknowledge this; for I remember when a boy at school I had the greatest desire to make a bonfire of every spelling-book in the world, and fancied how I would glory in seeing them blaze and turn to ashes. My spelling lesson at school was my especial aversion.

FRANK. Well, let Kate Preston ever find out that you are deficient in spelling, and she will spurn you *certain.* Beware how you write her any love-letters.

DAVID. To tell the truth, Frank, half my bad spelling does result from carelessness; but I confess that, with such words as *receive*, I never know whether the *e* or the *i* comes first, and I was twenty years old before I knew how to spell *separate ;* and this minute, if I were called upon to spell the word *niece,* I would not know where to place the *i* and *e.*

FRANK. Well; I will introduce you to Kate Preston, and then leave you to fight your own way.

DAVID. I think it would be a silly reason for a woman to give for rejecting a lover, that he happened to misspell a word.

FRANK. Yes; but you can put that to the score of a thousand other silly things women are guilty of. For my part, I intend to marry a wife beneath me in intellect, for I have a horror of blue stockings.

DAVID. Well, for my part, I intend to marry Kate Preston, if I can get her consent; for I am not afraid of her. She has no more talent by nature than I have.

FRANK. You may succeed, Doctor, and I hope you will, from my heart, for you deserve a good wife; but take care not to *write* to Miss Preston—do all your courting by *talking.* [*Both rise.*] But it is time we were starting to the theater. The young ladies will be impatient. So, let us be off. [*Exeunt* FRANK *and* DAVID.]

( *Curtain falls.*)

## SCENE II.

*Home scene.* NANNIE *seated near a table sewing. Enter* KATE.

NANNIE ( *rises ; offers a chair*). Come, Kate, and be seated. I was just thinking of you. I can work faster with your voice to cheer me.

KATE ( *takes seat*). O, Nannie! behold in me the most miserable of all women. I am utterly undone!

NANNIE. Why, Kate, what can be the matter? Have you heard bad news from home? Is your mother ill?

KATE. No! no!

NANNIE. Then, what ails you? Caressed and flattered as you are, what can trouble the belle of the season? Besides, does not the world say that you have won the heart of the brilliant Dr. Wellington?

KATE. You will drive me mad, Nannie! do not mention the creature's name.

NANNIE. The creature! Why, Kate, I begin to think you are crazy. Why do you apply such a name to *him?*

KATE. I tell you, do not mention Dr. Wellington again in my presence. I never, *never* can be his wife.

NANNIE (*surprised*). You love him, Kate? This you dare not deny.

KATE. Aye! that is just what distresses me. To think I have poured out my heart's best affection upon a man who—but, O, my heart is breaking! [*Puts her hand on her heart.*]

NANNIE. What does all this mean? What has Dr. Wellington done? Relieve my mind of this horrid suspense. Has he committed some crime? Has he been guilty of defalcation? I tell you, Kate, if such a report has reached your ears. it is a base fabrication. Dr. Wellington is honorable; he is noble; he is worthy the love of any woman. He may, perhaps, have killed some one in a moment of passion, but—

KATE (*lifting up her hands*). O, Nannie, do stop! I have *heard* nothing, but I have proof that he is totally unworthy of my notice.

NANNIE. Where is the proof?

KATE (*draws a letter from her pocket*). Here! I wrote to him, Nannie, as I promised, *first*, before he wrote to me, giving him a long account of my trip to the Mammoth Cave; and, in return, what have I received? Look here. [*Opens the letter; reads.*] "I am happy to know that you so much enjoyed your *t-r-i-p-e* to the Cave." Just to think, Nannie, he spells *trip, tripe!* O, my heart will burst! [*Covers her face with her hands.*]

NANNIE. Why, Kate Preston! I am overwhelmed with amazement. It may have been an oversight. Would you reject the man you love for this?

KATE. It was no oversight. [*Throws the letter toward NANNIE.*] Read for yourself. You know it was understood that when we were married we would take a tour through Europe, and, in alluding to that, he spells voyage *v-o-i-a-g-e!*

NANNIE. Well, suppose he does! Must a man be expatriated, exiled, *confiscated*, because he can't *spell?*

KATE. How can you jest, Nannie, when the happiness of my life depends on this.

NANNIE. Forgive me, Kate, I did not intend to wound you; but it is so silly, so ridiculous, for you to reject Dr. Wellington on such a plea.

KATE. *I have rejected him!*

NANNIE (*clasps her hands*). O, Kate!

KATE. I wrote to him that, as I was not fond of *tripe*, he must pardon me for wishing to be released from our engagement.

NANNIE. How could you wound his noble nature by any thing so cruel!

KATE. Well, it is too late now. The die is cast. The letter is on its way to New Orleans.

NANNIE. You have known Dr. Wellington nearly a year, Why did you not discover this unpardonable defect sooner?

KATE. How could I? I had never seen a word of his in writing, and he converses so brilliantly that I never suspected the truth. I will die an old maid before I will marry him!

NANNIE. Kate, how can you forget his devotion since the night of your birthday party? And don't you remember how Frank says he loved you all the time, at first sight, before he knew your position? How can you cast off one so generous, so devoted?

KATE. I have much respect, Nannie, for your opinion; but, in choosing a husband, I must be my own judge. When Dr. Wellington left us for his Southern home, last fall, I promised to become his wife; but, in my opinion, it will be more honorable to retreat now than to make him and myself miserable for life. I can not marry a man I think my inferior. My husband *must* command my respect, love, and reverence, and how could I look up to a man who is deficient in spelling? But

"We will not quarrel, my beloved friend,
    Opinions all must have—there let it end!"

NANNIE. I will not quarrel, dear Kate; but I can not forbear condemning your course. As sure as you are now alive you will repent such rashness!

KATE (*rises, throws her arm about* NANNIE's *neck and places her hand upon* NANNIE's *mouth*). Not another word,

Nannie—not another word! I can not marry a man who does not know how to spell.

(*Curtain falls.*)


SCENE III.

KATE *and* NANNIE, *surrounded by the different articles liable to be seen in a mantua-maker's department preparatory to a wedding—white tarlatan, satin, ribbons, flowers, etc., etc.;* KATE *twirling a wreath of white flowers in her hand;* NANNIE *holding a case of jewels.*

NANNIE. It seems so strange, Kate, that only a short time ago I was full of the idea of assisting you in preparing your bridal wardrobe, and now you are helping me!

KATE (*sighs*). Yes, Nannie, but we never know the changes that may take place!

NANNIE. I have never mentioned Dr. Wellington's name in your presence, Kate, since you told me how cruelly you replied to his letter. It has been so long ago that I feel justified in broaching the subject. I have always wanted to know how he received your answer.

KATE. I have avoided mentioning any thing in connection with the affair between Dr. Wellington and myself to you, Nannie, because I came painfully conscious of having recklessly thrown away my life's happiness, and indeed I have tried never to think of it.

NANNIE. And have you succeeded? Do you ever think of him?

KATE. Think of him! It is the only real pleasure I enjoy! I carry his answer to my letter always about me, and, although I richly deserve every word he has written, still there is an indefinable solace in reading the words traced by *his* hand. [*Draws a letter from her pocket.*] Here it is. Let me read it for you. No, I can not. Take it and read it to me.

NANNIE (*takes the letter*). Certainly, if you desire it.

KATE. Yes, I believe I want to hear it.

NANNIE (*opens letter; reads*). "Miss Preston—Your command I obey. The return of your picture to its fair original no doubt sets your restless heart at ease. You are free

9

from your hated engagement. I am very sorry you were not as much pleased with my letter as I am with your charming effusion, whose pages can almost rival the poetry of Shakespeare or the immortal Byron! The wonder still grows with me, how 'one small' sheet of paper can hold the knowledge therein contained. Such sublime eloquence! such *generous* sentiments! such noble *forbearance!* displaying all the grandeur of your Grecian mind. Alas! all is lost to me! HOPE, the lovely goddess of the unfortunate, even refuses her aid and sympathy; but FORTITUDE stands my noble friend and whispers she will lend her assisting hand. I believe I can survive the shock, and I am the better able to bear it as I have sufficient of this world's goods to sustain me, even should my days be prolonged to the length of our ancient friend, Methuselah. Perfectly excusable are you, my brilliant friend, not to throw away your towering talents for a man who, unfortunately for himself, *can not spell.* I am quite aware I am not a Demosthenes, Clay, or even a Noah Webster! Neither is every lady a Minerva! I have dared to love you, with all your august attainments, but I stand not alone, for all men admire coquettes and flirts. Farewell! I shall attend the lectures the ensuing winter. Fear not, I shall not intrude upon your regal beauty. Best wishes for your happiness until you can find a companion for life who can spell better than Your most devoted serv't, DAVID WELLINGTON."
[*Folds letter, hands it to* KATE.] Every word in this letter is spelled correctly. You can find no fault with this.

KATE. This letter has made me more unhappy than the first.

NANNIE. Why?

KATE. It proves for what a trifle I threw away my life's happiness.

NANNIE. But you do not love him now. You are too gay to be heart-broken. You are the life of society.

KATE. Do you suppose that I would make a public display of my feelings? I would never have alluded to the subject to you, Nannie, dearly as I love you, but the human heart longs for sympathy. O, Nannie! the night after the medical students received their diplomas, (I mean, of course, the graduates,) my father requested me to accompany him to hear the valedictory. I went, and when Dr. Wellington arose the chosen orator for the evening, so graceful, so handsome, so noble in his bearing, I trembled and must have turned deadly pale, for my father asked if I was ill, and handed me a glass of water. I had a conspicuous seat, and, fearing to attract attention, and above all *his* notice, I made a violent effort and controlled my emotion. But I came very near fainting. Ah, Nannie! you told me I would repent, and I have in "sack-cloth and ashes!" David Wellington will never know how my proud heart has been humbled; he will never know how much, how fondly, I loved him!

*Enter* DAVID *and* FRANK.

FRANK. Indeed, he will know it, and does know it; for as we were about entering this room we were stopped on the threshold of the door by the cadence of your voice, Miss Kate. I will do the Doctor the justice to say he was not a willing eavesdropper, but he was a delighted listener. [KATE *covers her face with her hands.*] Come, Katy, darling, [*takes* KATE'S *arm and draws her toward* DAVID,] you understand each other now; and, by the living piper, [*to* NANNIE,] sister, we will have a double wedding! Shall it not be so?

DAVID (*approaches* KATE, *draws her hand through his arm.*) Let Kate answer; my fate is in her hands!

KATE. I do not deserve—

FRANK (*interrupting* KATE). You do *not* deserve such a noble husband, Miss Kate, after your behavior to my friend; but if we never received any good but such as we *deserve*, I fear we would all be in Davy Jones's locker.

NANNIE. With nothing to eat, Kate, but *tripe!*

(*Curtain falls.*)

———————◆———————

## COSTUMES.

KATE PRESTON and NANNIE FOSTER. Becoming home dresses, varied in each scene according to the taste of the performers.

FRANK and DAVID. Plain citizens' dresses.

# THE PEA-GREEN GLAZED CAMBRIC.

## CHARACTERS.

NELLIE DALE.
Mrs. GREY, *Grandmother to* NELLIE.
Miss JULIA HOSKINS, *an Heiress.*
Miss SUSAN HOBBS, *a Spinster.*
Mrs. STUART, *Mother to* JAMES.
JAMES STUART.
DOXY, *a Servant.*

## SCENE I.

*A sitting-room.* Mrs. GREY *knitting, seated in an arm chair.*
NELLIE *seated near, with a half-worn white Swiss dress
across her lap.*

NELLIE (*throws the dress on the floor*). This old muslin
will never do. I have worn it till it is threadbare. Julia
Hoskins's birthday party comes off to-night, and I must
make a raise of some sort. [*Rises from her seat.*] Say, old
miss. give me the key of the red chest up-stairs; there may
be a handsome silk or something stored away in it.

Mrs. GREY. You can have the key, but, my poor child, I
fear it will be a fruitless search. Your mother's wedding-
dress was taken from that very chest; yes, and almost all
the finery she ever had, for your grandfather died soon
after his last sea-voyage, when he brought it to me. There
may be some ribbons and laces left, but I doubt it. This
muslin dress you have worn so often was the last dress pattern I had.

NELLIE. But, old miss, 't will do no harm to look; besides, it is my only chance. Where is the key?

Mrs. GREY. You will find it in the glass drawer, but be
careful and do not rumple my caps.

NELLIE.  Can't you throw an old shoe after me for good luck?  [*Exit* NELLIE; *hums a tune.*]

MRS. GREY.  When her poor grandfather returned from India and brought so many nice things, I little thought of the dark days that were to come.  Her mother was what Nellie is now, and when I look at her I almost fancy I have my first Nellie back.  Poor child! she ought to have a new dress.  Let me see.  [*Stops knitting.*]  Mrs. Stuart owes me ten dollars for sewing, and Nellie is entitled to it, for she worked day and night helping me.  But then to-morrow is rent-day, and market-day, too, and I have only two dollars in the house!  Can't I—

*Enter* NELLIE.

NELLIE (*holding up a roll of goods*).  See! old miss— Eureka!  A fine green glace silk!

MRS. GREY (*wipes her glasses, replaces them.*)  Am I dreaming?  Bring it closer.  I remember no green silk being in that chest, and you have been needing a party-dress so long, too.  Bring it nearer, I say.

NELLIE (*approaches;* MRS. GREY *takes the end of the cloth in her hands.*)  Dear child, did you think this was silk?  Why, it is nothing but green glazed cambric!    •

NELLIE.  I know it, old miss, but I intend to make folks think it is silk.  [*Draws from beneath the cambric some fine ribbon and lace.*]  Just see this elegant ribbon! and here is lace enough to flounce it to the waist, and that is the fashion now.

MRS. GREY.  You are not in earnest, Nellie?  If you wear a glazed cambric to the party, Miss Hoskins will feel insulted.  Always avoid any thing of this sort.

NELLIE.  But, old miss, I tell you they will never suspect it.  With *real* lace and this ribbon it will look exactly like silk.  Julia Hoskins will think her blue tarlatan totally eclipsed.

MRS. GREY.  And if they detect the imposition you will be mortified.

NELLIE.  I tell you they will never know the difference. I intend to risk the chances, at any rate.

MRS. GREY.  Will Susan Hobbs be at the party?

NELLIE.  Of course.  Julia Hoskins can not take snuff without Miss Susan sneezes, and you know she will be there.

Mrs. Grey. Then I know you can never pass off that stuff for silk.

Nellie. Do n't fear, old miss. If I do n't slip between Miss Susan Hobbs's fingers before she can feel the texture of this goods, I 'll agree that I am not smart enough to be called your granddaughter.

Mrs. Grey. But, Nellie, the idea of cambric! What would—

Nellie. It is no use, old miss, to argue the question. You know that every body in the village is aware of your high notions about things; because, if you are poor, you are as proud as Lucifer.

Mrs. Grey. I have reason to be proud, for—

Nellie. O, yes; I know the blood of a host of heroes flows in your veins and in mine; and for that very reason the people will never imagine that *your* granddaughter would wear a glazed cambric. I am sure that our *aristocratic* blood, and the *real* lace will put me through this evening. But I must go to work if I have to perform such wonders. [*Takes up the Swiss skirt; begins to measure off the widths of the green cambric.*]

(*Curtain falls.*)

## SCENE II.

Hobbs's *parlor*. Miss Susan *seated engaged in cutting quilt-pieces.* Enter Julia Hoskins.

Julia. Good morning, Miss Susan. How do you feel after last night's dissipation?

Miss Susan. Why, Miss Julia, is that you? Do have a seat, and let me compliment you on the success of your party. It was splendid! The tables were so beautiful. *Every body* said it excelled any thing of the kind that was ever in this town; and you, too, Miss Julia, I never did see you look so well. Indeed, I feel highly honored to be entertaining the belle of the place.

Julia. O, Miss Susan, you flatter me. [*Takes seat.*] Do not call *me* a belle after the sensation Nellie Dale made last evening.

MISS SUSAN. Lack a day! Miss Julia, did you notice the way she was dressed? A real fine new green glace silk!

JULIA. Notice! I think I did! It is a shame for Nellie Dale to wear such a dress when her poor old grandmother has to work so hard. It must have cost upward of fifty dollars. Did you look at that lace?

MISS SUSAN. I guess I did, and took hold of it too; and was just going to feel the quality of the silk, but she felt me pulling at the lace, and she jerked away from me as if I had been a rattlesnake; and *such* a look!

JULIA. I wonder! Miss Susan, you know people say that my father is rich, but *I* can not afford such a dress as that, and if I could I wouldn't. She looked for all the world just like a stage actress.

MISS SUSAN. I do wonder where she got it, for there are n't a piece of silk like that in this town; for I know what is in all the stores. Well, now, maybe Mrs. Stuart gave it to her. You know she is a great favorite with Mrs. Stuart.

JULIA. That would be worse than ever. If I had to go to parties in charity clothes, I'd stay at home forever. But she is so anxious to catch that young lawyer that I suppose she would raise heaven and earth to get a dress for the party. I, like a simpleton, told her he would be there, and I judge she thought to take him by storm.

MISS SUSAN. Old Mrs. Grey is monstrous proud, and I guess she had a hand in it. You know she sets up for aristocracy.

JULIA. O, yes, her family *is* good; but, law, she is as poor as dirt, and blood is nothing these days without money.

MISS SUSAN. That's a fact; and I guess you are right about her wanting to catch Jim Stuart for a husband; for I never did see any body as frisky as Nellie Dale was last night. I can't tell you the times I tried to feel of that dress, just to see the quality of the silk, and I do believe she "smelt a rat," for, as sure as I got close to her, just that sure she'd commence skipping about like a wild deer. I tell you, she were n't still one minute.

JULIA. Yes, and I know Mr. Stuart was disgusted with her.

MISS SUSAN. I'd say!

JULIA. Why, she just as good as asked him to go home with her.

MISS SUSAN (*clasps her hands*). You don't tell me, Miss Julia, that Nellie Dale asked a young man to go home with her?

JULIA. She had just as well said, straight out, Mr. Stuart, please go home with me, as to have asked as she did.

MISS SUSAN. What are we all coming to! What did she do? [*Small bell rings outside.*]

JULIA. He was conversing with me, as he had been trying to do all the evening, whenever Nellie Dale let him alone, and he appeared very much interested in the conversation, when, just at the most engaging point, up she comes, as brazen as you please, and said: "Mr. Stuart, I am ready." He looked at her like he could look her through, and said: "Do you wish to go home?" and don't you think she took his arm and led him off.

MISS SUSAN. Now, Miss Julia! and what did you say?

JULIA. I had nothing to say. I could have boxed her jaws; and I know Mr. Stuart felt ashamed of her behavior. But if I had I might have [*bell rings again, louder*] rubbed off some of the paint from her cheeks. I tell you, she is a fast one. But she isn't fast enough for me. I will knock all the sand from under her arrangements. See if I don't.

MISS SUSAN. O, Miss Julia, you will make me laugh for a week to come; you are so funny.

*Enter* JAMES STUART.

JAMES. Excuse me, ladies, for interrupting so interesting a *tete-a-tete*, but I rang the bell several times, and as you seemed to wish not to be disturbed, I would have retired, but my aunt, Mrs. Stuart, was particularly anxious that you, Miss Hobbs, should receive this little package. [*Hands Miss Susan a bundle.*] I believe it is something for the charity school. She said you would know all about it.

MISS SUSAN. O, yes, I understand it. Tell Mrs. Stuart I am very much obliged to her. But do have a seat. Just think of my keeping you standing at the door so long. But you must excuse it, for Miss Julia here made herself so interesting that I forgot every thing else.

JAMES. I'll excuse you, certainly, knowing Miss Hoskins's fascinations in conversation. [*Bows.*]

JULIA (*looks confused*). O, Mr. Stuart!

MISS SUSAN. And you listened to all we said? Ha! ha! that is a good joke. You know, Mr. Stuart, ladies will be gossipers when they get together.

JAMES. I did listen, Miss Hobbs, but assure you I was an unwilling listener. It was purely accidental; you would not be made conscious of my presence. And, as long as I heard a part of your conversation, allow me, Miss Hoskins, to correct you on one point. You were mistaken about Miss Dale asking me to accompany her home. I had previously engaged myself to take her home whenever she was ready to go, and begged her to inform me when it was her wish to retire. So, you will perceive, she did not "as good as ask me."

JULIA (*tosses her head.*) It makes no difference to *me* whether she did or not. It is so much like her that I thought it very probable. She has a very strange disposition.

JAMES. She appeared to me to be witty, agreeable, accomplished, and is a charming dancer.

JULIA. What a string of wonderful traits! Please, Mr. Stuart, spare my nerves. You almost stun me.

JAMES. Indeed! My presence has the same effect, then, upon *you* that Miss Nellie Dale's has upon me.

JULIA. I had given you credit for more brains than you seem to possess. I see that Miss Dale has blinded you with her arts already.

JAMES. Her devotion to her aged grandmother is a proof at least of her amiability.

JULIA. Yes, when she calls her "old miss!"

JAMES. That is one of the proofs of her affection. It is the wish of her grandmother that she should call her "old miss." She learned it from the servants when a child, and Mrs. Grey prefers the title, if I may call it such.

JULIA. Servants! They never had but one old negro, and she is dead now. But I haven't time to discuss Miss Dale's amiability or her pedigree. Remember, I warn you in time. She is a flirt! So, good morning. [*Starts.*]

JAMES. You will permit me to see you home?

JULIA. O, certainly. I will be glad of your company. Good-by, Miss Susan. Come and see us.

MISS SUSAN. And you come again, Miss Julia. I suppose

I may look for you, Mr. Stuart, when your aunt sends another package. [*Tries to look sentimental.*]

JAMES. I shall be the bearer of it with pleasure.

[*Exeunt* JAMES *and* JULIA.]

Miss SUSAN. I never like to hear the kettle call the pot black. If Julia Hoskins did n't do the same thing she accused Nellie Dale of doing, I ain't here! She as good as asked that young man to gallant her home; for if she did n't start home *first* just to make him go with her, I do n't know nothing. If I had been in her place, I would have sat here till judgment-day before I would have started first. He would have served her right if he had stayed here with me instead of gallanting her, but young men are so blinded to their own interests. They must be eternally running after some young giddy thing that knows no more about keeping house and raising a family than a "hog knows about holiday!" Well! well! there 's only this world and one more, and then we are done!

(*Curtain falls.*)

### SCENE III.

Mrs. STUART *and* JAMES STUART *seated in a neatly-furnished apartment;* Mrs. STUART *employed in some light needle-work.*

Mrs. STUART. James, come tell me about Miss Hoskins's birthday party. Did you enjoy it?

JAMES. More, dear aunt, than I usually do at such places. Miss Nellie Dale is a charming girl.

Mrs. STUART. I wish you could think well enough of Nellie to ask her to be your wife; that is, if she would receive you as a suitor.

JAMES. There was but one thing that prevented my proposing to her last evening.

Mrs. STUART. What?

JAMES. Her dress.

Mrs. STUART. You surely, James, could not think less of a young lady because she is not able to dress elegantly. I know you are fastidious, but I never thought you so weak-minded as to allow a plain dress to influence you in the choice of a wife. You should respect her more for her economy.

JAMES. Economy! you do not know what you are talking about. She was the most expensively-dressed lady in the room last evening, and it was this extravagance and apparent want of thought for her grandmother that kept me silent. She can not have a good heart if she can spend that old lady's hard earnings on finery, and this she must have done to be dressed as she was last night. Why, she looked like a queen!

MRS. STUART. You astonish me, James. Nellie Dale has but one party-dress, a white muslin. This I know. What kind of a dress did she wear to Miss Hoskins's party?

JAMES. A magnificent green silk, trimmed in rich lace and ribbons. I noticed particularly, because my heart was in the matter.

MRS. STUART. You mistook her for Julia Hoskins. Nellie has no such dress as you describe. If she had I am confident I would know it. You have made some mistake.

JAMES. Aunt, I tell you I went home with her. How could I be mistaken?

MRS. STUART. O, I forgot. You told me before.

JAMES. And I took her into supper, danced with her, and promenaded all with this same green silk dress.

MRS. STUART. And that dress prevented you from proposing?

JAMES. It did.

MRS. STUART. I am still not convinced. There is a mystery somewhere. Wait till I test the matter. [*Rings a bell.*] I shall not be satisfied until I see for myself. [*Enter a small servant.*] Go to Mrs. Grey's and ask Miss Nellie Dale to be kind enough to let me see the fine green silk she wore to Miss Hoskins's party last evening.

SERVANT. Yes, 'um. [*Exit Servant.*]

MRS. STUART. Now we will see the true state of the case. If what you say is true, I can never respect Nellie as I have heretofore; but it can not be. She is so thoughtful *always* about her old grandmother; so self-sacrificing.

JAMES. I do not dispute all this, but what I tell you is true. I hope there is something that will clear up the mystery, and that we may find her internal as pure and beautiful as her exterior appeared last night, for I do assure you she is very fascinating. [*Looks toward the window or door.*] But here comes Doxy full tilt. Perhaps she can tell us something cheering. I see that Miss Nellie has not trusted her with the dress. But here is Doxy; let her speak for herself.

[*Enter* DOXY.]

MRS. STUART. Well, where is the dress?

DOXY. Miss Nellie say she ain't got no green silk. She say she wish she did.*

MRS. STUART. I told you to ask her for the dress she wore last night, you stupid creature!

DOXY. Waal I did, and she say she never wore no green silk to the party.

MRS. STUART. What can it mean? You did not tell her what I said, I know.

DOXY. Yes 'um, I 'clare I tell her, and she say she wish she did hab a green silk for to look at herseff.

MRS. STUART. I am more and more puzzled.

JAMES. And I am sorry that what Doxy says goes to prove that Miss Nellie is trying to cover her extravagance by deceit. I am sorry, indeed, I repeat. [*Looks toward the window.*] But, as I live, there is Miss Nellie now, tripping along, looking as gayly and bright as if she had never been guilty of a deceitful action in her whole life!

DOXY. Dat was what she say. She say she was comin' herseff to tell you all about it.

MRS. STUART. Why didn't you tell this before?

DOXY. 'Kase you never axed me.

MRS. STUART (*to* JAMES.) I want you to step into the other room before Nellie gets here. You can overhear all we say, and if she does not vindicate herself then I'll give up that she is not a wife worthy of my nephew.

JAMES. If you insist, dear aunt; but I confess I have the luck of having to listen to ladies' conversations.

MRS. STUART (*excitedly*). Quick, James—she is coming!
[*Exit* JAMES.]

*Enter* NELLIE.

NELLIE (*throws herself on a chair*). My dear Mrs. Stuart, I came over to make you an explanation, as you deserve it. It is due you as my friend.

---

* Pronounced *deed.*

MRS. STUART. Excuse me, Nellie, if by sending for your dress I have—

NELLIE. No apologies from you now. I will tell you the "unvarnished truth" without preliminaries. Yesterday I was in despair at having nothing to wear to Miss Hoskins's party. My white muslin was threadbare. What to do I did not know, when grandpa's old India chest occurred to me. You know it has been the receptacle of odds and ends for years, and in our palmiest days revealed many a rich treasure in the way of foreign silks, and so forth; but, alas! on searching through it, even to the very bottom, I could find nothing but a piece of *pea-green glazed cambric*, which I made into a dress, and covered it so completely with some fine old lace that was once my mother's, that every one thought it was silk. Some rich ribbon from the same source completed my costume. And now I have confided to you the secret. Do not expose my poverty, for—

MRS. STUART. I think your ingenuity and taste deserves commendation, and you are entitled to—

*Enter* JAMES.

JAMES. My love and admiration, Miss Nellie. Can you ever forgive me for doubting your sincerity?

NELLIE (*rises, surprised*). Mr. Stuart! were you a listener to my—

MRS. STUART. Nellie! [*Comes forward toward* NELLIE.] Nellie, it is myself, and not my nephew, who is to blame for his being a listener to our conversation. I was determined he should hear your vindication from your own lips. You had been accused of extravagance and ingratitude, and I knew the charge was false.

NELLIE. I am satisfied; but—

JAMES (*interrupting* NELLIE). I am not satisfied, and never will be, Nellie [*takes her hand*], until you are Mrs. James Stuart.

NELLIE. O, but grandma. Mrs. Stuart [*looks at* Mrs. STUART], it is so sudden. [*Looks down, confused.*]

JAMES. O, my little Nellie, if you are calling upon grandma and Mrs. Stuart, I know where I stand; and I shall always remember THE PEA-GREEN GLAZED CAMBRIC, as it has been the cause of making me the happiest man alive.

(*Curtain falls.*)

# THE ELOPEMENT.

## CHARACTERS.

NORA, *Daughter of* Mr. COURTNEY.
MARIA, *Cousin to* NORA.
Aunt MARY, *Sister to* Mr. COURTNEY.
LILLIAN, *a Gay, Fashionable Girl.*
AGNES, *a Servant.*

## SCENE I.

*Room.* NORA *seated near a table reading a letter.* *She folds it, then opens it, rises, walks to and fro.*

NORA. To-day is Christmas. O, how different from this time a year ago; *then* I was happy, *now* I am miserable! [*Clasps her hands.*] It is a fearful thing to be in love, and to think my fondest hopes can not be realized. [*Sighs; seats herself and reads the letter.*]

*Enter* LILLIAN.

LILLIAN. Why, Nora, what ails you? Your face is as long as the moral law. I see you have a letter. Any bad news?
NORA. No, Lillian, but I am miserable!
LILLIAN. Miserable! What can make a girl of your wealth miserable?
NORA. Lillian, were you ever in love?
LILLIAN. Ha! ha! A thousand times!
NORA. O, how can you be so thoughtless? No person can love but once.
LILLIAN. You silly girl, without joking, I have been in love at least one dozen times. Let me see. [*Looks down thoughtfully.*] There was Joe Smallacres, a dandy little fellow, my *first* love. He used to pass up and down the street in sight of my window when I went to school in New

York, and would lay his hand so [*mimics him*], and look so
woe-begone, and at last succeeded in sending me a love-letter
by one of the "helps;" but the monitress intercepted the
missive, and thus blasted all his hopes; for I was reported,
of course, and only escaped the public disgrace of being
expelled by promising, with tears in my eyes, never to en-
courage Mr. Smallacres's attentions while I remained an
inmate of the Young Ladies' Seminary; and I shall ever
feel grateful to dear Mrs. Rigid for her timely interference,
as this same fellow Joe, my *first* love, is at Sing-Sing, work-
ing out a felon's term for stealing money from "the old
Governor," as he affectionately dubbed his father. Then
there was handsome Ben Crossfield, with his adorable mus-
tache; and Edward DeCourcy, too; his name was enough of
itself to turn my head. Mercy! how I did love him; but—

NORA (*impatiently*). O, Lillian, you are such a rattle-
brain. *I* never could love but *one!*

LILLIAN. You'll get over *that*. I have had it, and it
will not hurt you. But are you really in love? [NORA
*looks down; twirls the letter and sighs. Aside.*] I do believe
the girl is touched. [*Approaches* NORA.] Come, Nora, tell
me all about it. Who is the favored suitor of the young
heiress?

NORA. I am afraid to tell you.

LILLIAN. Do you doubt me?

NORA. No. I can trust you; but I am afraid of your
ridicule.

LILLIAN. Lay aside your scruples, dear Nora. I never
ridicule my friends. I must know the name of your hero.

NORA. Well, then, it is Clarence Orfield!

LILLIAN (*raises her hands in surprise*). The exquisite! I
loved him once myself. Poor Nora!

NORA. What do you mean?

LILLIAN. I mean just this, that, with all Clarence Orfield's pretensions, he is a humbug!

NORA (*deprecatingly*). O, Lillian!

LILLIAN. It is all a fact. Mr. Orfield wears inimitable
whiskers, dresses unexceptionably, and sports the darlingest
little cane, but—

NORA (*impatiently*). But what?

LILLIAN. Why, simply that he is not worth the powder
and shot that would kill him.

NORA (*angrily*). I do not thank you for speaking in this manner. Mr. Orfield is a *gentleman!*

LILLIAN (*carelessly*). If fine clothes and a dashing outside constitute a gentleman, then he is one. But, you know, he is dissipated, and has already squandered the property left him by his father. The greatest curse, in nine cases out of ten, that can befall a young man, is to inherit a fortune. It has made a profligate and gambler of Clarence Orfield.

NORA. I do not believe it. He told me that all these reports about him were vile slander, created to set my father against him. If you knew how I love him you would not talk so.

LILLIAN. Love, indeed. No doubt you think you love him; but it is impossible for any true woman to even *respect*, much less *love*, such a man. And, aside from all this, you are too young to marry.

NORA. I will be sixteen next May, and many girls marry at that age.

LILLIAN. And but for Mrs. Rigid's kindly interference I would have been now a miserable victim. I was just sixteen when she warned me of the evil consequences of an ill-assorted marriage. I shudder now when I think of the awful fate she averted, and will always thank God that such a noble and exalted woman had the care of 'my early education.

NORA. Plague take "Mrs. Rigid" and "early education." I know plenty of women who were married young and are happy. Look at Mrs. Greenleaf, and she was only *fifteen*.

LILLIAN. She is one in a thousand. Besides, she has a model husband; he is more like a father than a husband. He is a gentleman and a good man.

NORA. Yes, and Clarence is good, too. [*Takes a miniature from her pocket; hands it to* LILLIAN.] Look on that face, and say is it not angelic? Could a cross word ever pass such lips? [LILLIAN *looks at picture.*]

LILLIAN. O, Nora, you are sickening! I am sorry this thing has happened. Does your father know it?

NORA. Yes, and has forbid my meeting Clarence, or speaking to him—a command I can not find it in my heart to obey.

LILLIAN. Your father is right. He knows the wily fortune-hunter.

NORA. Some one has prejudiced my father against him. I am fully convinced that a better acquaintance would change his opinion of Clarence.

LILLIAN. Nora, let me *entreat* you not to hold any sort of communication with this man.

NORA. You are highly set up, giving advice. You are but little older than myself.

LILLIAN. I know this; but I am old enough to know that it takes something beside a handsome face and fine figure to make a woman happy.

NORA. You speak sagely. To hear you one would think you had had a lifetime experience.

LILLIAN. I shall never marry until I can find a man I can *trust*.

NORA. You may be deceived, after all.

LILLIAN. True. One thing is certain, however, I will study the character of the man I choose, and if I find that he makes his living by gambling, as Clarence Orfield does, you may be sure I will drop him, to use a vulgarism, "like a hot potato!"

NORA (*contemptuously*). What a pattern of prudence!

LILLIAN. You may sneer, Nora, but I know Mr. Clarence Orfield. He *courts* every pretty girl he sees, but intends to marry for *money*, and he has singled you out as a victim. Listen to my warning. Avoid this man as you would a pestilence, for nothing but misery can result from a connection with him. I do hope something will occur to thwart his base designs. [*Exit* LILLIAN.]

NORA (*looks after* LILLIAN). Humph! She would make a good tragedy queen. I see I can not trust *her*. If she finds out that I am going to elope with Clarence, she will betray me. But what must I do? I can not get out of the house at midnight without using stratagem. [*Looks toward the door.*] But here comes cousin Maria; I'll find out her sentiments, and if I can enlist her in my behalf all will be well. [*Conceals the letter and picture.*]

*Enter* MARIA.

MARIA. O, I have had so much fun! I got up at daylight and knocked at my uncle's door so loud that I roused him out of his morning's nap, and he was as mad as blazes. But I claimed my Christmas gift!

NORA. And pray, what did he give you?

MARIA. Nothing yet; but he has promised me a gold pen and a portfolio. You see I intend, some day, to be an authoress.

NORA. *You* an authoress?

MARIA. Yes, indeed; but you ought to hear uncle laugh at the idea of my being an authoress. I have not seen him laugh as heartily since the time I told him about Clarence Orfield making love to me!

NORA (*starts*). Clarence Orfield make love to *you!*

MARIA. Why not? Am I so frightful? But law! did I never tell you about it?

NORA (*sharply*). No!

MARIA. O, it was too funny! Do you remember when uncle took me over to Mr. Todd's?

NORA. Why, that was six months ago.

MARIA. To be sure; and when we got there who should be in the parlor but Mr. Clarence Orfield? I was introduced to the *exquisite*, of course; and when we all went into the conservatory Mr. Orfield gathered a handsome bouquet, and, as we were returning to the house, he said, as he handed me the flowers, "Miss Courtney, these rose-buds are like yourself, young and beautiful, and this sprig of box speaks the language of my heart—*constancy!*"

NORA (*indignantly*). You are making every word of this!

MARIA. Indeed, I am not. But this was not half. Listen, Nora. [*Takes* NORA *by the arm.*] He threw himself into a theatrical attitude and said: "I love you dearly, Miss Courtney; but perhaps you do not believe in love at first sight?"

NORA. Mr. Orfield did not say this to you?

MARIA. O, but he did; and I would have been covered with confusion, for I never had a gentleman to compliment me before, but I saw what he was after.

NORA (*eagerly.*) How?

MARIA. Why, he thought *I* was *you!*

NORA (*releasing herself from* MARIA's *hold*). How do you know he did?

MARIA. Because, would you believe it? I laughed in his face, and I said: "Mr. Orfield, I think you are caught!"

His face turned very red, and he asked how. "Why." replied I, "you have mistaken me for Miss Nora Courtney, the great heiress. I am nothing but a poor niece of my uncle, dependent upon his bounty."

NORA. What did he say?

MARIA. He said he thought Mrs. Todd introduced me as Miss Courtney. "So she did." said I. "but don't I tell you I am a poor relation of Miss Courtney!" Only think of the fellow's impudence! He tried to laugh, and said he knew all the time who I was, but he wanted to see how I would bear a little flirtation. This made me indignant. and I told him he could not deceive me. for I knew it was my uncle's *money*, and not my uncle's *daughter*, that he wanted.

NORA. How could you be so rude?

MARIA. Rude. indeed! If I had been a man I would have given the little dandy a good thrashing! As it was. my tongue was the only weapon I could use.

NORA. It was all a joke on the part of Mr. Orfield to quiz you. But suppose he had been in earnest, would you not have loved him?

MARIA. Why. Nora! Love Clarence Orfield?

NORA. Why not? He is very handsome.

MARIA. He is handsome. but such a villain!

NORA. How do you know?

MARIA. Because uncle told me that he was a designing villain, and I heard him tell Lillian that he would rather see you dead than to see you the wife of as base a man as Clarence Orfield! But I told uncle he need not fear. for I am sure you have too much sense to be gulled by a shallow-pated fortune-hunter. But I must go. You are so dry. Nora, and I am not half done catching Christmas gifts.

[*Exit* MARIA.]

NORA. And Maria. too, is against me! Agnes is now the last chance. Though she is a servant. she is a shrewd girl. and I know will assist me. I must go and pack my trunk and be ready at the appointed time. Clarence is to meet me at midnight. O. how my heart beats! [*Goes out.*]

(*Curtain falls.*)

## SCENE II.

*A period of three years has elapsed. Same apartment.* NORA
*seated in an arm-chair; her face pale and sorrowful.*

NORA (*looks around*).   How strange, and yet how fa-
miliar every thing looks to me here!   After an absence of
three years to find myself again in the house where my in-
fancy was cradled!   But there is one object I look for in
vain—my father!   O, my father!   And the bitterest pang
is that I did not receive his forgiveness before his lips were
closed in death!   [*Leans back in the chair, covers her face
with a handkerchief.*]

### *Enter* Aunt MARY.

AUNT MARY (*draws a chair close to* NORA *and seats herself*).   Now, my dear Nora, I am at leisure to hear your
wonderful story.   I am interested in all that concerns you;
but be as brief as possible, as you are very weak.

NORA (*takes handkerchief from her face.*)   I will try, in as
few words as possible, to give you an account of the life I
led after I left this house.   It is almost needless to say that,
with the assistance of Agnes, I fled from the home of my
childhood on that fatal night, without interruption, and
Mr. Orfield received me at the carriage in an ecstasy of joy—
joy which I foolishly supposed was occasioned by love for
me.   We were married, and the day following he urged
me to write a conciliatory letter to my father.   I did so.
The letter was returned, unanswered and unopened.   Mr.
Orfield seemed perplexed, and paced the room in great agitation.   After a while he became more calm and said to
me: "I reckon the old fellow will relent when his passion
is over!"   I had never heard my father spoken of disre-
spectfully, and at that moment I felt a peculiar veneration
for him, and I said: "If you wish me to love you, Clarence,
you must not speak in this manner of my father."   He
mumbled out something about not wishing to be catechised
by a woman, and left the apartment.   The next day I received a note from my father, stating that if I would permit him to get a divorce he would forgive and receive me,
but that he would never allow such a man as Clarence Orfield to become a member of his family.

AUNT MARY. And why did you not accede to the proposition?

NORA. Because Clarence had completely mesmerized me. I was totally blind to his faults, and believed he married me for love; besides, he kept up a show of affection, thinking my father would relent. I had not been married long before I discovered that Clarence did make his living by gambling. His humors were governed by his success at play. Whenever he won he was in glee; if unsuccessful, his temper was terrible. When he became convinced that my father would not give him any money, he said he could not afford the expense of a city boarding-house, and removed me to a small house in the country, where I remained a long time without many of the necessaries of life.

AUNT MARY. Poor child!

NORA. He would often leave me for days in this lonely place, and what I suffered from fear and anxiety words can not tell; and even when he was with me he was so ill-natured that, but for the fear of being left alone with only one servant, his absence would have been a relief. Some time after this he took me to Radway, a town where he wished to attend the races, and placed me in an indifferent boarding-house. He paid me little or no attention, and yet, so great was my partiality, I would make excuses for him, until, one day, I overheard a conversation between him and a dashing young man who boarded at the same house. I was seated at my window, which overlooked a grass-plat and rude arbor underneath. He and this Granville were smoking, and I heard Granville ask him why he did not introduce his wife into society? Clarence answered: "The truth is I don't want to show her. She is plain, and she was nothing more than a school-girl when I took up with her." "I think," replied Granville, "you underrate Mrs. Orfield. I have seen her several times, and she is graceful in her movements, and I would like to know her. She seems very much in love with her husband." "O, well," said Clarence, "I will introduce you. You certainly admire her more than I do, for indeed I have no affection for her, and in fact never had any. Her father was a rich old fool, and I, being over head and ears in debt, with the sheriff at my heels, married the creature solely for her money."

AUNT MARY. The perjured villain!

NORA. I thought I would faint, but nerved myself to listen, and he continued: "The old fellow has never given me a cent, and refuses to see his daughter unless she consents to a divorce; and this I would insist upon, for I am tired of looking at her pale face, but I have a lingering hope that the old governor will shell out yet!" I could hear no more, but rose from the window, and, flinging myself upon the bed, found some relief in tears. My eyes were at last open to the true character of my husband, and my love was that instant turned to hate. I did not tell him that I overheard the conversation. A few days afterward he proposed introducing me to Granville, and I indignantly declined. They both left Radway next day upon a gambling expedition. I then wrote to my father, acceding to his proposition, and begging his forgiveness, but never received an answer.

AUNT MARY. He never got that letter. He would have rejoiced in receiving you on the conditions mentioned.

NORA. I then lost all hope. After my husband's return he entered my room highly excited, and, throwing a newspaper in my lap, exclaimed, "There! your rascally old father has pegged out, leaving you a shilling for a dowry, and hereafter you may shift for yourself, for I'm cursed if I maintain you!" I did not comprehend him at first, but too soon the paragraph met my eyes, announcing the sudden death of my beloved father. I gave a shriek and fainted. I can never forget the agony of the moment when I recovered. I had lived in the hope of one day meeting my father's forgiving smile. I cared not for the loss of fortune. The world was to me a blank! I forgot to tell you that Clarence was gone, no one knew where. About ten days after my father's death Mr. Orfield returned; but, O, how changed! His spirit was cowering under some direful disease. I exerted myself and rendered him all the assistance of which I was capable. He grew worse and worse, and it was then that I wrote to you. I nursed him eight days faithfully; the ninth he died. I was of course miserable and destitute, and was almost in despair, as the funeral procession of my husband moved from the door. Just then your carriage drove up, and I knew you had received my letter. You know the rest.

*Enter* AGNES.

AGNES. Miss Mary, there is a lady below wants to see you.

AUNT MARY (*rising*). Calm yourself, child, I will return directly. [*Exit* Aunt MARY.]

AGNES. Law, Miss Nora, is that you? I'm so glad to see you. [*Approaches* NORA.] We had rare times that morning after you run off to be married. Your father and Miss Maria found out, somehow, that I had a hand in it, and they told me to pack my things and move. Well, Bill Howard, my sweetheart, thought this was rough treatment after I had helped you off so kind, and so he said I was not dependent on the Courtneys, and so he married me right away. So, you see, I killed two birds with one stone—got a husband for you and one for myself. But, law, they do tell me poor Mr. Orfield—

NORA (*nervously*). Do n't mention his name! I am thinking of my poor father. My conduct was the death of him. [*Clasps her hands and weeps.*]

AGNES. O, miss, do n't say that. Every body knows Mr. Courtney died with the pneumonia, and *you* had no hand in killing him. He wanted to see you when he was sick, and would have sent for you, but nobody knew where to find you.

NORA. O, Agnes, I would give worlds to recall that night when—

AGNES. Yes! yes! you did do wrong, but I could not see it then. It's a dreadful feeling to do a wrong thing that you can't undo. But it's a warning to you, miss, not to marry again. When a woman gets fairly rid of one husband she is a born fool to marry another.

NORA. Does your husband treat you ill?

AGNES. W-e-l-l, I can't say exactly. But, miss, a *hus-band* is one thing and a *sweetheart* another.

NORA. What do you mean?

AGNES. Why, I mean what I say. Afore one is married the man is all politeness. When Howard was courting me, if I dropped my handkerchief, he would pick it up as quick as a wink; and now, if I was to drop my head, he would n't turn on his heel to pick it up. Ah, miss, there is a monstrous difference! I tell you, marrying is n't what folks think it is.

*Enter* Aunt MARY *and* MARIA.

MARIA (*approaches* NORA). Dear cousin, welcome home again. [*They embrace.*]

NORA. Would to heaven I had never left my home!

MARIA. Do not indulge in vain regrets. You have youth, and will recover your health and see many happy days.

NORA. Never! never! The death of my father without his forgiveness is a sorrow that throws a shadow gloomy and dark over my soul! Life's glitter can never impart warmth to my desolate heart!

MARIA. Come, dear Nora, away with such gloomy thoughts. You must live for the sake of surviving friends. An attorney is waiting below in the library, and your presence is necessary.

NORA. For what?

AUNT MARY. Your cousin here wishes to make over the right to your father's estate.

NORA. Maria must not. It will be unjust.

MARIA. Rather say it would be unjust for me to keep that which is really yours. My dear uncle was afraid to leave the property to you lest your husband should squander it. Mr. Orfield, was the object of his detestation, and not you, Nora. Your father left the property to me, feeling assured that you would get the benefit of all put in my hands. Therefore you must submit to my will.

NORA. I can not allow you to do this.

MARIA. You can not prevent me.

NORA. But you have a husband? What will he say?

MARIA. He thinks it highly improper for me to keep your estate, and wishes me to have it permanently secured to you.

NORA. O, if Clarence had only been thus disinterested, how happy I might have been!

MARIA. Come, no more words, cousin; let us go and settle this business. I wish you to be present.

[*Exeunt* NORA, MARIA, *and* Aunt MARY.]

AGNES (*coming forward*). Well, well! just think, but a few years ago Miss Nora was as lively as a bird, and now how pale and sorrowful she looks! They say that husband of hers did n't treat her well. I would n't have the sins of men's treatment to their wives to answer for, no, not for the whole enduring world! Howsomever, it is a warning to girls, and 'specially school-girls, not to marry afore they gets an education; and not to be having beaux no way; and not to be taking up with every man that talks love to them; and not to be running off to get married in general. For my part, if a woman could make up her mind, it is best, I *do* think, not to marry at all!

*(Curtain falls.)*

## COSTUMES.

### SCENE I.

NORA. Dress of crimson silk velvet, trimmed in point lace; pearl ornaments. In this scene NORA should look as blooming and fresh as possible, so as to make the contrast (when she appears in the last scene) as striking as possible.

LILLIAN. Dress of Marie Louise silk, trimmed with blonde (or a mazarine blue silk, trimmed with ermine); brilliant ornaments. This part should be sustained with life and gayety or spirit.

MARIA. Dress of gay-colored French merino, trimmed in black; coral ornaments.

### SCENE II.

NORA. Dress of deep mourning; a widow's cap on the head; no ornaments. She presents in this scene a faded appearance. This can be done by whitening the face well, and then apply faintly under the eyes a little burnt cork, and a few faint lines under the lower lip. For a better description refer to "the Sociables," as in that book the "making up" of the various expressions requisite in stage acting is fully described.

AUNT MARY. Home dress, suitable for a maiden lady.

MARIA. Dress, morning wrapper, open in front, fastened at the waist by heavy cord and tassel; embroidered petticoat.

AGNES. Dress, calico; an apron of white, with pockets— as a white apron always suggests the idea of a chambermaid; a jaunty muslin cap on the head.

# MRS. VATICAN SMYTHE'S PARTY.

## CHARACTERS.

Mrs. VATICAN SMYTHE.
Mrs. PETROLEUM.
Mrs. SHODDY.
Mrs. General ALLFIGHT.
Mrs. SALLY BROWNE.
Aunt PEGGY LIGHTFOOT.
Ladies in attendance.

## SCENE I.

*Room. A well-furnished chamber;* Mrs. VATICAN SMYTHE *standing before a mirror, in full party dress, arranging her toilet; throws a hair-brush down; indignantly advances to front of stage.*

Mrs. SMYTHE. This is *too* bad! Just to think I have invited all those fashionable people here this evening, and now I am to be mortified by the presence of old Aunt Peggy Lightfoot! I do think it is an outrage! She *always* comes at the very time I least want her. [*Puts her hand to her head.*] Let me see, I must fall upon some plan to prevent these fine folks from seeing her. It will *never* do for Mrs. Petroleum to meet her; and Mrs. General Allfight is such a make-game, she would never be done talking of Aunt Peggy's peculiarities. O, I do think it is such a bore to have poor relations. [*Looks toward the door.*] But here comes the old lady now: I must try and compromise the matter with her in some way.

[*Enter* Aunt PEGGY; *starts with surprise as she looks at* Mrs. SMYTHE.]

AUNT PEGGY. Sakes alive, how you are dressed! You must be going to a party.

Mrs. SMYTHE. Not exactly. I have only invited a few select friends to spend the evening with me.

AUNT PEGGY. O, ho! that's the way of it. I thought the house looked mighty light as I drove up to the door, but I didn't dream about a party. Well, I come, then, just in the nick of time!

Mrs. SMYTHE (*wincing*). Y-e-s, but I did not think you cared about meeting *fashionable* people.

AUNT PEGGY. O, I've no objection to fashionable people, provided they don't put on too many airs. Who is to be here?

Mrs. SMYTHE (*pretending to study*). Let me see. There is Mrs. Petroleum, Mrs. General Allfight, and—O, I do not know how many.

AUNT PEGGY. And Sally Browne—of course she will be here?

Mrs. SMYTHE (*confused*). W-e-l-l, n-o. You see, Aunt Peggy, Sally has a house full of little children, and it is not convenient for her to leave home at night.

AUNT PEGGY (*excitedly*). You don't tell me that Sally Browne is not *invited*—your own born sister!

Mrs. SMYTHE (*plays with her fan, and looks down*). Aunt Peggy, you know Sally's circumstances, and that she is not able to dress much, and I knew that she had nothing fine enough to wear to meet Mrs. Petroleum and—

AUNT PEGGY (*raises her hands indignantly*). Jane Smythe, I am astonished at you, and did give you credit for some sense; but I see that living in the city has made a plump fool of you! Who *is* this Mrs. Petroleum?

Mrs. SMYTHE. Her husband is *very* wealthy. You know he struck oil?

AUNT PEGGY (*impatiently*). No, I don't know. Struck fiddlesticks! I'll warrant that Sally Browne has more sense in a minute than this up-start has in a year.

Mrs. SMYTHE. Well, but you know we must all conform to circumstances. Mrs. Petroleum and Mrs. Shoddy, and all the other ladies who are coming here this evening, have fine houses in the upper part of the city, and they give elegant entertainments, and, in short, they are entirely out of Sally Browne's circle.

AUNT PEGGY. Yes, and I hope they will always stay out of her "circle," as you call it! I tell you, Jane, that your

finical airs do n't suit me.  It will be late in the day when
I throw off my own blood-kin because I am ashamed of
them.

Mrs. Smythe.  I am not ashamed of Sally; but I know
she would feel mortified if these fashionable people were to
see her, unless—

Aunt Peggy (*impatiently*).  Tut—nonsense!  Do n't talk
that way to me!  I know you are ashamed of her, and the
next thing will be that you are ashamed of me.  But I must
sit down, for I have been riding on the cars all day, and I
am tired.

Mrs. Smythe (*offers a chair*).  Excuse me, Aunt Peggy,
for I was so flurried when you came in that I did not think
to ask you to be seated.  [Aunt Peggy *takes a seat.*]  You
know it always excites one to have company.

Aunt Peggy.  Having company never excites *me*, for I
think what *I* can eat *they* can eat; and if they do n't like it
they can take the less of it.

Mrs. Smythe.  You will be very comfortable up here.  I
would ask you down in the parlor, but I know you prefer
being alone.  [*Aside.*]  I must flatter her, or she will suspect me.  [*To* Aunt Peggy.]  O, I have a present for you.
[*Goes to a drawer, takes out a dress-pattern.*]  See, I bought
this for you some time ago.

Aunt Peggy (*takes dress and lays it across her lap*).  It
is very pretty; but I forgot to tell you that I came to the
city to-day upon *particular* business, and I wanted to have
a little private chat with you.

Mrs. Smythe.  Mercy, Aunt Peggy! this is no time for
business.  The ladies are waiting below for me, and you
really must excuse me.  Amuse yourself the best you can,
and when they are all done eating I will send up for you,
as I know you would rather eat at the second table.

Aunt Peggy.  O, yes, I see! you do n't want an old-
fashioned body like me to be seen at your table with the
"*quality*," and I suppose you gave me the dress to pay me
not to be seen.

Mrs. Smythe.  N-o-t exactly!

Aunt Peggy.  Well, I promise on the word of an honest
woman not to go into the dining-room while your fine folks
are eating.

Mrs. Smythe (*aside*).  I am glad to hear that.  [*To* Aunt

PEGGY.] Law! I hope you do n't think that I feel ashamed
of you? Do try and be comfortable; I really *must* go
down. [*Exit* Mrs. SMYTHE.]

AUNT PEGGY. Hope I don't think that she feels ashamed
of me! I can see through a mill-stone as well as the man
who pecks it. I have a mind to pitch this dress into the
fire—but no, I will give it to Sally Browne. Ah, Mrs. Jane
Vatican Smythe, you little know what brought your old
aunt to town this day. But you will know soon enough.
I have promised not to go in the *dining-room*, but I did not
promise to stay out of the parlor. [*Rises, walks to and fro.*]
And I am to eat at the *second* table like a hireling. Well,
[*looks down,*] I will, at any rate, change my gown, for who
knows but I may yet see "Mrs. PETROLEUM"?

[*Exit* Aunt PEGGY.]

(*Curtain falls.*)


SCENE II. ⁻

*Room decorated. Ladies promenading, conversing in panto-
mime.* Mrs. SMYTHE, Mrs. PETROLEUM, Mrs. SHODDY, *and*
Mrs. General ALLFIGHT *seated near the front of stage.*

Mrs. SMYTHE. I am afraid we will have a dull party, as
all our husbands are absent.

Mrs. ALLFIGHT. As the General says, it is like bread and
hoecake—so much of a sameness.

Mrs. SHODDY. O, we 'll git along first-rate; for my part
I am glad they are not here, for I *despise* men.

Mrs. PETROLEUM. I do, too; I think men is so hateful.
[*Fans.*]

Mrs. ALLFIGHT. That is just what the General says; he
despises men, but he likes the ladies.

Mrs. SHODDY. The laws a me! did you all hear about
Miss Graham's little boy?

Mrs. SMYTHE. No! What?

Mrs. SHODDY. Why, he was burnt to death.

Mrs. SMYTHE. How on earth did it happen?

Mrs. SHODDY. His clothes cotch a-fire somehow.

Mrs. ALLFIGHT. As the General says, "horrible."

Mrs. PETROLEUM (*fans herself and tosses her head*). Yes,

indeed; I ain't afeerd to die, but I always thought I'd hate to be burnt to death.

Mrs. SHODDY.  So would I.  But, laws a me! there is the Miller family that's in a sight of trouble.

Mrs. SMYTHE.  What is the matter?

Mrs. SHODDY.  Matter enough.  Their son John was killed on that steamboat that blowed up the other day.

Mrs. SMYTHE.  Shocking!

Mrs. ALLFIGHT.  The General says that is what comes of tubular boilers.

Mrs. PETROLEUM.  Yes, indeed.  [*Fans herself.*]  I ain't afeerd to die, but I always thought I'd hate to be blowed up in a tubureau boiler.

Mrs. SHODDY.  They do say John's death will kill his sister; the one that's got the consumption.  But them Millers needed something to bring them down; they be so awful stuck up.

Mrs. SMYTHE.  I am really sorry for the family, and that poor girl with consumption.

Mrs. ALLFIGHT.  The General says it is a dreadful disease.

Mrs. PETROLEUM (*fans herself*).  Yes, indeed.  I ain't afeerd to die, but I always thought I'd hate to have consumption; it is sich a long, lingering disease.

Mrs. SHODDY.  And old man Miller has been struck with appleplexy, and that makes the matter worse.

Mrs. SMYTHE.  Misfortunes never come alone.

Mrs. ALLFIGHT.  That's exactly what the General says.

Mrs. PETROLEUM.  Yes, indeed.  [*Fans herself.*]  I ain't afeerd to die, but I always thought I'd hate to die with appeplexy, it is so suddent.

Mrs. SMYTHE.  Changing the subject, Mrs. Shoddy, where are your daughters?

Mrs. SHODDY.  Laws a me! we sent them off to school last fall.

Mrs. SMYTHE.  Where did you place them?

Mrs. SHODDY.  Why, at Abbott's, of course.  It's the dearest school; but money is no object with us since Mr. Shoddy struck ile.

Mrs. PETROLEUM (*fans herself*).  That's so.

Mrs. SMYTHE.  How long will the girls remain?

Mrs. SHODDY.  I can't tell exactly.  We will let them *graduate a year or two.*

Mrs. SMYTHE. I do not see how you can bear to be separated from them. [*Enter* Aunt PEGGY LIGHTFOOT *behind* Mrs. SMYTHE; *walks slowly across the stage; peers at the company.*] I really do— [Mrs. SMYTHE *perceives* Aunt PEGGY; *screams; falls from her chair;* Mrs. SHODDY *supports her.*]

(*Curtain falls.*)


SCENE III.

*A plain room.* Mrs. SALLY BROWNE *and* Aunt PEGGY *seated near a table.*

Mrs. BROWNE. It is not possible that Jane Smythe treated you in this way?

AUNT PEGGY. Yes, it is all true. I saw as soon as I got in the house that company was expected, and I would have come straight here; but I wanted to test Jane Smythe, so I staid. As I told you, she gave me the dress to pay me for not going down to supper, so I determined to mortify her.

Mrs. BROWNE. And you really went in the parlor, among all the fine folks?

AUNT PEGGY. Yes, and a bull in a china-shop would not have kicked up a greater fuss. Jane fainted, and the balance of the women squealed like so many young colts.

Mrs. BROWNE (*laughing*). And what did *you* do?

AUNT PEGGY. Why, I staid till the servants took Jane off to bed and all the company went home; and then I got one of the boys to bring my satchel, and I came over here.

Mrs. BROWNE. And did none of the company eat supper?

AUNT PEGGY. No! Jane had fainted and was carried off, and every thing was helter-skelter. So the *quality* left in a hurry.

Mrs. BROWNE. Jane will never forgive you, Aunt Peggy.

AUNT PEGGY. O, yes she will, when she finds out my business to the city.

Mrs. BROWNE. And, pray, if it is not impertinent, what is your business?

AUNT PEGGY. Nothing is impertinent from you, Sally, for you have always acted to me as a daughter, and, in spite of my old-fashioned notions, you have treated me with kindness and consideration, and you are entitled to my confidence.  I received a letter from England the day before I came to town, informing me that a great-uncle of mine has died, leaving me his sole heiress, and I am the mistress of seventy-five thousand pounds!

Mrs. Browne (*greatly surprised*).  Is it possible?

Aunt Peggy.  Yes, and I wanted to tell Jane of my good luck last night; but, no, she said it was no time to talk about business, and would not listen.

Mrs. Browne.  Perhaps she will be sorry she did not.

Aunt Peggy.  Yes; but she will be still more sorry when she hears that I intend to give *you* the bulk of my property.

Mrs. Browne (*confused and surprised*).  O, Aunt Peggy!

Aunt Peggy.  Why not?  If Jane had acted as a genuine woman ought, I intended dividing the fortune equally between you, as she and yourself are all the **near relations** I have.  As it is, I mean to give the greater part of it to you, and I'll warrant the next *quality* party she has you will be able to dress fine enough to meet all the *Petroleums* and *Shoddies* in the world.

Mrs. Browne.  But I feel sorry for Jane.  She will be so disappointed when she knows all.

Aunt Peggy.  It will serve her right for acting like a silly, vain, light woman, as she is; and I am in hopes it will teach her a lesson, and that is, not to despise plain, old-fashioned people because they are not used to the forms and customs of city life; for many an honest heart beats underneath the coarsest dress.

(*Curtain falls.*)

---

## COSTUMES.

Mrs. Smythe, Mrs. Petroleum, Mrs. Shoddy, and Mrs. Allfight.  Dresses made in party style, elaborately trimmed; jewels, flowers, and feathers, to complete the costume.

Ladies in Attendance.  Dresses in party style.

Aunt Peggy.  In the first scene she is dressed in a coarse alpaca, the skirt narrow and short; a cape of material differing from the dress; a very wide collar; no hoops; heavy shoes; a sun-bonnet of gingham, to which is attached a long black lace veil; a reticule on her arm. In the second scene, Aunt PEGGY wears an obsolete black satin dress; a cap with a very high crown, trimmed in bright ribbon; slippers; reticule; spectacles; sports a large, old-fashioned fan, or a turkey-wing. In the last scene, Aunt PEGGY is dressed as in first scene.

Mrs. BROWNE. Plain, but neat home dress.

Children can be introduced in this scene, at the option of the teacher or manager of the play.

# THE PERFECTION OF BEAUTY.

### AN OPERA FOR FEMALE SCHOOLS.

### PART I.

*Enter the Nine Muses—Opening Chorus of Muses.*

We are the loved Muses whose songs
  Can lighten the pressure of care;
To us the sweet mission belongs
  The spirit to soften and cheer.

From ancient Parnassus we bring
  Soft melody, floating in air;
Of external beauty we sing,
  Of beauties both brilliant and fair.

The kingdom of nature we greet,
  With all the rich treasures of time;
Variety making complete,
  From lowliest to the sublime.

O, come from the green mountain side,
  The forest, and meadows so gay;
O, come from the blue ocean tide,
  O, come and respond to our lay.

*Enter the Sun—Solo.*

I come forth as a glorious king,
  In royal robes arrayed,
With my crown of light, beaming bright,
  Of sparkling luster made.

At midday I display my powers
  In majesty and might,
Warming the earth with golden showers
  Of radiant heat and light!

At eventide I lay me down
  In a rich crimson vest,
To dream of day in other climes,
  While this good land may rest.

*Chorus.*

Hail! hail! thou splendid orb of day,
Traveling in thy might;
Making all nature fresh and gay
With lustrous heat and light.

*Enter the Rainbow—Solo.*

The Rainbow! the Rainbow, arching high,
Decking the brow of the evening sky
With colors of gold and purple hue,
And the flaming crimson tinged with blue.

Quite gracefully bending to display
Its gorgeous tints, and then away—
Away! away! and nobody knows
Where the bright, beautiful phantom goes!

*Chorus of Muses.*

Lovely Rainbow, stay, O, stay!
Why so swiftly pass away?
Let us touch thy golden wing.  [*Exit Rainbow.*]
See! 'tis gone! the pretty thing.

*Enter the Stars—Chorus of Stars.*

We come! we come! the Stars with their light,
Chasing the somber shadows of night,
Dwelling on high, and seen from afar.
All in the heavens—in the fresh air.

Twinkling and smiling on all below,
Greeting the flowers which nightly blow,
While sportive zephyrs around them play,
Kissing the dew from their leaves away.

*Chorus of Muses.*

Welcome Stars, so gently gleaming,
Thro' the misty veil of night,
On our earth so kindly beaming,
With your soft and humid light.

Like so many rays of glory,
From your pure and native skies,
And in ancient fabled story
Thought to be the angel's eyes.  [*Exit Stars.*]

*Enter the Birds—Chorus of Birds.*

We are the songsters of Summer and Spring,
So merry of heart, so light on the wing;
In native costume, variously dressed,
Too happy and free for cares to molest.

All sportive in ether the live-long day,
Or resting awhile on a leafy spray,
And filling the air with music that floats
On the breath of the gale in plaintive notes.

Here's the rich-colored bird of Paradise,
And the turtle-dove, with its soft, black eyes;
And the lark, in the bright and morning sky,
Resounding his Maker's praise on high.

And the goldfinch, coming in early Spring;
And the canary, who doth joyously sing;
The lively robin, with his cheerful notes;
And bluebirds, in pairs, all tuning their throats.

And the humming-bird, with its downy nest,
As warm and as soft as an angel's breast;
The carrier-pigeon, so swift and so light;
The wood thrush, with song so clear in the night.

### Chorus of Muses.

Welcome! O, welcome, ye bright, feathered throng,
Who sip the pure air and revel in song:
    O, come from the hill,
    O, come from the rill,
Come away from the dark forest trees!
    O, come from the glade,
    All in the cool shade,
Where the butterfly flits in the breeze!
    Come in broad day,
    With plumage so gay,
Blithely skimming the heavens along;
    Or come in the night,
    With the glow-worm bright:
Thrice, thrice welcome, ye children of song—
Thrice, thrice welcome, ye children of song!

*Solo—Genius of Beauty.*

See, all nature is blest,
And how tastefully dressed,
  By the Maker of sea and of land!
From the green mountain high,
To the small fire-fly,
  All made by His bountiful hand!

*Chorus.*

The golden fish in the limpid tide,
And the silver trout which nimbly glide
Down the rippling stream in mirthful glee,
And the finny tribe of the rolling sea ;
The graceful roe.in the forest dell ;
The little pet lambs and gay gazelle—
All made by his bountiful hand,
All made by his bountiful hand.
                    [*Exit Genius of Beauty.*]

*Enter the Trees.*

We are the Trees, the verdant Trees,
Waving our leaflets with the breeze;
The sturdy Oak, with branches wide,
  Defying the ruthless gale :
Evergreen Pines, with lofty tops,
  And the Willow of the vale—
The Weeping Willow, the mournful Willow,
  The Willow of the vale!

The Broad-leaved Palm, and Fir and Bay,
Catalpa, with its flow'rets gay :
The Fringe-tree, myrtle growing round,
  In the lone, retired cove;
Arbor Cælestis, and Sycamore,
  And the Aspen of the grove—
The trembling Aspen, the tender Aspen,
  The Aspen of the grove!

The Laurel, yielding rich perfume ;
Pride of China, with purple bloom;
And tropical Trees, with fruit so rare,
  The fertile Trees of the East;

The Orange, Lemon, and sweet Fig,
   With the Olive of the East—
The peaceful Olive, celestial Olive,
   The Olive of the East.

*Chorus of Muses.*

The Lord Jehovah his great power displayed
When *He* this beautiful creation made;
Let wide-spread Trees his blessed commands obey;
Bow your tall heads and grateful homage pay
To Him the source of every truth and good—
God of the desert and the cool greenwood.

                    *[Exit Trees.*

*Enter the Flowers—Chorus.*

The "perfection of nature" we are called,
   By one who loves us well,
Whether blooming at home, or growing wild
   Within the lonely dell.

Where Blue-bells are peeping thro' the long grass,
   So modest and so meek;
Where the Eglantine sheds its soft perfume,
   With flushes on its cheek.

And the Daisy white, and the Daisy red,
   To grace the garden spot;;
Where the Tulip looks down, with gaudy pride,
   And the "Forget-me-not."

Tube-roses and Pinks, in the gay parterre,
   Tuft with the ivy ground;
Where Lilacs can vie with the Snow-ball high,
   And "Love-lies-bleeding" round.

The Snow-drop and Crocus of balmy Spring,
   And Violets blue and white,
The Hyacinth white, and yellow Jonquil, ,
   And the pretty "By-night,"

And the Rose, the Rose, the queen of all flowers,
   In various colors seen,
Lilies-of-valley, all pure and white,
   Wrapped in their leaves of green.

Anemones and Madeira vines,
And fair exotics too,
With their delicate leaves and tender blooms
Of every class and hue.

*Chorus of Muses.*

Bright, bright are your charms, ye beautiful flowers,
Who love to recline in soft, shady bowers;
But for your blest aid our sonnets might tire—
Your sweetness elicits poetic fire.

There's a pathos and song where bright flowers meet,
Where woodbines entwine the magnolia sweet;
There's melody in the breath of the rose,
And concord where thyme with lavender grows.

The music of nature hath its own place
In the changing tints of the floral race;
So bright are your charms, ye beautiful flowers,
Made to embellish this low world of ours.

*[Exit Flowers slowly.]*

*Enter the Jewels—Chorus of Jewels.*

We are the brilliant and costly gems,
From the Andes high and foreign realms;
Coral and Pearl from the ocean bed,
The Emerald green and Rubies so red.

Amethyst purple, Agate pure white,
The Topaz yellow, the Diamond bright,
Polished by art, and brought from afar
To deck the city belles' glossy hair,

And make them so many pretty things,
With sets in gold, for their finger-rings;
Our richest and rarest are often seen
In the crown of a king or of a queen.

A much greater use yet we may claim,
Which gives immortality to our name;
We form a foundation for that abode—
The luminous City of our God!

*Genius of Beauty—Solo.*

With natural beauties the world doth abound,
Across the Atlantic, on Eastern ground;

In rich Southern climes many beauties are seen—
The North, too, can boast of its beauties, I ween.
Beyond where the green cliffs of Otter arise,
In freshness and grandeur, saluting the skies;
O, far, far away to the bright glowing West,
With pines of the mountains and alder-trees drest,
Where the rose of the vale and crab-apple bloom,
Diffusing a fragrance of mellow perfume;
Where the breezes of heaven are wont to impart
A glow to the cheek and good health to the heart:
Where wild flowers blow and pretty birds sing,
Where life is afloat and hope on the wing;
There, there we find *Beauty*, the offspring of Heaven,
On the rich landscape spontaneously graven.

[*Exit Jewels.*]

### Song of the Muses.

Good-night, good-night! ye beauties all—
  The evening twilight steals along;
When daylight peeps we will return
  And cheer you with our morning song.   [*Exeunt.*]


## PART II.

*Enter the Muses—Chorus by the Muses.*

Hail, hail to the morning, the spring-time of light,
The air is all dewy and healthful and bright;
While nature is busy and sportive and gay,
We come from Parnassus to welcome the day.

Of beauties around us, on earth, we have sung,
With music adapted to a mortal tongue;
But more spiritual themes are wont to inspire
The magical notes of a seraph's gold lyre.

*Enter Angel of Eternity.   Angel of Eternity—Solo.*

That God who made the natural sun to shine
  And cheer our hearts with genial warmth and light,
Can cause the sun of righteousness divine
  To rise upon the spirit clear and bright.

And He who in the cloud hath set his bow
Can radiate the darkness of the mind;
Reflecting thus His image to restore
Upon our souls affections good and kind.
Yes, He who framed this outward world or time
Can form with greater beauty that within;
For what are all the riches of this clime
Compared with those beyond the sphere of sin?

*Enter Angel of Time.  Angel of Time—Solo.*

The beauties of nature all fade, fade, fade,
For the fairest are often laid, laid, laid,
In the cold, cold tomb,
Never more to bloom,
On this low changing and imperfect earth—
The sad, sad doom of evanescent birth!

*Angel of Eternity—Solo.*

But beauties that are more holy and high,
They live in the mind, which never can die;
From heaven's blest court all beauty descends
And beauty with goodness, with right, ever blends.

They live self-existent in the divine,
Yet too pure with Him in mortals to shine;
Tempered to suit us, they come from above
In thoughts and affections of wisdom and love!

Thoughts and affections no good can bestow
Till brought into forms of uses below—
Forms which the seekers of virtue will find
Made to embellish the heart and the mind.

[*Exit Angels.*]

*Enter Honesty and Decorum—Duet.*

Order is God's first law, and we
Are missioned to impart
*That* beauty which should ever be
The mentor of each heart.

Civility to all extend,
The justice due perform;
An honest motive be the end,
Decorum its bright form.

[*Exit Honesty and Decorum.*]

*Enter Devotion and Gratitude—Duet.*

To us the beauteous forms of use are given
To elevate the soul and open Heaven;
Its bright pellucid glories to reveal,
And to impart the bliss which angels feel.

When in their bright abodes beyond the skies,
Freed from all worldly care and selfish ties,
'Tis ours the virtue of this faith to prove
By acts of duty and by works of love.

*Chorus by Muses.*

Love and light to man revealing
   Thro' the gentle power of prayer;
Softly o'er the spirit stealing,
   Releasing from unholy fear.

Then in praise to God returning
   For the mercy He imparts;
With a flame of glory burning
   On the altar of our hearts.
              [*Exit Devotion and Gratitude.*]

*Enter Temperance—Solo.*

See Temperance with her crystal bowl,
   From nature's limpid springs,—
A beverage nice to poise the soul
   From all unholy things.

Which surely is a beauteous grace
   To keep the pious mind
From lawless passions, and erase
   Excess of every kind.

*Chorus by Muses.*

Come on, ye sons of Bacchus, come!
   Her banner is unfurled;
She holds aloft the sacred pledge,
   Inviting all the world.     [*Exit Temperance.*]

*Enter Patience and Resignation—Duet.*

When storms of affliction encompass the life,
   O'erwhelming the sorrowful soul,
Resignation will quell the horrible strife,
   And Patience the storm will control.

Tho' boisterous the wind, and heavy the sea,
And clouds overhead looking dark,
Those beautiful handmaids the pilots will be,
And moor into port the frail bark!

*Chorus by Muses.*

As these lovely guides contending,
Yielding to His will,
See! the Lord the bark defending,
Crying, "Peace, be still!"
[*Exit Patience and Resignation.*]

*Enter Chastity and Innocence—Duet.*

Ye licentious, come not near us!
We are unblemished, pure and fair;
Avaunt! *you* can not revere us,
Your presence might our beauty mar.
One unhallowed touch might harm us,
And thus despoil our matchless fame;
Spheres of truth and goodness charm us
Where evil lust can not inflame.

*Chorus by Muses.*

Chastity! thou precious boon,
So beautiful and rare,
Thine is the power to bind in one
The fond "conjugal pair."
While innocence doth crown their days,
Devoid of selfish strife,
The stream of life takes smoothly on
The husband and the wife!
[*Exit Chastity and Innocence.*]

*Enter Humility—Solo.*

I am the meek-eyed and lowliest grace,
So timid, so mild, and serene;
With the vile and impure never have place,
But dwell with the holy and clean.
For what I possess give honor and praise
To HIM the great Giver divine,
Tho' filled with all good my spirit still says:
"The kingdom and glory be thine!" [*Exit Humility.*]

*Enter Sincerity—Solo.*

They call me beautiful and very fair,
With open brow, and free, ingenuous air;
O, say, what peerless virtue can surpass
That bosom, though 'twere transparent glass!

Thro' which strict Truth might look with piercing eye,
And not one atom of concealment spy;
An artless spirit, free from all disguise,
Nor would a mantle throw to blind the wise.

*Chorus of Muses.*

The sun is pompous in his strength and might,
And gilds the rainbow still with softer light.
The birds are charming, and the bright stars shine;
The flowers are lovely, and their rich wreaths twine

In clusters sweet, around our garden trees,
Waving their green tops in the gentle breeze;
And precious stones of many sparkling hues,
Among the beautiful their place can choose.

Say, ye impartial, say! can all of these
The virtuous mind and holy angels please,
Like one with "free-born look" and honest smile,
An Israelite in whom there is no guile! [*Exit Sincerity.*]

*Enter Faith, Hope, and Charity. Faith—Solo.*

I am the rock on which the Lord
His glorious church hath built,
A sure foundation to redeem
Repentant souls from guilt.

*Chorus of Muses.*

Faith, the gift of God extending
To the children of his love;
From all evil thus defending,
His redeeming power to prove.

*Hope—Solo.*

On this unshaken rock I stand,
A beacon to the soul;
Still upward pointing to the land—
The Christian's wished-for goal.

*Chorus of Muses.*

This gospel, Hope, supports the mind
Firm thro' misfortune's blast;
On it the Christian still may lean,
An anchor sure and fast!

*Charity—Solo.*

See, Charity cometh with dove-like cheek,
So gentle, so loving, and kind;
Of faults and of failings never will speak,
But always some virtue can find;
Over the erring her mantle will throw,
Excusing, tho' others assail;
All, all may forsake and leave to the foe,
But Charity never can fail.

Charity! Charity! brightest and best
Of all the rich treasures of Heaven,
O, how our world would be favored and blest
To all could thy spirit be given.
[*Exit Faith, Hope, and Charity.*]

*Enter Mercy and Truth—Duet.*

And Mercy is the matchless, beauteous grace
Which moved the everlasting God to come
As Truth, and save a wretched, fallen race,
That we, in Heaven, might find a blissful home.

If the good Lord his mercy doth bestow
On us, so far beneath his holy name,
How much forbearance should we ever show
To the offending, tho' they be to blame.
[*Exit Mercy and Truth.*]

*Enter Righteousness and Peace—Duet.*

These lovely Graces are;
The fruits of Righteousness,
When loved and cherished, fill the mind
With pure and perfect Peace.

Peace, Peace! thou child of Heaven,
How dear, how sweet thou art!
O! that thy motto might be graven
On every human heart!

*Chorus in full.*

This pure transparent Righteousness
    Belongeth to the Lord,
And he, the only source of Truth,
    Shines glorious in his word.

In every dot, and every line,
    JEHOVAH GOD doth dwell,
Who did assume the human form
    To rescue man from hell,

Where all is ugly and deformed,
    And loathsome, and impure,
Where not a trace of Beauty will
    Be seen for evermore!

Thus all may learn the world above
    *Is Beauty's native home,*
Where HEAVEN and BEAUTY, GOD and LOVE,
    Exist as only ONE.

Then let us raise our anthems high,
    To Heaven's immortal King.
Sounding his praise thro' earth and sky,
    And with the Psalmist sing:

"Beautiful for situation, the joy of the whole earth, is
Mount Zion, on the sides of the north the city of the great
King.  Out of Zion, the PERFECTION OF BEAUTY, God hath
shined."—PSALM xlviii, 2; and l, 2.

---

## COSTUMES.

The Nine Muses are represented by nine girls dressed in
flowing robes of airy material, each bearing a musical instrument, or a garland of flowers, or some badge of science.  The
Muses are generally represented crowned with palms, but a
crown of gems, or one of leaves or flowers, would be appropriate.

CALLIOPE, who is esteemed the most excellent of all the
nine, should be dressed in manner to distinguish her from the
rest.

CLIO is so named from *glory*.

ERATO has her name from *love.*
THALIA, from her *gayety* and *pleasantry.*
MELPOMENE, from the excellency of her *song.*
TERPSICHORE has her name from her delight in *dancing.*
EUTERPE, from the *sweetness* of her *singing.*
POLYHYMNIA, from *memory, gesture,* and *action.*
URANIA was so called because she *sings of divine things.*

A lady teacher of refinement and taste can, from the above, soon determine a dress that will suit the different characters of the Muses, and also the most appropriate emblem for each one to bear. Perhaps a few suggestions relative to the dress of each character in this simple little opera will assist those who deem it worthy of imitation; and I will, therefore, mention the dress in connection with each character as they succeed each other, for, to make the play attractive to the audience, too much taste can not be displayed in the arrangement of the stage, or the appearance of the actors.

THE SUN. Represented by a young lady. Dress of thin white or red illusion, spangled properly.

THE RAINBOW. Dress of silk tulle, in which all the colors of the rainbow must be regularly combined.

THE STARS. Dresses of blue or white tarlatan, dotted with stars cut out of gilt or silver paper, and placed at regular distances upon the tarlatan. The stars are put on with common thin paste, and dried immediately by passing a warm iron over each star as it is placed upon the tarlatan. It is easily done, and the effect is beautiful. A crown made of pasteboard and covered with stars should be added.

CHORUS OF BIRDS. Dresses of various hues, and made of light material. The best singers should be chosen to represent this chorus. Each girl ought to wear a bandeau upon her head with the name of the bird she represents in gilt letters upon it. To make the tableau more effective, the girls should be arranged in *pairs.*

GENIUS OF BEAUTY. The prettiest girl in the school should be chosen for this character. Dress of airy texture, trimmed tastefully about the skirt with gay ribbons, or looped over a satin petticoat with bunches of delicate flowers. The berthe and sleeves trimmed to correspond with the skirt. Hair curled and a wreath of trembling flowers.

CHORUS OF TREES. The girls who represent this should wear dresses of different shades of green, ornamented with leaves of brown and green, of a lighter or darker shade than the dress itself. These can be pasted on in wreaths or rows around the lower part of the skirt, or in regular distances, (as the stars are in the dresses above.) Wreaths of *leaves*, intermingled with green and brown, with buds and blossoms for the hair.

CHORUS OF FLOWERS. These must be arranged with regard to the color of the flower each girl personates. Blue-bells, blue; Roses, red and white; Tulip, variegated, etc., etc. A wreath of the flowers, corresponding to each character, ought to be worn by all means. If natural flowers can not be procured, artificial can. In arranging this tableau the teacher must decide the characters, for a bold, showy girl ought not to personate a violet; neither would a timid, shrinking girl do to represent a gaudy flower. All these little things must be taken into consideration, for it requires a good deal of tact to arrange *trifles* in a way to make the general effect of an exhibition striking. I have known some very amusing and ridiculous scenes to occur from this very want of tact on the part of teachers.

CHORUS OF JEWELS. The young ladies who compose this should, if it is practicable, wear a set of the gems they personate. The color of the dress ought, at any rate, to correspond with the jewels they represent. Emerald, green; Ruby, red; Topaz, yellow; Amethyst, a bluish violet color; Carbuncle, a deep red, etc., etc. The Chorus of Jewels makes a brilliant and effective tableau if properly arranged.

## PART II.

ANGEL OF ETERNITY. Dress of crimson satin; a tunic of white satin, embroidered with gold; an ephod of white satin, brought from behind the neck over the shoulder, crossed over the bosom, and studded with gems. A crown upon the head, formed of brilliants.

HONESTY, DECORUM, DEVOTION, and GRATITUDE. Dresses of white, light material, each bearing a badge, either upon the head or in the hand, on which must be inscribed the names of each in gilt letters.

TEMPERANCE. *Pure* white dress, bearing in her hand a glass pitcher or goblet of clear water. There must not be a particle of color in the dress—all white.

PATIENCE and RESIGNATION. Dress of simple white, with wreaths of green leaves on the hair. All the above characters should be chosen with reference to the expression of countenance possessed by the different scholars. The meekest looking must be chosen to personate these latter.

CHARITY and INNOCENCE. Dresses of pure white, with

wreaths of white flowers. Girls with the most innocent expression of face must be chosen for these two characters.

HUMILITY. An orange-colored dress, without ornament, made of tulle, or some other light fabric. Hair perfectly plain.

SINCERITY. Dress of light blue, with ornaments to correspond. A very fair girl should act this part.

FAITH, HOPE, and CHARITY. Faith—Dress of white silk or satin, with pearl ornaments; a white wreath formed of small buds or trembling flowers; a crucifix in her hand. Hope—Dress of blue satin, embroidered with silver; a diadem of stars upon the head; an anchor in her hand. Charity—Dress of crimson satin; a mantle of white satin, falling loosely and gracefully over the shoulders, or carried on one arm; a crown of jewels.

# THE OLD MAN'S POCKET-BOOK.

## CHARACTERS.

Mr. HARRY FOPPY.
FRANK.
NED.
SUSAN, *the Broker's Daughter*.
LILY, *Sister to Susan*.
EMMA.
MARIA.

## SCENE I.

*A Parlor in a Hotel.* HARRY FOPPY, FRANK, *and* NED *seated at a table on which is a backgammon-board;* FOPPY *and* FRANK *engaged in the game,* NED *looking on. After the curtain rises, they continue to play a few minutes.*

FRANK (*throwing the dice*). Sixes, I declare! Well, Foppy, that gammons you.

FOPPY. I give it up. Suppose we stop and take a smoke. [*Takes a cigar-case from his pocket and offers it to* NED *and* FRANK, *who take a cigar.*]

*Enter* LILY (*unseen by the young men; takes a seat at some distance*).

NED. Foppy, what news is this I hear of you? They say you are really courting Miss Susan, the daughter of the rich broker, Jones.

FRANK. I can not see what there is to admire about *her*. I assure you she is not *my* style. [*Puffs cigar.*] Well, Foppy, I think Ned and I are entitled to your confidence. Come, tell us all about it.

NED. Yes, Foppy, speak freely—we are all friends.

FOPPY (*strokes his chin with his hand pompously*). Well, boys, I will be candid. It is true that I am courting Miss

Susan Jones, but the fact is I care nothing for the girl. The old man's pocket-book is all that I am after.

NED (*discovers* LILY). I would advise you not to speak quite so loud, for there is the young lady's sister.

FRANK (*looks at* LILY.) Yes, and she has heard every word that you said.

NED. Little pitchers have long ears, Foppy.

FOPPY. Never mind. [*Winks knowingly at* NED *and* FRANK.] I'll make it all right. [*To* LILY.] Come here, my little miss. [LILY *approaches* FOPPY, *who takes her on his knee.*] Did you hear what I said just now about your sister Susan?

LILY (*sharply*). I guess I did.

FOPPY (*aside*). The nation you did! [*Aloud.*] See here! will you promise not to tell any body what I said if I will give you a shinplaster?

LILY. Yes.

FOPPY (*puts a dime in the child's hand.*) Now, remember, you are not to tell.

LILY. I will.

FOPPY (*kisses* LILY *and places her upon her feet*). Run along now, that's a good child. [*Exit* LILY.] It's all right with her now.

FRANK. Don't be too certain.

NED. As I said before, little pitchers have long ears.

FRANK. And long tongues, too, sometimes.

FOPPY. I have no fears on that score, boys.

FRANK and NED. We will see.

(*Curtain falls.*)


SCENE II.

*Room.* SUSAN, EMMA, *and* MARIA *seated, sewing. Enter* LILY.

LILY. O, girls, see what Mr. Harry Foppy gave me! [*Shows the money.*]

MARIA. How did this happen?

SUSAN. You should never accept money from young men.

LILY. You was the cause of it.

SUSAN (*in surprise*). Me! What do you mean?

LILY. Ma sent me to the hotel to take a note to a lady,

and while I was waiting in the parlor Mr. Foppy and Mr. Frank and another man was there, and they asked Mr. Foppy if he wasn't courting *you?*

EMMA. My goodness! and what did Mr. Foppy say?

LILY. He said yes; but he didn't care for sister Susan—the old man's pocket-book was all that he was after, and he gave me this not to tell!

EMMA. And you took the money, and then told!

MARIA. You are a fast one!

SUSAN. Never mind, girls; I am glad Lily has told. I will now know how to treat the young man the next time he calls.

(*Curtain falls.*)


## SCENE III.

*Same room.* SUSAN *seated near a table; knocks heard outside.*

SUSAN. Come in. [*Enter* FOPPY.] Mr. Foppy, good morning. [*Rises, offers a chair.*] Pray, be seated.

FOPPY (*with an embarrassed air*). Miss Susan, excuse me—but—I—you must be aware, Miss Susan, that my frequent visits to you have not—[*puts his hand on his heart, bows profoundly*]—been without an object.

SUSAN. Really, Mr. Foppy, I would be very stupid if I did not comprehend the object of your frequent visits.

FOPPY (*with earnestness*). Dare I hope that my fondest wishes are about to be realized? [*Bows.*]

SUSAN. You may, indeed! I understand from a most reliable source that all you are after is the old man's pocket-book! Allow me to present it to you—[*gives him an empty, dilapidated pocket-book*]—and, at the same time, to bid you a very good evening. [*Exit* SUSAN.]

FOPPY (*twirls the pocket-book round and round*). Well, well! this is what I call putting a fellow through in double-quick!

*Enter* FRANK *and* NED.

FRANK and NED. Ha! ha! ha! Sold, Foppy—sold!

(*Curtain falls.*)

# ARAMINTA JENKINS.

## CHARACTERS.

ARAMINTA JENKINS.
SUSAN.
LOUISE.
ANNA.

## SCENE I.

*Room plainly furnished.* ANNA *and* LOUISE *standing at
right side of stage. Enter* SUSAN—*L.*

SUSAN. O, girls, we have a new scholar.
ANNA. What is her name?
SUSAN. Her name is Araminta Jenkins.
LOUISE. Mercy! what a name!
ANNA. Where did she come from?
SUSAN. Fresh from the country.
LOUISE. No doubt a real greenhorn.
SUSAN. You will think so when you see her.
ANNA. How is she dressed?
SUSAN. O, so queer; and then she talks so outlandish.
But, hush! she is coming.

*Enter* ARAMINTA—*L.*

ARAMINTA. Plague take them servants with their white
aprons. I wonder if they have packed in all my baggage.
LOUISE. How much baggage have you?
ARAMINTA. Why, two trunks, one bandbox, a carpet-
sack, a round basket, a pair of Injin rubber overshoes, and
an umbrella.
ANNA. How do you think you will like our school?
ARAMINTA (*tosses her head and walks about*). Don't
know. Maw told pap he ought to send me here a spell to

qualify myself, else I would n't marry soon; but the idea of being shut up here nearly *slays* me!

SUSAN. Have you been used to much company?

ARAMINTA. Much company! I should say I had. I went to lots of storm parties, and quiltings, and all that sort of thing, last winter. But pap said I needed one more quarter at school to polish me off.

LOUISE. What do you expect to study?

ARAMINTA. O, I'm done with 'rithmetic and all that. I am just going to be a parlor boarder, and look after music and French a bit, and spelling. You see, pap wants me to be a kick above the common run, because he's rich. He makes five cents every breath he draws, and he draws a powerful lot of breaths every day.

ANNA. What profession is your father?

ARAMINTA. Sakes alive! he ain't no professor.

ANNA. I mean, what does he do for a living?

ARAMINTA. O, I see what you mean. Well, pap was an army contractor till he struck ile. I tell you what, pap is one of the 'stocracy, if he does live in the country.

SUSAN. What do you call 'stocracy?

ARAMINTA. Laws! do n't you know? Why people that lives in four-story houses and has marble mantel-pieces, and keeps a girl to cook, and one to clean house, and a man to do extras. I've got an aunt that lives in Cincinnater, and *she* is 'stocracy, and so is pap. He is none of your mush-a-rooms!

ANNA (*smiling*). What are mush-a-rooms?

ARAMINTA. Why people that lives in two-story houses, and has n't got no marble mantel-pieces, and do n't keep but *one* girl.

LOUISE. Are you fond of reading?

ARAMINTA. Reading! I should say I was. Did n't I bring a perfect cord of yaller back novels in my trunk? [*Tosses her head.*] O, I could *live* on novels. [*Turns suddenly to* SUSAN.] Look here! Did you ever read the Children of the Abbey?

SUSAN. O, yes.

ARAMINTA. I was named out of that book. You see, when I was a baby maw called me Rachel, but you better believe when I got old enough to read the Children of the Abbey, I changed my name to *Ar-a-minta*.

Susan. I wonder you did not call yourself Amanda Fitzallan, after the heroine.

Araminta (*with disdain*). O, she was so hateful and stuck up. She always had a lot of men in love with her; and all the time she did n't love nobody but Lord Mortimore. You see *I* know all about these things. Jim Smith, he come over to our house purpose to court me; but I knowed all he was after was pap's money, and you better believe I sent him up the spout. [*Points upward.*] I know them Smiths from A to izzard, and they are the peskiest people you ever hearn tell of.

Susan. Well, changing the subject, did the war affect your part of the country?

Araminta. The war! I should say it did. That very Jim Smith I was talking about just now, went right straight and joined the army as soon as I jilted him. and the very first battle he got into he was shot plum through the arm. [*Strikes her left arm with forefinger of right hand.*]

Susan. Did he die?

Araminta. Die! I should say he did n't. The bullet has got to be molded yet to kill Jim Smith. He got well as soon as the ball was *amputated*.

Susan. I want to know if the war affects your society?

Araminta. I should say it did. All the fellers that belonged to the debating society went off into the army, and knocked the whole thing into *fits*.

Susan. I did not allude to any particular society. I wanted to know how the war affected the people generally.

Araminta. O, I see what you mean. I should say it has scared half the girls in our neighborhood out of their seven senses.

Susan. How?

Araminta. How! Why men are getting as scarce as hen's teeth, and they are afraid they will all die old maids. I heard pap say that by the time the war was over, wid-*ows* would n't be worth ten cents a car load.

Susan. You must live in a lively neighborhood?

Araminta. I should say I did. But, laws a mercy! I must go and dress for dinner, for maw said if I did n't dress three times a day you *town* folks would n't know I was 'stocracy! [*Exit with a flourish—R.*]

Susan. Poor girl! She thinks *money* is every thing.

But, tell me, girls [*addressing* LOUISE *and* ANNA], would you not rather have more brains and less money?

LOUISE and ANNA. More brains!

SUSAN. Very well, then; let us learn a lesson by knowing Araminta Jenkins; and, as long as none of us are wealthy, let us strive to be intelligent, for it is far better to be *sensible* and *humble* than to be *rich* and *arrogant*.

LOUISE (*comes forward*). As Miss Araminta Jenkins would say, "I should think it is."

(*Curtain falls.*)

## COSTUMES.

SUSAN, LOUISE, and ANNA. Neat home dresses.

ARAMINTA JENKINS. A gaudy colored dress, made awkwardly; an ill-fitting basque; tawdry ribbons about her neck and hair; a very high comb.

# THE DANCING DUTCHMAN.

## CHARACTERS.

| | |
|---|---|
| MASTER. | SERVANT. |
| TRAVELER. | DUTCHMAN. |
| JUDGE. | SHERIFF. |
| ATTENDANTS. | |

## SCENE I.

*An out-door scene.* Master *walking to and fro, as if in deep thought. Enter* Servant.

SERVANT. I beg pardon for interrupting you, but I would like to speak with you.

MASTER (*halts suddenly; frowns*). Well, what may be your pleasure?

SERVANT. It's no use to be looking so black about it, for the honest truth is the honest truth.

MASTER (*impatiently*). Have done with your canting, and speak your errand.

SERVANT. Ah, well; my errand is soon spoken. I have served you now faithfully for three long years, and think I ought to be paid my wages. Be so good as to give me what I deserve; for I wish to leave and look about me a bit in the world.

MASTER. Yes, my good fellow, you have served me industriously, and therefore you shall be cheerfully rewarded. [*Aside.*] The fellow don't know a twenty dollar gold piece from a copper cent. I will fool him—pay him off and let him go. [*Takes three coppers from his pocket; hands them to* Servant.] There; I give you three twenty dollar gold pieces, one for each year, which is much more than you would have received from most masters. Go! and make the best of it.

SERVANT (*takes coin; bows low*).  Thank you, thank you
a thousand times.  May your shadow never grow less.

MASTER (*shakes* Servant *by hand*).  Farewell, and may
you always find as kind a master as I have been to you.
[*Exit* Master.  Servant *walks about and whistles; shakes the
coin in his pocket.*]

*Enter* Traveler.

TRAVELER.  Whither away, merry brother?  I see you do
not carry much in the way of care.

SERVANT.  Care!  Why should I be sad, with the wages
of three years in my pocket?

TRAVELER.  How much is your treasure?

SERVANT (*takes out coin*).  Three twenty-dollar gold
pieces; all honestly counted.

TRAVELER.  Well, I am a poor, needy old man—you
are young and able to work for more—give me the gold.

SERVANT.  For heaven's sake, take it.  [*Hands coin to*
Traveler.]  You certainly look as if you need it.  I am
more able to do without than you.

TRAVELER (*takes coin; looks at it*).  My merry brother,
this is not gold.  You have been cheated.

SERVANT (*surprised*).  Not gold!  Well, heaven knows I
worked for it honestly, and ought to have been paid honestly.  I would n't swap places with that old curmudgeon
of a master.  However, keep it, keep it.  You are welcome to it.

TRAVELER.  I see you are a noble fellow, and will reward
you accordingly.  [*Draws a fiddle from under his cloak.*]
See, here is a fiddle that possesses wondrous powers.  No
matter who comes within the sound of it dances.

SERVANT (*surprised*).  Whether he wills or not?

TRAVELER.  Even so.  No person can hear the sound of
this fiddle and refrain from dancing, except the one who
plays upon it.  I give it to you.  [*Hands fiddle to* Servant.]
Use your power, young man; but do n't abuse it.

SERVANT (*turns fiddle over and over; looks at it; tunes it
slightly*).  You say every one who hears this fiddle is *bound*
to dance?

TRAVELER.  What I tell you, young man, is true.

SERVANT.  Then, by the piper, I'll try it on your spindle
shanks!  [*Plays fiddle;* Traveler *dances off the stage.*]

*Enter* Dutchman.

SERVANT (*ceases playing; starts back*). Halloo!

DUTCHMAN. Halloo, myself!

SERVANT. Who are you? Where did you come from? Where are you going? What are you going for? And do you expect to get it?

DUTCHMAN. Ugh! Von question at a time, and dey will lasth te longer. My name ish Shacob Hoffen-boffen-steiner, shoost from Californa, mit mine pag of kold. [*Shows bag of gold.*] I ish goin' home to marry Katrin Squeeshilfauter. O, Katrin is one great gurl! She can tance like one top.

SERVANT. And can't you dance, too?

DUTCHMAN (*puts his hands on his breast and puffs*). O, no! I ish not much to tance. I ish too heavy.

SERVANT. O, I think you could dance.

DUTCHMAN. O, no; you mishtake. I can not tance. I ish too fat enough. [*Servant begins to play the fiddle slowly; Dutchman begins to dance slowly.*] O, vat ish te matter mit mine feet? [*Servant plays faster; Dutchman dances faster.*] O, I vish you would shtop dat feedle. I ish not vish to tance. [*Servant plays still faster; Dutchman dances still faster.*] O, shtop dat leetle fiddle! O, mine pack! [*Puts hand to his back.*] O, shtop, shtop dat—von lee-tle—fid-dle and [*pants*] I give you all dis kold. [*Holds up the bag. Servant ceases playing.*]

SERVANT. You say you will give me all the gold?

DUTCHMAN (*ceases dancing; pants*). No! drink my lager if I do. I prake dat von leetle fiddle. [*Servant plays briskly; Dutchman dances furiously.*] O, yes! O, yes! Shtop—and—I geeve—you—all—mine—kold! [*Throws the bag down angrily.*]

SERVANT (*stops playing; stoops; takes up the bag and walks away*). I thank you kindly, Mr. Hoffen-boffen-steiner: but I must say you dance as if you had been bred to it. Farewell, and good luck to you. [*Exit Servant.*]

DUTCHMAN (*looks after Servant in amazement*). Dunder und blixin! He ish got mine kold und gone mit it! Murther! murther! Roppers! roppers! Fire! fire! fire! O, vere ish poor Katrin und te papies now? [*Strikes his hand to his forehead; shakes his fist after Servant.*] Nix com roushe! O, you plack varmint! you leetle mug of spiled

peer! I'll report you to head-quarters, und have you tried
midout habeas corpus by de court-martial, und shot to
death mit a rope round your ugly neck on de gallows!
I'll show you vat it ish to play on von leetle fiddle! You
shall dance von leetle jig on te tight rope! O, Katrin!
Katrin!

(*Curtain falls.*)


## SCENE II.

*A court-room.* Judge, Lawyers, Sheriff, *and people in attendance.* Enter Dutchman *in haste.*

DUTCHMAN (*approaches* Judge). O, Shudge, I ish got one
sorry tale to tell you! I vash coming home mit mine pag
of kold from Californa to marry Katrin, und shoost as I
get to de edge of town I meets a man dat ask all apout
mine beesness, und I tell him; und ten he pegin to play him
leetle fiddle, und make me tance till I promise him mine
bag of kold. I tance und tance, und ain't mooch to tance
neitder, because I ish too heavy enough; but de more he
play te more I tance, till mine pack pegin to fall off my
clothes, und I git so tired dat I shoost as lief live as die, I
pe so tired muchly.

JUDGE. This is a strange story, my good fellow. Was it
a soldier who treated you in this way?

DUTCHMAN. No, it vas no soljer! I tell you it vas one
beautiful leetle fiddler, und I vant to catch de tog mit mine
kold. He make me to tance, und den he peat me, und I
vant him put in de jail-house und den hang him till he
give mine kold pack.

JUDGE. Would you know him again?

DUTCHMAN. Yaw, I would know him one tousand times!

JUDGE (*to* Sheriff). Sheriff, go with this man and bring
the fellow to justice. If he has been guilty of committing
such an outrage upon the public road, he must be punished.
[*Exeunt* Dutchman, Sheriff, *and others.*] This is a highly
improbable story; but one side is always good till we hear
the other. We will not make up an opinion until the matter undergoes a strict investigation. It is not always best
to jump at conclusions. [*Looks pompously around.*] The

office of judge is not only a trying one, but, in many cases, thankless; and it requires great deliberation and much consideration in all litigation to win the approbation of—[*looks toward entrance*]—but I see they have caught the offender. [*All look outside.*] He struggles manfully, but the Dutchman holds a tight grip. [*Outside a voice heard.*]

DUTCHMAN (*outside*), O, yaw! by tam, git up mit you. I told you, you squealin tog, I'd preak dat von leetle fiddle! Come, und let de law make you tance to anoder fiddle. [*Enter* Dutchman, *dragging* Servant, *followed by* Sheriff *and others.*] Here he is mit his fiddle and mine kold in his pocket. [*Looks exultant.*]

JUDGE. Sheriff, search the prisoner.

DUTCHMAN. Dat ish right! Pring him round! pring him round! O, you von pig tog!

JUDGE. Silence in court! [*To* Servant.] What charge is this brought against you? Robbing and beating a poor, inoffensive Dutchman on the public highway!

SERVANT. I never touched the Dutchman, and did not steal his money. He gave it to me, of his own free will and accord, to pay me to cease fiddling.

DUTCHMAN. Dat ish a lie! I tell you, Shudge, he can tell lies faster an I can catch flies on de wall.

SERVANT (*looks contemptuously at* Dutchman.) I tell your honor I did not lay the weight of my finger on his Dutch carcass.

DUTCHMAN. Dat ish a bigger lie an de udder. He peat me und peat me till mine pack drop off my clothes, und shoost as I was about to git a fence off de rail to knock his shoulders off his head, he begin to play dat von leetle fiddle und make me to tance. De Shudge can see; und de ting speak for itself! Where ish mine money, hey?

JUDGE (*to* Servant). Your defense will not do; for no Dutchman would give away a bag of gold of his own free will. You have committed a robbery, and that on the public highway; and for such an offense our law says you must be hung! Sheriff, take the prisoner into custody. [Sheriff *takes hold of* Servant, *hands the bag of gold to* Dutchman.]

DUTCHMAN (*takes gold, dances about in glee*). O, yaw, you von pig tog! you go board at de jail-house, und I bet de jailer put one lock pehind you so tight dat you never git

loose no more. Besides, ve git you hung so high de Gov'-
nor can't pardon you in time to save you proken neck. [*Exit*
Sheriff *and* Servant. *All retire to back of stage;* Dutchman *comes forward, flourishing gold.*] Now, Katrin, Shacob
vill puy de farm, und ve can raise pigs und shickens und
tings, und pe so happy as de day ish long! [*Sings.*]

### FINE OLD DICHER GENTLEMAN.

TUNE—"*Fine Old English Gentleman.*"

I 'll sing you now a Dicher song 'bout Hans von Crouplegate,
Vot kept a lager-beer saloon right in de Bowery Schtreet;
He eat de swine beef-steak and slouk and every kind of meat—
   [*Spoken*]. And I swear mit mine goot gracious pon top of de people as so
much as a barrel of sour krout and—
Two bushels of lager-beer every morning he would eat;
He was a fine old Dicher gentleman, one of de real sthock.

By his fire-stove in his beer saloon every morning he would stand,
Mit a bottle of schnapps down by his side and a glass up in his hand,
And by himself he drinks dis toast "Och, die, de Faderland!"
   [*Spoken*]. And midout you could Dicher versa as he would say nix Eng-
lish—
Gasper hoskle spikle beef-steaks you nix could understand,
Dis fine old Dicher gentleman, one of de bestish kind.

His nose was red as beetle—yaw, by tunder dat was true!
His mouth 'bout sixteen inches wide, his eyes was plack as blue,
An' he belong to de Sangerbund, and he was a Turner, too—
   [*Spoken*]. But in politics make nix difference mit him, but den you come
round mit de Maine liquor law—
And takes away his lagerbeer, den by tam dat was someting near to
Dis fine old Dicher gentleman, one of de real sthock.

Dis fine old Dicher gentleman to his bed went every night,
And when comes round elections mit oder fellows he did fight,
And sthrike mit a double-barreled bowie-knife, but I do n't tink dat was right—
   [*Spoken*]. And run one of dem peoples, hit his head, breaked into his
nose all over his face, and he was drowned mit a big sthick—
I tell you right away—just now—it was a sorry fight
To dis fine old Dicher gentleman, one of de bestish kind.

But by and by den comes some troubles, he must fight with all his main,
Dough he was kilt two as six eight dozen couple times, he jumps up and
    fights again,
Dough his head was split open down his back, and de blood come down like
    rain—
   [*Spoken*]. And in comes a cor'ner mit de jury and sets on his pody twenty-
four hours as three-quarters and den dey—
Brings in a verdict dat he died mit brandy and vater on te brain—
He was a fine old Dicher gentleman, one of de real sthock!

(*Curtain falls.*)

## SCENE III.

*A gallows erected on the stage. A mixed crowd.* Sheriff conducts prisoner *(bearing his fiddle) to the ladder;* Servant *mounts to the top round;* Sheriff *stands with rope in hand.* Dutchman, Judge, *and* Lawyers *in attendance.* Servant *turns to* Judge.

DUTCHMAN *(shakes gold at* Servant). O, you von pig dog! you steal my money, did you?

SERVANT *(to* Judge). Will your honor grant me one request before I die?

JUDGE. If you do not ask your life, I will.

SERVANT. I do not ask my life; all I ask is to be allowed to play *one* tune upon my fiddle.

DUTCHMAN. Murder! murder! Don't, for de world, let him play on dat tam ting—don't!

JUDGE. Why not? It is almost over with the poor fellow.

DUTCHMAN *(grasps* Judge's *arm).* For de love of your life, don't let de pig tog give a schrape of de bow on dat tam ting!

JUDGE *(shakes* Dutchman *off).* Off with you! I will grant this last request. Be off! [Servant *tunes fiddle.*]

DUTCHMAN. O—O! Murder! fire! Somepody hold me! Tie mine feet, somepody—tie me—tie me! O, I pe a dead man!

[Servant *plays softly at first; the rope drops from the* Sheriff's *hand; the feet of the whole crowd begin to move simultaneously; as the* Servant *plays faster all begin to dance; the faster he plays the higher they all jump, until, exhausted, the* Judge *cries out piteously.*]

JUDGE. For the love of Heaven, stop—cease—your—fiddling! [*Pants.*] Do—you—hear? I—will grant—your—life—if you will—on-ly—s-t-o-p!

SERVANT *(ceases playing).* Did your honor say you would spare my life?

JUDGE *(with others, ceases dancing).* No, you vile deceiver! you shall be hung as high as Haman!

DUTCHMAN *(panting).* O. yaw! you villain loafer—hear dat? Shudge, hang him so high dat de buzzards can't find him! Make him tance von leetle jig on de tightrope! [Servant *begins to play a lively air; all fall to danc-ing.*]

JUDGE (*at the top of his voice*). Yes, yes! Only stop, and you shall live, on my honor as a judge!

DUTCHMAN (*dancing furiously*). Yaw, Shudge—let him live—let him live—te pig tog! O, hold me, somepody!—O—O!

(*Curtain falls.*)

# THE RELIEF AID SEWING SOCIETY,

## Or Mrs. JONES'S VOW.

### CHARACTERS.

Mrs. JONES.
Mrs. MILLPOST.
Mrs. DAFFODIL.
Mrs. JOHN SMITH.
Mrs. BRIGGS.
Mrs. MARTIN, *an old Woman.*
Mrs. BURKE.
Mrs. McBRIDE.
Miss UPSTART, *an old Maid.*
PHILIP JONES.

### SCENE I.

*Stage, arranged with chairs and a table, on which is piled different articles of clothing, cut ready for sewing. Mrs. Mc-Bride and Miss Upstart seated near the table, engaged in preparing the work for the Society.*

Miss UPSTART. I wonder what is detaining the members of our society so late? [*Takes out her watch.*] It is past seven.

Mrs. McBRIDE. I'm sure I don't know. It is a wonder Mrs. John Smith and Mrs. Briggs are not here, for they are generally the first.

Miss UPSTART. Yes, for they are always afraid something will be done without their having a finger in the pie. They think our Relief Society would tumble to pieces if they were not here to hold it together. I despise meddlers!

Mrs. McBRIDE. So do I; and it is just as you say, Mrs. Briggs and Mrs. Smith both believe that if they had had the management of affairs that the South never would

14

have been defeated. For my part I never want to inter-
fere with other people's concerns.

Miss UPSTART. O, every body knows you, Mrs. McBride;
but I just wanted to ask you: Did you see that hat of Mrs.
Burke's last Sunday? It was a bed of flowers. Where is
that gusset? [*Stoops and looks under the table.*] O, here
it is.

Mrs. McBRIDE. O, yes, I noticed it. I couldn't listen
to the sermon for looking at that and Miss Miller's shawl.
For my part I can't see how Mrs. Burke can afford a twenty-
dollar bonnet, when her husband is nothing but a carpenter. Hand me the thread.

Miss UPSTART (*hands thread*). Mrs. Burke would blow
you sky high if she heard you call Burke a carpenter. *She
says he is an architect.*

Mrs. McBRIDE. Archifiddlesticks! I do think Mrs. Burke
is the most affected, stuck-up person I ever saw. [*Looks toward entrance.*] But, mercy! here she comes, with old Mrs.
Martin. Miss Upstart, loan me your scissors—I forgot mine.
[*Miss UPSTART hands scissors.*]

### *Enter* Mrs. BURKE *and* Mrs. MARTIN.

Mrs. BURKE. Good evening, ladies. [*Sinks into a chair
in an affected manner.*]

Mrs. MARTIN.* Why, nobody here but you? I thought
we would be the last, for I had to wait for Mrs. Burke.

Mrs. BURKE. Well, you know, Mrs. McBride, I have to
humor Mr. Burke to death. He must have supper before I
could get off. He is regular. The sun, moon, and stars may
vary, but Mr. Burke *never* does.

Mrs. McBRIDE. You know the old saying: "Talk of the
Old Boy, and his imps will appear!" We were just talking
about you [*to* Mrs. BURKE] before you came in.

Mrs. BURKE (*elevates her brow*). Indeed! Nothing bad,
I trust.

Mrs. McBRIDE (*winks at* Miss UPSTART). O, no. We
were speaking of your new hat, and how very becoming
it is.

Miss UPSTART. What did it cost?

Mrs. BURKE. O, it was a bargain—only twenty dollars!

---

* The girl who acts this must imitate the voice of an old woman.

Mr. Burke wanted me to purchase one at thirty, but I am too economical for that.

Mrs. McBRIDE. I have always admired your economy. [ *Winks at* Miss UPSTART.]

Mrs. BURKE (*looking round*). Where are all the other ladies?

Miss UPSTART. They'll be along presently. I know Mrs. Millpost is coming. I saw her at one of the store doors in that old barouche of hers as I came down street.

Mrs. McBRIDE. I would be ashamed to ride in that old rattle-trap. You can hear it a mile before you see it, and the curtains go flip-flap like a hound dog's ears.

Miss UPSTART. And that old horse looks as if he had n't seen a curry-comb for an age.

Mrs. BURKE. Mrs. Millpost is able to purchase a new, fashionable equipage.

Miss UPSTART. Her excuse is, that her husband would never be willing for her to ride in a new one. It would be always too muddy or too dusty. [*Looks toward entrance.*] But here they all come. Do, pray, do n't tell her what I said. We must n't make her mad, for she sews so fast; and the fact is I like Mrs. Millpost—she's so lively.

Mrs. BURKE. Well, give Mrs. Martin and myself some work. [Miss UPSTART *hands them a garment; they seat themselves and sew.*]

*Enter* Mrs. JONES, Mrs. DAFFODIL, Mrs. JOHN SMITH, Mrs. MILLPOST, *and* Mrs. BRIGGS.

Miss UPSTART. And so you are all here, at last. Come, hurry and take off your things and get to work, for I am afraid the poor southerners will suffer for clothing if we do n't work faster. [*All seat themselves and begin to sew.*]

Mrs. MILLPOST. You are right, Miss Upstart. If our needles were to move as fast as our tongues we would get along better.

Mrs. BRIGGS. That is just what Briggs says, and that he would n't be compelled to listen to all we say for ten dollars an hour.

Mrs. JOHN SMITH. I would n't risk offering it to him, and I'll warrant he would not hear half the gossip from us that he would if as many men were to meet together.

Mrs. BRIGGS. That's exactly what I told him.

Mrs. Daffodil. Yes, and it is true; for I just *laughed* at Mr. Daffodil, the other night. He came home and told me the longest rigmarole that happened down town, and I asked him how he heard it, and he said that John F.* heard Silas W. tell Mr. S. that A. told him that Jim H. heard Judge somebody and Dr. R. discussing the matter, and it was true without a doubt. Now if that is not gossip, what is gossip?

Mrs. John Smith. I have a curiosity to know what these gentlemen were gossiping about. Do you remember?

Mrs. Daffodil. Mercy on me! I don't exactly remember—something, I believe, about Judge Lynch. Mrs. McBride, please clip this thread; my scissors are so large. [Mrs. McBride *cuts the thread.*]

Mrs. Briggs. It seems to me [*looks around*] I miss somebody. Who is it?

Mrs. John Smith (*looks around*). Why, it is Mrs. Mansfield; and she won't be here, for her husband is on another spree.

Mrs. Briggs. I didn't know Mr. Mansfield ever drank too much.

Mrs. John Smith. O, yes, the old man gets on a bender every once in a while.

Mrs. Millpost. I do not see how she does to stand it; for I'm sure if my husband were to get drunk it would kill me. I wouldn't know what to do.

Mrs. Briggs. Well, if Briggs were to get drunk I know mighty quick what *I'd* do.

Mrs. Jones. What would you do?

Mrs. Briggs. Why, I would tar and feather him.

Mrs. Burke. If Mr. Burke were, by any accident, to become inebriated, he would long for the sound of my voice like birds long for Spring; for I would never speak to him again, I am sure.

Mrs. McBride. Well, you had better believe, *I'd* speak, and act, too; for if ever my husband gets drunk I will sew him up in a bag and whip him with a good cowhide until he becomes sober.

Mrs. John Smith. I would not be as severe as that, Mrs.

---

* Wherever this is performed the names introduced should be taken from life, as such a local introduction will make it more laughable, especially if dignified gentlemen's names are used.

McBride, but I think if John Smith were to come home drunk, I would lock him up and feed him on bread and water till he came to his senses.

Mrs. DAFFODIL. Well, I would neither whip Mr. Daffodil or starve him; but if he were to contract the habit of drinking, I would get a bottle of whisky, and every time he took a dram I would take one too, and disgust him so that he would be glad to keep sober.

Miss UPSTART. Well, I never had a husband; but if I am ever unfortunate enough to be entrapped into matrimony, and I should get a drunken husband, I would duck him in Edmonds's pond till I cooled him off.

Mrs. JOHN SMITH. Well, here is Mrs. Martin [*looks toward* Mrs. MARTIN]. who has not spoken a word. Now, what would you do if Mr. Martin were to get drunk?

Mrs. MARTIN (*pushes up spectacles*). I have been listening to you young folks, and none of you know as much about the world as I do. I'll tell you what I'd do if my old man should forget himself and drink too much whisky.

Mrs. BRIGGS and Mrs. SMITH. What, Mrs. Martin?

Mrs. MARTIN. Well, just this: I would say nothing to him or any body else; but I would tuck him in the bed and cover him up, and hide it from the world if I could.

Mrs. MILLPOST. Are you in earnest, Mrs. Martin?

Mrs. MARTIN. Yes, child; it do n't pay to lay open each other's failings, and a woman ought never to expose a fault in her husband to the world, especially if she has children. For their sake and her own she ought to keep quiet.

Mrs. JONES (*approaches front of stage*). Do n't talk to me. Mrs. Martin, about a woman keeping quiet if her husband gets drunk. I do not believe that doctrine; and you all hear me say it, if Philip Jones were to get drunk I would not live with him another day.

Mrs. DAFFODIL. O, yes; you say that because you know Philip is a member of the church, and a sober man, and there is no danger.

Mrs. MARTIN. And you ought not to be so positive; you might rue it.

Mrs. JONES (*scornfully*). Rue it! I intend here to make a solemn vow before you all. that *if my husband gets drunk I will not live with him another day.*

Mrs. MARTIN (*comes forward; takes* Mrs. JONES's *arm*).
Janey, do n't say that; you will be sorry for it, maybe.
Mrs. JONES (*shakes off* Mrs. MARTIN's *hand*). It is too
late to take it back. I have said it, and I will stick to it,
so help me—
Mrs. MARTIN (*seizes* Mrs. JONES's *uplifted hand*). Do n't,
Janey! do n't!

(*Curtain falls.*)

### SCENE II.

*Room furnished as a family room.* A *table with books and
a work-basket on it; a lounge, chairs, etc.* Mrs. JONES
*walking to and fro; stops, walks again, comes forward to
front of stage.*

Mrs. JONES. I wonder what keeps Philip out so late. I
never knew him to act this way before. [*Looks at her watch.*]
It is nearly twelve o'clock. What can detain him? [*Walks
to and fro.*] I believe I will sew and pass off the time.
[*Seats herself; takes work-basket on her lap and sews a second
or two, throws down the basket, rises, walks to and fro.*] I
can not work; I am too uneasy. [*Looks out; returns.*] I
do not hear a soul stirring. Where can Philip be? [*Sighs.*]
I will read. [*Takes seat, reads a moment, throws down book,
rises, walks, wrings her hands.*] O, I can not read. I can't
fix my mind on any thing. What on *earth* can be the matter? Surely nobody has murdered him! O, this suspense
is awful! I will call the servants, he may have had a
spasm. [*Starts to go; stops, puts her hand to her ear.*] I
hear a noise! [*Slight noise of footsteps heard outside.*] That
is not *his* footstep—it is too irregular. [*Whistle heard outside.*] It can not be Philip; he *never* whistles. [*Singing in
a half-drunken tone heard outside.*] I am more puzzled, for
Philip does n't sing. [*Looks out.*] And yet I see, by the
moonlight, it is his overcoat, and his hat; but how he
walks! I do believe he is staggering! Yes, yes [*claps her
hand in glee*]; it *is* Philip. [*Starts forward.*]

*Enter* PHILIP JONES; *staggers across the stage, almost knocking* Mrs. JONES *down. Rights himself; leers at* Mrs. JONES.

PHILIP. Is that you, my duck? Why [*hic*] arn't you in bed. hey?

Mrs. JONES (*indignantly*). Philip Jones!

PHILIP. I am here to answer. That is my name. And now [*hic*] is there any thing that Mr. P. Jones can do to [*hic*] accommodate Mrs. P. Jones? [Mrs. JONES *puts handkerchief to her face; sinks into chair.* PHILIP *looks at her; staggers toward her.*] I say [*hic*]. Mrs. P. Jones, is there any thing Mr. P. Jones can do [*hic*] to ac—

Mrs. JONES (*rises indignantly*). Don't come near me, you brute—don't pollute me by touching me! [*Aside.*] O, how can I speak cross? [*Covers her face with handkerchief; looks up.*] Are you not ashamed of yourself?

PHILIP (*looks down at himself*). Me! ashamed of yourself? No, Mrs. P. Jones, you are not ashamed of myself.

Mrs. JONES (*sobs*). O, Philip, did I think I would ever see this? [*Aside.*] He *is* drunk.

PHILIP. See this? Yes, Mrs. P. Jones [*hic*]. and much more. [*Takes a green glass tickler, half filled with whisky, from his pocket; looks at it. holding it between him and the light.*] Jack-ee! [*Approaches* Mrs. JONES.]

Mrs. JONES (*shrinks*.) The horrid. miserable stuff!

PHILIP. Don't put on [*hic*] airs, now. You know. Mrs. P. Jones, that a [*hic*] little will do you good. For by pouring *sperrits* down [*hic—staggers*] we raise our *sperrits* up. Jackee!

Mrs. JONES (*aside*). O, isn't this terrible! [*To* PHILIP.] Philip Jones, do you *dare* to insult me by offering me whisky?

PHILIP (*turns bottle over and over in his hands. takes cork out, smells it*). Yes. Mrs. P. [*hic*] Jones, it *is whisky.*

Mrs. JONES (*excitedly*). The idea of such vulgarity! If I were so low down as to drink whisky, I would not disgrace myself still more by drinking it from a green glass tickler! Bah! [*Tosses her head and walks to and fro. Aside.*] O, I shall die, I know I will!

PHILIP (*looks at bottle*). Yes. Mrs. P. Jones, it is a grass-green tickler: but [*hic*], but are you aware of one fact, that [*hic*]. [*Approaches* Mrs. JONES. *She curls her lip, folds*

*her arms, looks defiant.*]   Allow me to [*hic*] inform you, Mrs.
P. Jones, that the article called [*hic*] whisky—this [*hic*]
article—[*puts it to his mouth*]—tastes just as good out of a
grass-green tickler [*hic*] as it does out of a—[*staggers around
stage*]—jackee!

Mrs. JONES (*desperately*).   Philip Jones, you have for-
feited the respect of all decent people!  [*Aside*].  How can
I talk to him?  [*To* PHILIP.]  You have disgraced yourself
and me; and now, for Heaven's sake, go to bed before the
servants find it out, and it is all over town that you are—
[*Covers face with her hands.*]

PHILIP.   Speak it out; don't be [*hic*] afraid.  Say it.
Gen-tle-man-ly in-e-bri-a-ted—hey?

Mrs. JONES (*stamps her foot*).   No, sir!  Not gentlemanly
inebriated; but beastly—  [*Sobs.*]

PHILIP.   Say it, Mrs. [*hic*] P. Jones, say it; but before
you *do* say it [*hic*] take a little.  [*Hands bottle.*]

Mrs. JONES (*recoils*).   *Dare* to hand *me* that vulgar bottle!
You are a brute!

PHILIP (*staggers back; rights himself up; in a loud tone*).
Mrs. P. Jones, don't you [*hic*] believe the Bible, hey?

Mrs. JONES.   Of course I believe the Bible.

PHILIP.   Well [*hic*], then; ad-mit you believe the Bible.
Don't Paul say to Tim-[*hic*]-othy, take a little for your
[*hic*] stomach's sake, hey?

Mrs. JONES (*approaches* PHILIP; *takes his arm*).   Philip,
dear, won't you go to bed?

PHILIP (*loosens himself from* Mrs. JONES's *hand*).   Damn
the bed!

Mrs. JONES (*starts back, amazed*).   O, Philip! and you a
member of the church!

PHILIP.   Yes, Mrs. P. Jones, one of the [*hic*] pillars of the
Sanc—tu—*a*-ry!  Jack-*ee!*

Mrs. JONES (*aside*).   What shall I do?  [*To* PHILIP.]
Philip, you *must* go to bed.

PHILIP.   Mrs. P. Jones, answer me [*hic*] this.  Why do
you [*hic*] go to bed, hey?  For the simple reason that [*hic*]
the bed won't come to you.  Do ye see, hey?

Mrs. JONES.   O, Philip!

PHILIP.   I say, like the [*hic*] immortal Toodles, emphati-
cally [*hic*], religiously, morally, damn *the* bed!  [*Noise
heard without.*]

Mrs. JONES (*terrified, runs to* PHILIP, *jerks off his hat, pulls the collar of his coat back, and pushes him in the direction of the lounge*). Philip Jones, you *shall* go to bed. It is nearly day, and the servants will soon be up, and if they see you the whole town will know it.

PHILIP (*seats himself on the side of the bed*). Mrs. P. Jones, you are my lawful, wedded wife—ain't ye?

Mrs. JONES (*covers her face with handkerchief*). Yes, Philip.

PHILIP. And I am your [*hic*] lawful, wedded husband—ain't I, hey?

Mrs. JONES (*aside*). This will kill me. [*To* PHILIP.] Of course you are.

PHILIP. Well, then, as you are [*hic*] my lawful, wedded husband, and I am [*hic*] your lawful, wedded wife, answer me this: which has [*hic*] the right to put [*hic*] t'other to bed—hey?

Mrs. JONES. Please, Philip, stop talking and go to bed.

PHILIP. I will compromise. Now [*hic*], listen. If you have the right to [*hic*] make— [*Noise heard without.*]

Mrs. JONES (*desperately*). Philip, for Heaven's sake, go to bed—

PHILIP. Well, Mrs. P. Jones, as you [*hic*] appear so anxious for me to [*hic*] retire, I will do so if you will promise [*hic*] one thing.

Mrs. JONES. What, Philip, what?

PHILIP. Why, that you will [*hic*] *not leave me.*

Mrs. JONES. I will not leave you, Philip.

PHILIP. 'Pon honor [*hic*], hey?

Mrs. JONES. Upon honor, Philip.

PHILIP. That won't do, Mrs. P. Jones. You [*hic*] must swear!

Mrs. JONES. Well, I swear. I'll do any thing if you will *go to bed.*

PHILIP. You say [*hic*] you'll swear?

Mrs. JONES (*impatiently*). Yes, I swear. [*Aside.*] O, mercy! [PHILIP *rises, throws off overcoat, and falls heavily on the lounge.* Mrs. JONES *covers him carefully with the coat; takes a seat and buries her head in her lap; sobs.*]

PHILIP (*from the bed*). I say, Mrs. P. Jones, did [*hic*] you swear you wouldn't leave me?

Mrs. JONES. Yes, Philip, I did. Please go to sleep.

PHILIP. Well, going to bed [*hic*] is one thing, and going to [*hic*] sleep is another thing. Jack-ee!

Mrs. JONES. I know it. [*In a second or two* PHILIP *breathes or snores heavily.* Mrs. JONES *comes forward softly; takes a seat near front of stage; clasps her hands.*] The greatest trouble of my life has come upon me. [*Looks toward bed.*] What shall I do? [*Looks toward audience.*] Old Mrs. Martin was right. It is better to keep quiet. What will Mrs. McBride, and Mrs. Briggs, and all of them, say? [*Looks toward bed.*] I wonder if they will find it out? [*Looks toward audience.*] I wish I knew if any one saw him as he came home. I can never hold up my head again. Yes, as old Mrs. Martin said, I'll hide it from the world if I can. O, how can I bear the disgrace? It will kill me! [*Buries her face in her handkerchief; sobs.* PHILIP *rises softly in a sitting posture, and looks quizzically at* Mrs. JONES. *She raises her head and looks toward the bed.*]

PHILIP (*in a natural tone*). Are you the woman, Janey, who, only last evening, vowed that if your husband got drunk you would not live with him another day?

Mrs. JONES (*rises and approaches* PHILIP; *puts her hand on his forehead.*) And are you not drunk, Philip?

PHILIP (*rises, takes* Mrs. JONES's *hand, and leads her to front of stage*). No, Janey, I am not; and, thank Heaven, I never was drunk. I was only quizzing you, to prove how foolish was the vow you made against your husband.

Mrs. JONES. So foolish, Philip, that I will now promise never to make another like it. Ladies, take warning.

(*Curtain falls.*)

- -

## COSTUMES.

No costume is needed in this play, but walking and home dresses.

# HEALTH *vs.* RICHES.

## CHARACTERS.

Mrs. BROWN.
CARRIE, *Daughter to* Mrs. BROWN.
SUSAN SLATE, *a Sewing Girl.*

## SCENE.

*Room poorly but neatly furnished.* Mrs. BROWN *seated near
a table at work.* Enter CARRIE.

Mrs. BROWN. How did you enjoy your walk, my dear
daughter?

CARRIE. O, mamma, I enjoyed it very much at first; but
while I was running so happy, gathering flowers, Colonel
Bloomington's fine carriage came along, and in it was his
daughter Lulie. She was dressed in silk, with a velvet hat
and feathers, and had two or three servants waiting upon
her. She stopped and made the footman gather some blue-
bottles and daisies, and sat so grand in the carriage, giving
orders just like a queen.

Mrs. BROWN. Well, my child, what of all this?

CARRIE. O, nothing; only I wondered why she should
be so rich while I am so poor. She is no larger than I am;
and not half so good.

Mrs. BROWN. Indeed; and how did you make this dis-
covery?

CARRIE. Why, she was too lazy to get out of the carriage and run after the flowers for herself. But I know one
thing, she has got to die some day, as well as myself.

Mrs. BROWN. Why, Carrie, I am surprised to hear you
talk in this manner. Why should it fret you because Lulie
Bloomington is rich?

CARRIE. I don't know; but it made me mad to think

about it, and I threw my bouquet away and came home. I
wonder why *I* can't have a fine house and ride in a carriage? I felt ashamed when I saw this girl looking at my
homespun dress, for she just gazed at me.

Mrs. BROWN. It is not only very foolish, but extremely
wicked, for you, my daughter, to indulge in feelings of
envy and discontent. The Lord knows what is best for
every one. He gives riches to those whom it will not injure,
often; and others he permits to remain poor in accordance
with his divine wisdom.

CARRIE. Well, it don't look right to me for one person
to be set up above another. I have just as much right to
be rich as Lulie Bloomington, and I know she made fun of
my coarse dress.

*Enter* SUSAN SLATE.

Mrs. BROWN. Good morning, Susan. I have not seen
you for some time. Have a seat.

SUSAN. No, thank you; I haven't time to stay. I was
on my way from Colonel Bloomington's, and thought I
would stop a minute.

CARRIE. O, Susan, do tell me about all the fine things
they have there; for I am sure they must be very happy.

SUSAN. Indeed, you are very much mistaken. I would
rather be you than Lu. Bloomington.

CARRIE. O, Susan! Why, she has every thing that heart
can wish; a fine house, and fine clothes, and a fine carriage,
and—

SUSAN. Not so fast, Miss Carrie. You see, I went to
Colonel Bloomington's this very morning, to take home
some work I had been doing for them; and while I was
there they brought Miss Lulie in the house and laid her on
the sofa, and I never felt so sorry for any body in my life.

CARRIE. What was the matter; was she sick?

SUSAN. No, not exactly sick; but you see she can't walk
the first step that ever was ordered—

CARRIE (*in surprise*). Can't walk?

SUSAN. No, not a living step. She was born lame; her
feet are deformed in some way, and her mother says the
poor child is never well.

CARRIE. Is it possible?

SUSAN. Yes; and what's more, she was crying like her

heart would break. She said that while she was out riding she saw a beautiful, rosy little girl, just her own age, running about gathering flowers so happy, and that she would give the world if she was as well and happy as that little girl. Her mother tried to comfort her, but it were n't no use. Her mother said, well, Lulie, the girl you saw was poor, for you said she had on a homespun dress, and you are rich and wear silk dresses, and ride in a fine carriage. At this she cried harder than ever, and said she would be willing to be poor and wear homespun all her life if she just had the use of her limbs like that little girl. Her mother then told her it was the will of the Lord for her to be lame, and she must pray to him to make her contented with her lot, and she told her mother she would try; but, as I said before, I left her crying. But, law, I am overstaying my time. Good-by, Mrs. Brown; good-by, Miss Carrie. · [*Exit* Susan.]

Mrs. Brown. Now, you see, my dear child, while you were envying this poor girl her riches, she was wishing to be like you, healthy and active. I hope this will be a lesson to you, to be content with your lot.

Carrie. I hope that God will forgive me for my wicked feelings, for it was very wrong for me to speak as I did: and now I would rather be poor and have to sew for my living, like Susan Slate, than to be deformed and sickly, like Lulie Bloomington, with all her money.

(*Curtain falls.*)

# THE MINISTER'S GUESTS.

## CHARACTERS.

Mr. ALLSTON GRANGER, *the Minister.*
ELINOR, *the Minister's Wife.*
Aunt PEGGY, *the Minister's Aunt.*
Rev. ASA DOWNE.
Mrs. ASA DOWNE.
ABEL,
NICODEMUS, } *Children of* Mr. DOWNE.
PRISCILLA,
BRIDGET, *an Irish Servant Girl.*

## SCENE I.

*A family room, or reception room. On a small table is a China mug, a candlestick, with a candle in it, a photograph album, and a hair brush, with inlaid pearl handle.* ELINOR *and* Aunt PEGGY *seated opposite each other.*

AUNT PEGGY. Elinor, I don't blame you, child, because I know you love Allston, and he is a good husband and a clever gentleman; but a woman who marries a minister is, in my opinion, doing a poor business.

ELINOR. But, Aunt Peggy, Allston is so kind, and so thoughtful of my comfort in every particular.

AUNT PEGGY. Yes, yes, I know all that; but I know, too, the trials that a minister's wife is subject to. Upon my word, if I were compelled to make a choice between a gambler and a minister for a husband, I should take the gambler.

ELINOR. Why, Aunt Peggy! A woman of your age and noted morality to make such a speech! I am astonished!

AUNT PEGGY. I am not surprised at your being shocked; but, Elinor, I only speak the truth when I say that ministers' wives are the greatest slaves on earth. A minister is expected to keep a hotel, and that, too, without money and without price. His house must be open day and night. Hot meals must be served at all hours. People who are too low to stay at the tavern are sent to the minister's. Tract-peddlers, book-peddlers, lecturers, agents, every body goes to the minister's; and then if he pleads an over-worked wife and poor salary, he is *piously* reminded that St. Paul and St. Peter, and all those fellows, never would receive a salary. But whether these saints kept tavern and entertained all creation, *free of charge*, does n't appear.

Elinor. We have been keeping house only a month, and I am sure we have not had a great deal of company.

Aunt Peggy. You have n't? Who went from here only this morning? Why, three ministers and one book-peddler. You waited on them until your head aches fit to burst now. And, Saturday night as it is, I would n't wonder if some one else comes to sponge on you till Monday morning.

Elinor (*puts her hand to her head*). I hope not.

*Enter* Mr. Granger.

Mr. Granger (*approaches* Elinor). Well, Elinor, I have finished my sermon, and, with a good night's rest, can deliver it to-morrow in a manner acceptable to our congregation. [*Takes sermon from his pocket ; puts it on the table.*]

Aunt Peggy. I can't see how you did to write it with the house full of company.

Mr. Granger. But the company is gone now, and we shall be able to get every thing in order by church time.

Aunt Peggy. Do n't hollo till you get out of the woods.

*Enter* Bridget.

Bridget. Misther Granger, there is a gintleman below stairs wishes to see ye.

Aunt Peggy (*triumphantly*). I said so!

Mr. Granger (*to* Bridget). A gentleman! Who is it?

Bridget. An' shure, how can I tell, plaze yer worship, when I niver saw his ugly face before. An' there's a leddy beside, as big as the side of a house, and three childer in the bargain.

Elinor (*puts her hand to her head*). O, mercy! and my head aching as it is !

BRIDGET. Faith, and what I tell you, ma'am, is all thruc. And thin there are iver so many thrunks, and boxes, and bundles, and a saucy poodle dog for good maisure.

Mr. GRANGER. This is unaccountable. [*To* BRIDGET.] Go and invite them up. [*Exit* BRIDGET. *To* Aunt PEGGY.] Who can be coming here this time of night? There must be some mistake.

AUNT PEGGY (*bridling*). I'll warrant there is no mistake; and if you and ELINOR permit yourselves to be imposed upon in this way, you can entertain your guests yourselves without my assistance. [*Exit angrily.*]

*Enter* Rev. ASA DOWNE, Mrs. DOWNE, ABEL, PRISCILLA, *and* NICODEMUS, *the latter bearing a poodle in his arms.*

DOWNE (*approaches* Mr. GRANGER; *grasps his hand cordially*). Dear brother Granger, I am the Reverend Asa Downe, traveling itinerant, and this [*points to* Mrs. DOWNE] is my wife, and these [*points to children*] are my children, Abel, Nicodemus, and Priscilla. We came directly to your house, because we knew you would be mortally offended if we didn't. My wife is a great invalid, a dreadful sufferer; been sick for seven years; and, while I think of it, we *must* sleep where there is a fire. I wouldn't have my dear Eliza Jane to sleep without a fire for a thousand dollars; and I want your wife to have the sheets well aired. My wife is nervous, *very* nervous, exceedingly nervous. She wouldn't sleep a wink in coarse sheets—would you, my dear?

Mrs. DOWNE. No, indeed; I would die before day if I were to sleep in coarse sheets. I came very near going to my last home, about a week ago, from sleeping on an unbleached pillow-case. They thought I *was* dead for two hours! Dear me! [*Looks around.*] Have you a stuffed chair? I can not sit on an uncushioned chair. [*Looks at* ELINOR.] And I will take a cup of tea and a bowl of oyster soup, or some mince-pie. I feel so faint. [*Sinks on the easy chair.*]

DOWNE (*sits*). And, sister Granger, I will trouble you for a cup of coffee. It will be a stay for my stomach till supper is ready. What time do you have tea?

ELINOR (*aside*). Supper has been over two hours.

ABEL. And I want some gingerbread and milk and

honey, and cold pie.   I 'm half starved.   Where is the cup-
board?   I can help myself.

PRISCILLA.   And I want a doughnut and some pickle.
Pickle and cake is so good together; and if I can't have
that rocking-chair to sit in, I won't stay here.   You see if
I do.

NICODEMUS (*looks around*).   W-h-e-w!   What a mean
little room, by crackee!   What's that on the table?   O,
golly! if it ain't a mug just like one I used to have.   [*Goes
to table; takes the mug in his hand; lets it fall and breaks
it.*]   How!   [*Looks down.*]   It is slippery!   [Mr. GRANGER
*stoops; picks up the broken mug; looks grave.*]

Mrs. DOWNE.   O, it's no matter, brother Granger.   You
can mend it with Spalding's glue.   I mended a bowl with
it not long ago, and it was as good as new.   [*To ELINOR.*]
You don't look much like a preacher's wife.   I see you
have a red ribbon on your head—too stylish, too stylish;
and ear-rings, too.   Now, I never wear such things, but try
to be as plain as possible.

ELINOR (*aside*).   You needn't try very hard, I 'm sure.

DOWNE.   My wife is a model, brother Granger.   Would
there were more like her.   Eliza Jane, love, you ought to
have a bath.   Will you see, sister Granger, that she has
one?

ELINOR (*takes candle in her hand*).   Allow me, Mr. Downe,
to show you and Mrs. Downe and the children to your
room, where you can take off your things and rest till supper is ready.

ABEL.   Good for that.   I 'm tired of this old room
already.   [*They all prepare to go.*]

PRISCILLA.   So am I.   I wonder how long we shall have
to wait for supper.

NICODEMUS (*to ELINOR*).   Is our room any nicer than this
one?   Because if it ain't I don't mean to stay.

Mrs. DOWNE (*looks back*).   Silence, Nicodemus.

[*Exeunt Mr. and Mrs. DOWNE, ABEL, NICODEMUS,
PRISCILLA, and ELINOR.*]

Mr. GRANGER.   Well, this is an unexpected trial upon
poor Elinor.   I do not know what it will result in; but this
comes of being a minister.

(*Curtain falls.*)

## SCENE II.

*Same room. Mr. and Mrs. Downe seated near each other. Abel, Nicodemus, and Priscilla seated on the floor. Abel has a pair of scissors cutting Mr. Granger's sermon into various forms. Priscilla has a photograph album, turning the leaves in a careless and destructive manner. Nicodemus is holding a restive kitten, stroking its back with Elinor's pearl-handled hair-brush. Enter Mr. Granger.*

Mr. Granger. Good morning, Mr. Downe. I hope you and Mrs. Downe rested well during the night?

Downe. Indeed, I never spent a more wretched night. I think, however, some fresh eggs, soda-crackers, dry toast, and some coffee and cream and honey for my breakfast, will make "Richard himself again." Eliza Jane, love, how do you feel this morning?

Mrs. Downe (*rolls up her eyes*). Dear me; I never slept a wink the *whole* night. I am sure the bed was filled with hens' feathers, and I never *could* sleep on hens' feathers; they always stuff me up so. I feel as if I were smothering.

Mr. Granger (*discovers his sermon; snatches a piece of it from Abel*). Why, child! this is my sermon you have cut to pieces. How dare you—

Mrs. Downe (*interrupts Mr. Granger*). Law, sakes! Don't take on so; they did n't mean any harm, bless 'em.

Mr. Granger (*in a provoked tone*). I think, madam, children should be taught not to meddle with such things.

Mrs. Downe. Well, you need n't swallow me, brother Granger. For my part, I did n't know that ministers ever lost their temper. Asa *never* does; and I guess our children have cut up twenty of his sermons. What does it matter? You no doubt have plenty of other sermons, and children *must* have amusement; *they require it!*

Mr. Granger (*perceives Priscilla with the album; approaches her, and attempts to take it from her*). My dear, give me that album; it is no plaything for you. It was a bridal present to my wife, and she prizes it very much. [Priscilla *clasps album to her breast and runs between* Mr. Downe's *knees, whining.*]

Downe. Priscy, dear, give brother Granger the album; do, dear. [Priscilla *screams and hugs the book closer.*]

Mrs. DOWNE. O, Asa, let the poor child alone. You make me nervous! Suppose it *was* a bridal present. Brother Granger has been married long enough for the honeymoon to be over; and when that happens, bridal presents are played out. Besides, what is a photograph album? They are as common as kraut.

ABEL. I wonder if that dogon old breakfast ain't ready. I'm so awful hungry. [*Looks toward* NICODEMUS.] Mother, make Nic give me that kitten.

NICODEMUS (*throws cat at* ABEL). Take the old cat and go to thunder.

Mrs. DOWNE (*looks around alarmed*). O, that reminds me! Children, where is Fan?

Mr. GRANGER. Who is "Fan?"

Mrs. DOWNE. Why, my lap-dog; where *can* it be?

ABEL (*grins*). We've had a funeral!

Mrs. DOWNE (*half shrieks*). A funeral! What do you mean?

NICODEMUS. I'll tell you, mother. Fan is in Mrs. Granger's work-box, buried in the garden.

Mrs. DOWNE. What! Fan! My precious Fan! Buried?

NICODEMUS. Yes, indeed! Abe preached the funeral, and Pris and I went as mourners. and Abe was sexton, too. O, crackee! wasn't it jolly! [Mrs. DOWNE *rocks to and fro; wrings her hands; moans.*]

DOWNE. You naughty boy; go this instant and bring the box here, before your mother has spasms.

[*Exeunt* ABEL, NICODEMUS *and* PRISCILLA.]

Mr. GRANGER. Your children do not seem to be under much control. I am sure they would be much happier if they were trained to be orderly and obedient.

Mrs. DOWNE (*recovering*). Brother Granger, I am astonished; there never were more obedient, *lovely* children than mine. Did you observe how readily Abel obeyed his father when he told him to bring the work-box and dog?

DOWNE. Yes, brother Granger, and I attribute it all to my dear Eliza Jane. She is a pattern wife and mother. Would there were more like her.

Mr. GRANGER (*aside*). Heaven forbid!

*Enter* ABEL, NICODEMUS, *and* PRISCILLA. *They put the box on the floor, open it; dog jumps out.*

Mrs. DOWNE. O, gracious me! I am dying! To think

of my poor Fan being buried! It is too much for my weak nerves. Farewell, Asa. [*Falls back in chair.*]

NICODEMUS (*in front of stage, to* ABEL). Abe, Abe! Say, if mother dies sure enough, this time, call me. I want to go out and play with the kitten. [*Exit* NICODEMUS.]

DOWNE (*supports* Mrs. DOWNE.) O, dear! O, dear! She is dying at last. My poor Eliza Jane! Get the camphor! Get some ice lemonade! (*Enter* Aunt PEGGY, ELINOR, *and* BRIDGET.) Wring some flannel out of hot, *hot* water. To think she's been sick for *seven* years, and now, after all, she's dead! She's dead! [*Weeps.*]

AUNT PEGGY (*comes forward*). If she is dead, I guess the sooner she is laid out the better. You've got rid of a great burden, Mr. Downe. A wife that has been seven years dying must be dreadful to get along with, and you ought to thank the Lord she is gone. Allston, go and get a plank to stretch her on. [*To* ELINOR.] Elinor, hand me the scissors. [*Takes hold of* Mrs. DOWNE's *head.*] I'll cut her hair off first. It will make somebody a waterfall; and the way hair sells, it will nearly pay for her coffin.

Mrs. DOWNE (*starts from the chair; seizes* Aunt PEGGY *by the arm*). You'll have my hair off, will you, and sell it to buy a coffin? I'll take your skull-cap off first, see if I don't! [*Jerks off* Aunt PEGGY's *false front*]. I'll peel your old pate faster than a Cherokee Indian would do it, you old Jezebel!

AUNT PEGGY (*runs to the broom; seizes it, and pummels* Mrs. DOWNE *off the stage*). I'll show you what it is to come into people's houses and find fault and put on airs. [*Turns upon* Mr. DOWNE, *who also retreats. Turns on* ABEL *and* PRISCILLA.] I'll let you know, you spoiled brats, what it is to cut up sermons and bury live dogs in work-boxes. [ABEL *and* PRISCILLA *retreat screaming.*]

BRIDGET (*pitching the band-boxes and bundles after them*). An' faith, Misthress Peggy, I'll be afther helpin' ye to turn the spalpeens out; for divil a bit of comfort is there in the house with the likes of them. [*Jerks the lap-dog from* ELINOR, *who, in the confusion, had picked it up; throws it after the boxes.*] And I'll sind the mite of a puppy afther ye for good luck.

(*Curtain falls.*)

# MARRYING A FORTUNE.

## DRAMATIZED FROM A MAGAZINE STORY.

### CHARACTERS.

KATE BARTON.
JENNIE CAMPBELL.
Dr. CAMPBELL.
Mr. FITZFOONE.
NED LELAND.
PHILIP OTIS.
Ladies and Gentlemen in attendance.
Servant.

### SCENE I.

KATE *and* JENNIE *seated near each other, one holding a fan, the other a bouquet. Home scene.*

JENNIE. Kate, since we have come to the city to live there is one thing that troubles me very much.

KATE. What on earth can trouble you?

JENNIE. Why, you know I have lately come into the possession of fifty thousand dollars, and as we are soon to make our *debut* into society, I dread the score of hollow-hearted admirers and scheming fortune-hunters that will be paying attention to me for the sake of money.

KATE. O, is that all? Well, my cousin, if you will aid me, I will take it upon myself to outwit all such characters.

JENNIE. What can you do?

KATE. If you and uncle Campbell will lend yourselves to the plot, I can soon test the sincerity of all the wife-seeking beaux that come about us.

JENNIE (*looks toward entrance*). Well, here comes my father, and you can explain yourself.

*Enter* Dr. CAMPBELL.

Dr. CAMPBELL (*seats himself*). Well, young ladies, what is troubling your heads this morning? Are you consulting about the dresses you are to appear in this evening at the party? I want, before you go, to give you some advice; and, my daughter, I wish you to be on your guard against fortune-hunters.

JENNIE. We were just speaking on that subject before you came in.

KATE. And I was telling Jennie, if you and she will assist me, I will deceive this class of individuals.

Dr. CAMPBELL. You must explain yourself.

KATE. It is soon explained. No one knows of Jennie's newly-acquired fortune, and it will be very easy to mislead all interested admirers.

Dr. CAMPBELL. Let us hear your plan.

JENNIE. Do, Kate; I am anxious to know it.

KATE. Allow me to assume a manner and dress entirely opposite to my real character. I can transform my person so that even you will not recognize me; and, when this is done, introduce *me* into society as *the heiress.* I will take upon me the style of an uncultivated rustic, and then if I succeed in making a conquest it will be for myself alone.

Dr. CAMPBELL. This is all very well if you can carry it out. But I fear you will betray yourself.

JENNIE. Do you think you can succeed?

KATE. I *know* I can if you and uncle Campbell will humor the joke.

Dr. CAMPBELL. You talk like a sensible girl; and if that is all depend upon me, for I think it will be a capital joke.

KATE. Capital, indeed! And by it Jennie will find out if there is a heart disinterested enough to love her for herself alone.

Dr. CAMPBELL. And if you are successful, Kate [*they all rise and come forward*], I will say I have seen what I never expected to see—a woman sharp enough to outwit a fortune-hunter.

(*Curtain falls.*)

## SCENE II.

*A ball-room. Ladies and gentlemen promenading at back and sides of stage, conversing in pantomime.* JENNIE *leaning on Dr.* CAMPBELL'S *arm; near them,* KATE. *In front of stage,* FITZFOONE, LELAND, *and* OTIS.

OTIS. Who is she, Ned [*looks at* JENNIE], that lovely girl with Dr. Campbell?

NED. O, that's the Doctor's daughter, Miss Jennie Campbell, and the other lady near them is his niece, Miss Kate Barton, an heiress of fifty thousand.

OTIS. She is decidedly plain, if she is an heiress. What horrid red hair, and that shocking yellow dress; and, then look, her cheeks are fairly daubed with paint. She certainly has no taste.

FITZFOONE. What a deuced pity now that that chawming cweature, Miss Campbell, had n't the money, instead of her tawdry cousin. I would cultiwate her acquaintance if she had. [*Turns to audience and struts about.*] But it would nevaw do for Mr. Fitzfoone to thwow himself away upon a poor girl. I think, though, I'll be intwoduced to the heiress any way. Fifty thousand is not to be gwind at.

NED. That's a fact, Fitz; so come and I'll introduce you. [*They approach* KATE, JENNIE, *and* Dr. CAMPBELL.] Miss Barton, allow me to introduce to you Mr. Fitzfoone, an English gentleman of rank, who desires to make your acquaintance.

FITZFOONE. I am happy to meet you, Miss Bawton. Hope you are well?

KATE. Pretty well, thank ye. [*Shakes* FITZFOONE'S *hand violently.*] I hope you 're well, though you do n't look much smart?

FITZFOONE. O, I assure you my health is foine.

KATE. I'm glad to hear it; but you do look 'mazin' slim. But, then, it 's the fashion to look like a candle, and I 'm going to eat pickle and stint myself till I get poor as a snake, for I want to look fashionable and citified, 'cause I 'm an heiress, you see, and have to catch a husband.

FITZFOONE. Will you allow me to bwing you some suppaw?

KATE. Pshaw! I aint hungry a mite. You see, I never was at a party before, and I don't feel like I'd ever eat another mouthful.

FITZFOONE. Perhaps you'd take an ice cweam or some jelly?

KATE. I hate ice cream; it makes my teeth ache. I've got a hollow in one of them, and when the cold strikes it, O, jiminy, how it jumps! What's the jelly made out of?

FITZFOONE. Calves' feet, I pwesume.

KATE. Calves' feet! Well, I believe I won't take none, for it can't be clean if its made out of them.

FITZFOONE. I pwesume you've lived in the country?

KATE. O, yes; I'm a real country bumpkin, and I don't believe I'll ever get used to city doings. You see, I always went to bed at dark before I come here. [*Yawns.*] Setting up late don't suit me. [*To* Dr. CAMPBELL.] Uncle, ain't it most time to go home? I'm powerful sleepy.

Dr. CAMPBELL (*suppresses a smile*). Any time that suits your convenience, my dear.

KATE (*takes* Dr. CAMPBELL'S *arm*). Well, Mr. Fitz-*fool*, or whatever your name is, we'll have to bid you good night. [*Courtesies low and awkwardly.*] Come round some time and take grub with us. Can't he, uncle?

Dr. CAMPBELL. Certainly, my dear. Mr. Fitzfoone, we will be pleased to see you on Walnut Street any time that suits your convenience.

FITZFOONE (*bows low*). Thank you, Doctaw. I'll do myself the honaw.

[*Exit* Dr. CAMPBELL, KATE *and* JENNIE.]

FITZFOONE (*comes forward*). She is gawky, but I can't stop to be squeamish now. I am bound to make a strike for money. Fifty thousand is a nice sum. I am so confoundedly in debt I can't stir without being dunned. There is the tailor, and the shoemaker, and that old rip of a washerwoman, all at my heels, like so many hungry dogs, and my landlord is getting suspicious. There is nothing for me to do but marry that dawdy country girl. But once let me get the fifty thousand in my pocket and won't I show a pair of light heels. It's a deuced pity for a fine-looking fellow like me to be sacrificed; but it can't be helped. I wish her head was not quite so bushy; but, never mind, money hides a multitude of faults. Before many days pass, Miss Kate Barton will be Mrs. Fitzfoone. [Bows.]

(*Curtain falls.*)

When Fitzfoone comes forward, after Dr. Campbell, Kate, and Jennie exit, all on the stage must fall back. Otis must join Jennie and appear engrossed with her.

## SCENE III.

*Same as first. Enter* Dr. CAMPBELL, KATE, *and* JENNIE.

Dr. CAMPBELL. Well, girls, a pretty rig you are leading me. Here is Kate making a fright of herself with that wig and yellow dress. No wonder she scared all the beaux away. I was diverted at the way the young fellows looked at her last night.

KATE. But you forget Mr. Fitzfoone, uncle. I am sure he played the agreeable, but it cost him an effort; and Jennie did not suffer for attention, for Mr. Philip Otis was devoted to her. I would give all her fortune, and the wig and yellow dress to boot, to have so disinterested a lover.

JENNIE. You make a fine country girl. I thought I would expire when Fitzfoone asked you to have ice cream and jelly. He looked so funny when you said it was not clean. He is taken with the fortune, I see, and will soon be an avowed lover.

Dr. CAMPBELL. A trifling puppy! And, Kate, I don't care how much you quiz him; he deserves it. [*Enter* Servant: *hands a card to* Dr. CAMPBELL.] By the living piper, it is the fellow's card. He is biting at the bait. [*To* Servant.] Go, invite him in. But, girls, I must leave you to fight your own battles. [*Exit* Dr. CAMPBELL—*L.*]

*Enter* FITZFOONE—*R.*

KATE (*advances*). Good morning, Mr. Fitz-*fool*. This is my cousin, Jennie. [*Presents* JENNIE. FITZFOONE *bows stiffly.*] Why don't you speak to my cousin Jennie? Don't you see her?

FITZFOONE. O, yes, Miss Barton, I see her.

KATE. Then why in the nation don't you speak and shake hands? Ain't that city fashion? [*To* JENNIE.]

16

JENNIE. Yes, but sometimes people omit the custom.

KATE. O, yes, it's only intimate friends that shake hands. Ain't that so, Mr. Fitz-*fool?*

FITZFOONE. I believe so—or those who are engaged.

KATE. But you shook hands with me at the party, and we ain't engaged. That is—not yet.

FITZFOONE (*aside to* KATE). Nobody knows *what* may happen, my adowable cweature.

KATE. O, Jennie, did you hear that?

FITZFOONE (*aside*). Don't tell her, Miss Bawton.

KATE. I will tell her. Jennie, he calls me his adowable cweature, and looks like he thought I was good enough to eat. Now, Mr. Fitz-*fool*, don't deny it. [*Points to* FITZFOONE.]

FITZFOONE. I don't deny, Miss Bawton. But, changing the subject, do you sing?

KATE. I sing like a martingale. I can't play on the piano yet, but uncle says I can learn. Jennie there can play, and sing, too. Sometimes I sing Old Hundred and the Doxologer. Maybe you 'd like to hear me. Zeb Hall used to admire to hear me. You see, Zeb wanted to set up to me after I got the fifty thousand; but I told our folks I didn't want a farmer, so I come up here to try some of the city chaps. But about singing—if you 'll pitch the tune I 'll sing Doxologer for you.

FITZFOONE. I nevaw sing.

KATE. Well, you dance, I guess?

FITZFOONE. No, miss, I nevaw dance.

KATE. Well, in the name of gracious, what do you do?

FITZFOONE. I converse.

KATE. Well, I 'll get Jennie to [*exit* JENNIE, *unobserved by* KATE] pitch the tune on the piano. [*Looks round.*] Bless goodness, she is gone. I guess she 's got the toothache, by her leaving in such a hurry. Well, I 'll try and sing anyhow.

FITZFOONE. Excuse me, Miss Bawton, but I have urgent business in the city, and must go.

KATE. Law, sakes! Why, you ain't set down yet. Is that the way city chaps spark?

FITZFOONE. Pardon me, but I merely came this morning to beg you to grant me a pwivate interview. [*Falls on his knees.*] I want to pour my heart out at your feet.

KATE (*starts back*). O, do n't, Mr. Fitzfool! You make me feel all overish like! But come to-morrow afternoon at four o'clock, and I will get all the folks out, and we can have a real nice time sparking, and saying all sorts of loving things to each other.

FITZFOONE (*rises*). Thank you, my angel. I will be punctual to the moment. [*Kisses* KATE's *hand. Bows to* KATE, KATE *bows to* FITZFOONE, *alternately, until* FITZFOONE *disappears from the stage.*]

*Enter* JENNIE.

JENNIE (*falls on a chair*). O, Kate, you will be the death of me yet.

KATE. Tell me; do I act the *role* of the country girl well?

JENNIE. *Act* well! You ought to go on the stage.

KATE. Do you think Mr. Ned Leland suspects me?

JENNIE. No. Why do you ask?

KATE. Because he looks so quizzical, and his manner to me is so courteous.

JENNIE. Ah, Kate! Take care. Ned is a charming fellow, and I see he has already made an impression on you. Take care that the biter is not bitten, my fair cousin. [*Exit* JENNIE.]

KATE (*comes forward*). Her warning comes too late. Alas! I am deeply interested in Mr. Leland. If I could know that he loves me for myself alone, I would be happy.

Dr. CAMPBELL (*outside*). Kate! Kate!

KATE. I am coming, uncle. [*Starts to go.*]

(*Curtain falls.*)

## SCENE IV.

*Same as first. Enter* JENNIE *and* KATE.

JENNIE. I begin to think, Kate, that Ned Leland does see through your disguise. He evidently admires you, and it is not natural that he can fancy, truly, the wig and that odious dress.

KATE. If I could only be convinced that he is disinterested.

JENNIE.  I do not think Ned Leland is a mercenary man. He is noted for being open and generous, and if he loved a woman I can not believe that he could be influenced by money.

KATE.  O, if he only loved me as Philip Otis loves you— for myself alone.

JENNIE.  For Philip thinks I am poor, and is willing to take me "for better, for worse."

KATE.  Ah, Jennie, you are a happy girl.  [*Looks to entrance.*]  But, as I live, there comes that simpleton, Fitzfoone, again.  I will give him a quietus this time.  [*Looks at her watch.*]  Yes, it is precisely four o'clock.  He *is* punctual.

JENNIE.  I will retire and give him a clear field.

[*Exit JENNIE—R.*]

*Enter FITZFOONE—L.  (KATE seats herself.  FITZFOONE approaches and seats himself near KATE.)*

FITZFOONE.  Ah, my dear cweature, were you really expecting me?

KATE.  I do n't know as any one else was expecting you.

FITZFOONE.  Yes, you are the only one, the only being whom I would wish to expect me, or desire my coming.  I have come, adowable cweature, to pour into your listening ears the secret I have kept in my heart of hearts since the night I first beheld you.  I can keep it there no longer. Like a caged lion, it must be released.  Can I hope that my love is returned by you, most chawming girl?  [*Falls upon one knee.*]

KATE.  There!  I knowed it.  I knowed you loved me; and, this morning, when uncle came in and told me that the bank had failed, and that my fifty thousand dollars had took wings and flew off, I said I knowed there was *one* that would always love me, and that's *you!*  [*FITZFOONE starts to his feet; KATE rises.*]  But what is the matter, my dear Mr. Fitzfool?  You look kinder flurried.  I'm afeard you are sick.  Is the cholera about anywhere?  Let me get some camphire, and maybe you'll come all right again.

FITZFOONE.  No, thank ye, Miss Bawton.  I am better already.

KATE (*approaches him*).  Then, let's set down and talk it all over—love in a cottage, and all that.  O, my dear Mr.

Fitzfool, you do n't know how jolly I feel to think, now that all the fortune is gone, you still stick to your Katy darling. Come, man, you do n't seem to understand. [FITZFOONE *stares like an idiot.*] What are you staring at ?

FITZFOONE. Indeed, Miss Bawton, you have made a mistake. I did not mean that I wanted to *marry* you.

KATE (*indignantly*). Not marry me! Did n't you get on your knees and look soft, and talk love, and swear I was your "adowable cweature"?

FITZFOONE. You have deceived me.

KATE (*stamps her foot*). O, you cruel, cruel man! [*Goes toward* FITZFOONE; *takes his arm.*] Is this the way city chaps do their courting? Come along with me [*pulls him to entrance*], and I 'll make my uncle show you what it is to crawfish.

FITZFOONE (*struggles to release himself*). Murder! Help! Fire! Damnation! Murder! O!

*Enter* Dr. CAMPBELL, JENNIE, NED LELAND, *and* PHILIP OTIS. (FITZFOONE *jerks away from* KATE *and runs off the stage.*)

Dr. CAMPBELL. Ah, Kate, it is out of the question for you to persecute that poor devil so. Come! come!

KATE. Never mind, dear uncle. we will not be troubled again with Mr. Fitzfoone. He has heard of my loss of fortune, and has taken to his heels to escape from his "adowable cweature."

Dr. CAMPBELL. You are a real mad-cap, Kate; and if you do not deport yourself differently in future I will expose some of your willful conduct.

LELAND. You may spare yourself the trouble, Doctor, for Miss Barton was not cunning enough to deceive me. I have known all along that she wore a wig and used paint; and though others were deceived, I saw through her disguise. Love has sharp eyes, you see, Miss Kate.

KATE. O. Mr. Leland, you, too, will change your opinion when you know all. Mr. Fitzfoone is not the only one who has been taken in. I not only borrowed the wig and yellow dress, but also the fifty thousand dollars with which to act the heiress. The fortune belongs to my cousin Jennie, and well have she and I carried out the plot to test the affection of our suitors.

LELAND. Ah, Miss Kate, you little know the depth of my affection. All I ask is to possess you. [*Approaches* KATE; *draws her hand through his arm.*]

Dr. CAMPBELL. Well, girls, I have had two consultations to-day without a single fee; both on your accounts, you "*creatures.*" But I administered the right potions and the patients are doing finely, and I think are strong enough to speak for themselves. [*Looks at* OTIS *and* LELAND.]

OTIS (*approaches* JENNIE *and puts her hand in his arm*). I for one can speak. Jennie, your father has consented to our union, and I was willing to take you without the money, but must say I have no particular objection to it.

JENNIE. Very likely. But as my cousin Kate has so well acted her part, and with her assistance I have proved the truth of your affection, I will not consent to be your wife unless my fortune is equally divided between myself and Kate.

OTIS. To this I have no objection; for I am sure Ned and myself have been fortunate indeed to join the hands and hearts of the girls we love best, without the addition of a fortune neither expected.

Dr. CAMPBELL. I think, myself, you are both extremely lucky. It is with my advice and sanction that Jennie divides her fortune with Kate, for both are equally dear to me. [*Takes his position between the couples.*]

KATE. I can find no words to express my gratitude to you, uncle and Jennie, for this unexpected kindness.

LELAND. And I—

Dr. CAMPBELL. Say no more, say no more! If my children are happy I am satisfied: and the little plot managed by these mischievous girls proves that there are various ways of MARRYING A FORTUNE.

(*Curtain falls.*)

# DECLAMATIONS.

## SALUTATORY.

SUITABLE FOR THE EXHIBITION OF A MIXED SCHOOL, SPOKEN
BY A BOY TEN OR TWELVE YEARS OLD.

Our programme we have put in print,
To give you all a friendly hint
Of what we each intend to do
Before the exhibition's through.
The boys are dressed in Sunday suits,
With buttons bright, and genteel boots;
And all the girls are decked so fine
That some of them look quite divine.
But you must not by this suppose
We 've thought of nothing but our clothes;
For some of us have studied well,
And learned to read, and write, and spell.
It 's true, the rules we 've often broke—
We 've eat in school, and sometimes spoke;
If we did not obey command
Our teacher then would reprimand;
But, to her credit, I 'll say this:
She never struck a lick amiss.
And now, before I go away,
There is one thing I wish to say:
We 've studied hard for many days,
Our speeches, dialogues, and plays;
If we should fail to act them well,
When people ask you—*please do n't tell.*

## SPEECH FOR A BOY NINE OR TEN YEARS OLD.

The subject of my speech is odd;
But, in these modern times,
A poet like myself can make
All sorts of funny rhymes.

We have a flesh-brush at our house—
It is about so—long;*
'T is shaped just like a paddle, smooth,
With handle straight and long,

Would you believe it, if I were
To tell you here to-night
That mother uses this flesh-brush
To make her chaps act right?

No general ever used a sword
Upon the battle-field
With half the skill that mother does
This awful weapon wield.

I did not want to speak to-night,
But mother frowned and said,
That if I did not come right out,
She'd box me on the head.

And so I thought it was no use
To show an angry flush;
I knew that if I did not speak
I'd feel that old flesh-brush.

---

## SPEECH FOR A GIRL EIGHT OR NINE YEARS OLD.

I never made a speech before,
But that's no reason why,
Because I never spoke before,
I ought not now to try.

There are some silly little girls
Who are afraid to speak,
For fear some one will laugh at them:
I think this very weak.

I hope I'll always have the sense
To do as I am told;
Then people will not laugh at me,
Or think I am too bold.

---

\* Puts the forefinger of his right hand near the top of his left arm.

## SPEECH FOR A VERY SMALL CHILD.

I am my papa's little pet;
I love my book right well;
I hope, before another year,
I'll learn to read and spell.

## ANOTHER SPEECH FOR A VERY SMALL CHILD.

I've been to school
And learned to spell;
I've said my lessons
Quick and well.

And now I'm glad
That school is done,
So I can play
And have some fun.

## SPEECH FOR A SMALL BOY.

I wish the time would ever come
When all the little boys
Can run and play, just as they please,
And make a sight of noise.

I can not even *whistle* loud
But some one says, "O, stop!"
And if I crack my whip, just once,
I'm sure to get a pop.

And if I come into the house,
And happen to forget,
And leave my hat upon my head,
It puts mam in a fret.

O, don't I wish I was a man,
So I could have some ease—
I'd crack my whip and whistle loud,
And do just as I please.

The boy who speaks the above should come on the stage with a whip in his
hand, and a jaunty-looking cap on his head.

## ANOTHER SPEECH FOR A SMALL BOY.

I am a very little boy,
　　As you can plainly see,
And as I stand before you now
　　I tremble in each knee.

But then I thought it would not do
　　For *all* the boys in school
To make a speech, and leave me out,
　　Like a poor, simple fool.

And so I plucked my courage up,
　　Determined to be bold,
And have come out upon the stage
　　To do as I am told.

I thank the ladies very much
　　For listening to my speech;
And, if they ask me, I am sure
　　I'll give a kiss to each.

## A SCHOOL-BOY'S TROUBLES.

Good people, listen to my speech,
　　And I will tell you true,
The troubles of a poor school-boy,
　　And they are not a few.

He has to be on guard each day,
　　As much as any picket;
For if by chance he breaks a rule,
　　He's sure to lose his ticket.

At home he's always in the way,
　　The family all kick him;
And when a lesson he recites,
　　Some girl is sure to beat him.

Nobody ever seems to think
　　The school-boy has a heart;
Nobody cares if to his eyes
　　The childish tears do start.

He is too young to be a man,
Too old to be a pet;
And as he plods his weary way,
No comfort does he get.
And so, between the kicks and cuffs
At home and then at school,
No wonder half the people think
The school-boy is a fool.

## SPEECH FOR A BOY TEN OR TWELVE YEARS OLD.

I did not want to speak to-night,
But could not have my way;
And now I've come before you all,
I don't know what to say.
I am so scared, you all can see,
That I can hardly talk;
So none of you need be surprised
If I do make a balk.
You don't know how a fellow feels,
Who is about my age,
When he gets up to make a speech
The first time on the stage.
His face turns white and red by turns—
He shakes from arm to heel;
And if a lady looks at him,
His head begins to reel.
I hope the effort I have made
This audience will admire,
And while you wish to criticise
Permit me to retire.

## SPEECH FOR CHILD SEVEN OR EIGHT YEARS OLD.

You all may think, because I am
So very small and young,
That I'm afraid to stand up here
And use my little tongue.

I'll let you know, in double-quick,
  That I've not learned my books
For ten long months, to now be scared
  By all these people's looks,

It would be very strange indeed,
  That chaps born in *this* State
Should put their fingers in their mouths
  And show a dastard trait.

Our fathers were as brave a band
  As ever lived, we know;
And we are "chips from the old block,"
  From head down to the toe.

The child, in the last two lines, must suit the action to the word. Too much pains can not be taken in drilling for an exhibition.

---

## SPEECH FOR A YOUNG GIRL.

If there's a thing that puzzles me,
  In all this wide creation,
It is the trouble people have
  To get an education.

First, all the *letters* you must learn,
  And then hard words to spell;
Then weeks and weeks of work to do
  To learn to *read* right well.

Then comes the art of *writing* next—
  Straight lines, and then "pot-hooks;"
And then a girl must turn from these
  To piles of awful books.

There's *grammar*, with its hateful words
  And all its horrid tenses ;
It is enough to drive one mad,
  And make her lose her senses.

*Geography* must then be searched
  Before we know the reason
Why, as the earth turns round and round,
  We have each yearly season.

Then *history* comes upon the list,
To make us understand
The constitution and the laws
That govern every land.
And then all have to learn that thing
They call *arithmetic;*
In trying to do a single sum
I sometimes get quite sick.
Then comes a string of other things,
Too tedious here to mention;
But if I live I'll study all—
At least that's my intention.
So, "take it all in all," I think
It does require great pains
To cram these studies all complete
In one small lot of brains.

---

## SPEECH FOR A SMALL BOY.

I'd rather take a whipping now
Than stand up here and make a bow,
And speak before a crowd like this;
For much I fear you all may hiss.
But then I thought that Henry Clay
Had been a boy once in his day.
And Daniel Webster had to crawl
Before he ever walked at all.
"Large oaks from little acorns grow."
And, though I creep along quite slow,
Who knows, but at some future day,
*I'll* be as great a man as Clay.

---

## SPEECH FOR A LITTLE BOY AND GIRL ABOUT THE SAME AGE.

*Girl speaks first.*

There was a little maid and she had a little bonnet,
And she had a little finger, with a little ring upon it:

She squeezed her little waist to such a little size
That it made the little blood rush to her little eyes.
This pretty little maid had a pretty little beau,
And he wore a little hat, and gloves as white as snow;
He said his little heart was in a little flutter,
That he loved this little maid like little boys love butter.
A little while, alas! and her little beau departed,
With all his little vows, and left her broken-hearted.
Now, all you little maids, a moral I will give you,
Don't trust to little men, they surely will deceive you.

*Boy speaks.*

There was a little fellow and he had a little coat,
And he had a little beard, just like a little goat.
This handsome little fellow did love a little lass;
He loved this little lady like little calves love grass.
But, ah! this little lassie did fool her little beau—
When he asked her if she'd marry she worked her fingers *so.*
　　　　　[*Puts his thumb on his nose and works his
　　　　　　fingers.  Points with the other hand to the
　　　　　　male audience.*]
Now, all you little men, mind what I say to you,
Don't court these little maids, they'll fool you if you do.

They enter the stage together.  In speaking, both suit the action to the word.

--------

## SPEECH FOR A GIRL TEN OR TWELVE YEARS OLD.

I am a gay and merry child,
　And love to dance and play;
I think that pleasure ought to be
　The order of the day.

I wish I was the President
　Of these United States;
I'd *veto* all the school-rooms,
　And burn the books and slates.

And then I'd give to all the girls
　Nice dolls and lots of toys;
I'd buy all sorts of whips and things
　And give the little boys.

If the great men of our day,
Who now cut such a "swell,"
Had never gone a day to school,
And learned their lessons well,
There never would perhaps have been
This cry of "dissolution,"
And all the people going mad
About the constitution!
The moral of my speech is this,
That men who've been to schools
Sometimes, with all their pile of sense,
Turn out the greatest fools!

## THE PRICE OF GOLD.

The times are very tight, we know,
And every day grow tighter,
And pap complains, when bills come in,
His purse is growing lighter.
If a new coat I want to buy,
Invariably I'm told
To do without, as there is now
A large per cent on *gold!*
And if I want a pair of shoes
To keep out mud and cold,
I'm told to make the old ones do
Till there's a fall in *gold!*
My gloves are nearly both worn out,
Together they won't hold;
But I must wear them, rags and all,
While premium's high on *gold!*
I asked my ma for a new hat—
Law, how her eyes she rolled!
"Why, child," she said, "have you forgot
The awful price of *gold?*"
It is enough to fret a saint—
My temper I can't hold;
I'm tempted sometimes to run off
Till there's a fall in *gold!*

## SPEECH FOR A VERY SMALL BOY.

A very little boy am I,
And yet to speak I mean to try;
Because I know a thing or two,
As small as I appear to you.

I know that millers have fat hogs,
I've seen them roll about like logs;
But where the miller gets his corn
I never knew since I was born.

I know that lawyers oft get rich
When into people's suits they pitch;
But how they get the money paid
I never knew since I was made.

I know that doctors all dress fine,
No matter how their patients pine;
But how they get so much to spend
I never knew, you may depend.

I know the boys all love the girls,
And talk about their "eyes" and "curls;"
But why the *girls* do n't like a beau
I never do expect to know.

I know some lady here will say,
"That boy's too fast—take him away!"
This trouble I will save you now
As thus* I make my farewell bow.

---

## SPEECH FOR A VERY SMALL BOY.

It is a trying thing to me
To get up here where all can see,
And make a speech before a crowd,
For you must know I can't speak loud.

But then I thought, as I was dressed,
I'd come and do my very best;
Some credit you will give me now
As to the ladies here I bow.

---

* Bows.

## SPEECH FOR A VERY SMALL BOY.

George Washington was once a boy,
  And had to learn to spell,
They say he was his father's joy,
  And that he learned right well.
He never spoke a lie, I'm told,
  No matter where he went,
And by behaving good and bold
  Became our President!
Then who can tell but that *I* may
  Become as great as *he?*
And if I do I hope that day
  You all may live to see.

## TURNING THE GRINDSTONE.

When I was quite a little boy,
  One winter morning cold
I started off to school, and felt
  All manly, fresh, and bold.
Just then a man accosted me;
  Said he, "My pretty lad.
Just look at this nice ax I hold,
  To grind it I'd be glad.
"Your father's grindstone stands quite near,
  Please turn it now for me:
For surely you're the nicest boy
  I ever yet did see."
Pleased with the compliment I said,
  "The grindstone's in the shop,
And tho' I'm on my way to school,
  For you, kind sir, I'll stop."
The man replied. "How old are you?
  For I am very sure
A finer fellow than you are
  I never saw before."
I listened to his wily words,
  And, like a simple fool,

I turned and turned the grindstone for
    The man to grind the tool.

I toiled and tugged and puffed and blowed—
    The ax, you see, was new;
At last 't was ground, and bitterly
    Did I my folly rue!

I thought the man would maybe give
    A penny for my work;
Instead of that he started off,
    And scowled just like a Turk!

"You little rascal!" then he said,
    "You have the truant played;
Be off, or else you 'll rue the hour
    That you from school have strayed!"

Alas! I thought 't was bad enough
    The grindstone thus to turn,
But to be called a rascal, too,
    With anger made me burn.

Since I've grown older, when I see
    A merchant very kind
To customers, I always think
    He has an ax to grind.

Or when I hear a lawyer's voice
    To blarney much inclined,
I'm sure to think his client finds
    He has an ax to grind.

And when I see a preacher bow
    And *humbly* speak his mind,
I fear his flock will soon find out
    He has an ax to grind.

Or if I hear a gambler say,
    "Here, boys, I go it blind!"
I know full well he has an ax,
    The dullest sort, to grind.

The moral of my speech is this,
    That those who seem most kind
Are often just the folks who have
    A new dull ax to grind.

## THE IRON SHROUD.

I 'll tell you now a horrid tale
  I read long months ago
About a man who was confined
  By one who was his foe.

The room in which this wretch was placed
  Was built of iron strong,
And in it seven windows stood,
  All narrow, high, and long.

But as the captive watched each day,
  He noticed, with great fear,
That almost imperceptibly
  The wall did disappear;

And as the days and hours passed,
  He anxiously did wait
To solve the dreadful truth that hung
  So darkly o'er his fate!

*Years* passed along, but as they went
  The room still smaller grew;
And often tears of anguish did
  The prisoner's eyes bedew.

He saw the windows, one by one,
  Vanish by slow degrees;
And as the fearful wall grew close,
  It made his heart's blood freeze!

But so it was, and the last ray
  Of light and hope was gone,
And silently the wretched man
  Awaited death forlorn!

It came at last, and with a shriek,
  So long, so clear, so loud,
The captive yielded his last breath
  Within the IRON SHROUD.

## AN OLD TRADITION IN A NEW GARB.*

One Summer eve young Cupid hied
To roam the shady woodland side,
To pass the time in merry play,
And gather flowers fresh and gay;
With wings of gold and purple hue,
And quiver full of arrows too,
Suspended by a ribbon blue,
Across the shoulder lightly swung,
To which a supple bow was hung.
And thus equipped he moved along,
Singing a soft melodious song;
With diamond eyes and blooming face,
And dimpled cheek and childish grace;
A polished forehead, golden hair,
Whose glossy ringlets kissed the air;
With rosy, pouting, parting lips,
The nectar from the violet sips;
And then his playful fancy tries
In chasing pretty butterflies.

  *  *  *  *  *

While thus amused, he spied Lord Orville Grey
Wending his pensive steps across the way;
With haggard look and many a deep-drawn sigh
He caught the laughing boy's mischievous eye.
"You little rogue," he said, and caught him by the arm,
"Your silly pranks have rendered me much harm."
"What have *I* done?" His lordship quick replies,
"You've pierced my heart through Clare's bewitching eyes.
Now know, proud boy, revenge is just and sweet,
And you shall pay for that malicious feat."
"O, let me go," the impatient urchin cried,
"And Lady Clare shall be your happy bride.
I swear, by Venus and the gods above,
She shall return your pure and ardent love;
Attend to-morrow Lady Melton's fete
And I'll be there the conquest to complete."

  *  *  *  *  *  *

---

* Published many years ago without the knowledge or consent of the author.

Wrapped in rich crimson robes of flaming light,
The sun retired beneath the horizon;
The soft air breathed his parting orison;
Then slowly came the somber shades of night.
    A soft retreat young Cupid found
    Within a rural, grassy glen,
    Far from the busy haunts of men:
Throwing his quiver careless on the ground.
Was soon reposed in slumber most profound.
While thus unconscious the unconscious beauty lay,
Old grim and ghastly DEATH beset his way,
Seeking, with hollow eyes and dismal moans,
A place to rest his weary, aching bones.
    In that warm, sultry clime,
    A fatal fever raged.
    Which kept him all the time
    Quite busily engaged
Stalking abroad, all day compelled to roam.
To summon mortals to their *long, last* home!
    On this momentous night
    He wished a short respite;
For well he knew, before the break of day.
Old Rowland must the debt of Nature pay;
From Jupiter the awful mandate came.
Which, if neglected, *Death* must bear the blame.
    Scattering his arrows all about,
    He stretched his fleshless carcass out,
    With a cold, heartless shiver;
He woke, and found no time to waste—
Gathered them up in breathless haste
    And put them in his quiver,
His orders to obey; selected thence a pointed dart,
Shot old Rowland thro' the heart,
    And strode his weary way.

Cupid arose with the morning air,
Laved his brow in the dewy air;
His arrows were all in confusion tost,
He counted and found that none were lost,
And carefully put them all away
In view of his pledge to Orville Grey.
When night came on with a smiling face
He bent his steps to the Melton place.

Lord Orville Grey was already there,
And so was the lovely Florence Clare;
A blaze of the beautiful graced the hall,
But the Lady Clare surpassed them all.
Lord Orville lingered close to her side
And whispered low, "Will you be my bride?"
"He speaks of love," thought Cupid; "now's the hour
To show Lord Grey my soft, seducing power,
        And make my promise sure!"
Twang! went the bow, sped well the fatal dart,
The life-blood curdles at her very heart;
Her cheek turns pale; she starts, and pants for breath;
Then sinks into the icy arms of Death,
        To speak and rise no more!
Cupid, amazed, beside the victim crept,
And wondered how it was, and then he wept
That youth and so much beauty could not save
Sweet Florence Clare from an untimely grave!

Meantime the angry god had summoned Death,
To learn why Rowland still preserved his breath.
Death met the accusation with surprise,
And to his frowning master thus replies:
"The deference due your majesty I make,
But must affirm it's all a great mistake;
I pierced old Rowland with my keenest dart
Right thro' the center of his sordid heart,
And can't imagine how the stroke he parried.
Not dead? You joke!"  "Why, no! the coon is married.
Instead of taking his detested life
You've blessed him with a young and handsome wife!"
Death scratched his skull and said he knew not why
He could not make the tough old villain die;
That he had *taken* many in his life,
But never *tendered* any man a wife;
And much he feared, could the whole truth be known,
*Young Cupid's* arrows mingled with his own
        On that dark, fatal night!
And what about the blamed affair he hated
    Both formed to conquer human hearts,
    So much alike the plaguey darts
Could not be separated,
        *And never would be right!*

*Cupid* and *Death* each other's weapons carry,
And thus we see the reason why,
As long as this wide world shall stand,
In every clime, in every land,
  The *young* and *beautiful* must *die*
And *foolish old men marry!*

## TRUE GREATNESS.

Some call that great which wealth can claim,
Some predicate it of a name,
And others deem it worldly fame;
While some by pomp, and power, and show,
Would let the world their greatness know.
While through *this* life we take our course,
*Such* greatness may be turned to use,
To aid us in the higher aims
Which the immortal spirit claims ;
Such greatness natural pleasure brings,
Merely confined to natural things.
*True* greatness, not to these confined,
In magnanimity of mind,
Declares itself of higher birth
Than gilded pageantry of earth !
We trace its noble origin
To HIM whose greatness is divine—
Whose glorious greatness is no less
Than pure essential HOLINESS.
He is called great, and conqueror, too,
Who earthly kingdoms can subdue;
*But he who can himself control*
Displays true greatness of the soul.
To make the proper estimate,
Then, to be *good* is to be *great!*

## TRUTH DIVINE.

O, truth divine, to mortals given
To ope the mind to peace and Heaven,

How precious and how dear thou art
To those who seek a change of heart!
From worldly love and passion freed
The Christian feels a bliss indeed.
When a pure state like this we find,
We think it strange the human mind
Can vain fallacious errors clasp
With Truth Divine within its grasp.
O, love of truth, who knows its worth,
A gem too pure for this low earth;
But if the soul this pearl would find,
All others must be cast behind.

## TRUTH AND LOVE.

Bright crystals of truth, O, how divine,
When midst bright flowrets of love they shine!
Bright jewels of virtue rich and rare
Will always glitter conspicuous there.

Jewels of virtue *seem* to be lost
When innocence yields to Death's cold frost;
But *truth is innocence,* and *love never dies*—
In the garland of virtue each ever vies.

## ON MUSIC.

Music, thy varying and harmonious power
Adapts itself to every mood and hour;
Thy full-drawn chords devotion can impart,
And elevate the Christian's drooping heart,
Above this sphere of sense and time,
To the celestial spirit clime;
And when in unison with those who weep,
Then pity moves the string with pathos deep.

But, Music, thou **canst merry** be,
And change thine **air** to suit thy company;

In quickstep cheerful, brisk, and loud,
Canst animate the reveling crowd,
Or on the sanguine battle-plain
Exhilarate with martial strain.
When rattling drums and clarion clear
Invigorate the soldier's ear;
Or thou canst with a pastoral lay
While the dull shepherd's time away.

And, Music, thou dost condescend
To be the smiling infant's friend;
Deigning thy soothing power to try
In the sweet, simple lullaby.

But most bewitching thou canst prove,
Should unsophisticated love
Breathe softly on the magic lyre,
Responding to some angel choir,
Whose highest notes can only swell
The melting power of LOVE to tell.

## CLOSING SONG.

TUNE.—*"Just Before the Battle, Mother."*

We now come forth to thank you freely
    For your interest so kind,
And to tell you that we'll ever
    Such attention bear in mind.
        *Chorus*—Farewell, then, for we may never
            Together meet on earth again;
            'T is painful thus for us to sever,
            And the parting gives us pain.

For our teachers we will cherish
    Love and friendship while we live,
And for the care of us they've taken
    Warmest thanks to them we give.
        *Chorus*—Farewell, then, for we may never
            Together meet on earth again;
            'T is painful thus for us to sever,
            And the parting gives us pain.
18

Farewell, classmates, we may never
   Meet again together here;
But our school association
   To each other will be dear.
      *Chorus*—Farewell, then, for we may never
               Together meet on earth again;
            'T is painful thus for us to sever,
               And the parting gives us pain.

---

## THREE LITTLE GRAVES.

'T was Autumn, and the leaves were dry
   And rustled on the ground,
And chilly winds came whistling by
   With low and pensive sound,

As through the graveyard's lone retreat,
   By meditation led,
I walked, with slow and cautious feet,
   Above the sleeping dead.

Three little graves ranged side by side
   My close attention drew;
O'er two the tall grass bending wide,
   And *one* seemed fresh and new.

As lingering there I mused awhile
   On death's long, dreamless sleep,
And opening life's deceitful smile,
   A mourner came to weep.

Her form was bowed, but not with years—
   Her words were faint and few;
And o'er those little graves her tears
   Distilled like evening dew.

A prattling boy, some four years old,
   Her trembling hand embraced;
And from my heart the tale he told
   Can never be effaced.

"Mama, what made sweet sister die?
   She loved me when we played.
You told me if I would not cry
   You 'd show me where she 's laid."

     *     *     *     *     *     *

"'T is here, my child, that sister lies
    Deep buried in the ground;
No light comes to her little eyes,
    And she can hear no sound."

"Mama, why can't you take her up
    And put her in the bed?
I 'll feed her from my little cup—
    And then she won't be dead.

"For sister 'll be afraid to lie
    In this dark grave to-night;
And she 'll be very cold, and cry
    Because there is no light."

"Your sister is not cold, my child,
    For God who saw her die,
As he looked down from heaven and smiled,
    Recalled her to the sky.

"And then her spirit quickly fled
    To God, by whom 't was given;
Her *body* in the ground is dead,
    But *sister* lives in heaven."

"Mama, won't she be hungry there,
    And want some bread to eat?
And who will give her clothes to wear
    And keep them clean and neat?

"Papa must go and take her some—
    I 'll send her all I 've got;
And he must bring sweet sister home—
    Mama, now must he not?"

"No, my dear child, that can not be;
    But if you 're good and true,
You may one day go up to her—
    She can not come to you.

"'Let little children come to me,'
    Once our dear Savior said;
And in His arms she 'll always be,
    And God will give her bread."

## TRUE DEVOTION.

The Sabbath morn broke bright and beautiful
　Upon the dew-bespangled earth;
*One* lonely heart bowed meekly dutiful
　In prayer to hail its hallowed birth.

With lifted hands, and eyes unclosed to aught
　Save that which now possessed her soul,
"Is there not grace in Heaven?" she inward thought,
　"And power the reckless to control?"

On that same morn the bright celestial choirs
　Awoke to sympathy and love;
In notes of praise attuned their *golden lyres*
　To HIM who rules the heaven above.

Life, light, and glory from the presence blazed,
　The chant swelled full and loud and high;
And cherub faces with sweet rapture gazed
　On HIM who made both earth and sky.

They hist! a tone of pure and fine-wrought feeling
　Vibrated through the blest abode;
From earth it came in mournful numbers pealing,
　Up to the very throne of God!

With deep and heavenly odors breathing,
　Athwart the glorious conclave swept;
A strain of *grieving love*, and so entreating,
　The happy angels paused and wept.

A peaceful answer quickly passed, returning
　That which gospel faith and love had won—
That holy prayer, still on the altar burning,
　*The mother's offering for an only son.*

---

## DIVERSITY OF CHARACTER.

There are hearts in this world so humble and meek
They would not the praise of the multitude seek,
But glide through their duties, both peaceful and still,
Like wild flowers twining near streamlet or rill,
Which fancy lone meadows so fertile and green,
And bloom in obscurity—sometimes unseen:

Disdaining the honor or plaudits of men,
Content to reside in their own native glen.
Another would soar on the pinions of FAME,
And labors intensely to get a great name;
A cringing and bowing popular minion
Who falsifies truth for public opinion ;
While others would sacrifice comfort and health.
And honor and conscience, to accumulate wealth;
Plodding early and late, increasing their store—
Could they gather up *all*, would want as much more!
Some, if they can, think it pleasant enough
To murder their time in *tobacco* and *snuff*;
And some with strong liquor their moments consume,
Although it may lead them to gutter or tomb!
Thousands, quite reckless, care not how they live—
To pleasure and sporting their hours they give;
Not reflecting, though happy and cheerful they seem.
That life is as short as a morning's light dream;
That existence thus wasted must set in a cloud,
When the shadows of Death shall their pathway enshroud.
Let others speak lightly, and think what they will,
My life I would choose by Virtue's soft rill ;
Sound reason would whisper, 't is happier, indeed,
To be like the wild rose that blooms on the mead.

## SUMMER FRUIT.

"Fine Summer fruit; come buy, come buy
    Sweet apples large and round,"
The market-man was heard to cry,
    As promenading round.

One selected from the rest,
    And paid the man his price,
And thought it surely was the best,
    So very plump and nice.

I put it carefully away
    Within a China jar,
To keep it for a Winter day,
    When fruit is sometimes rare.

One snowy eve, both dark and cold,
  The rarity in store
Was cut to eat; and then behold,
  'T was *rotten at the core!*

'T is thus, I cried, with favor sold,
  And he who pays the fee,
When he has parted with his gold,
  Will much resemble me.

We choose our friends by outward show,
  Because they promise well;
Their motives we are not to know,
  For who *the heart* can tell?

Bought friendship lasts like Summer fruit
  While all is bright and fair;
Long as the int'rest it may suit,
  And *then*—no friendship there!

When poverty's cold Winter blows
  And gloom is spreading round,
The heart must bear its throbs and woes—
  The friend can not be found.

Or if perchance he should seem kind
  And feign a friendly part,
Just push him close, and you will find
  Him hollow in the heart.

---

## ON SLANDER.

We mourn the selfish pride which now prevails,
And on our hapless erring race entails
  Care, misery, and death;
And what we all must own, by far, is worse,
That deadly, heavy, and malignant curse,
  Foul stains of SLANDER's breath,
Which often blasts the honest fame
Of many a true and virtuous name;
Which else might live in partial bliss,
*Even in such a heartless world as this!*

For what to man are golden stores of pelf,
Or roseate health, or even life itself,

When character is torn;
Leaving the hopeless, sad, and stricken heart
Without a friend, a cast-off, and apart
In solitude to mourn?
Bereft of that most pleasing source
Of life, sweet, soothing intercourse;
And, what is still more hard to bear,
In this his helpless children have to share!
Ye reckless spoilers of a neighbor's weal;
Ye manger dogs! too merciless to feel;
Too indolent to climb
Yourselves the mount which leads to fame,
You look with jealous envy and declaim
'Gainst him who spends his time
In active useful enterprise,
And falsify him in the eyes
Of those who would his cause defend,
And to his wise pursuits assistance lend.
And when the *blackish, fiendish* deed is done,
You smile and smile, and look quite calmly on.
To you we recommend
That golden maxim of the Holy Word,
As taught by Jesus Christ, our only Lord,
The wretched sinner's friend:
Unto another always do
As you would have him do to you;
And if you would for mercy pray,
O, sin, O, "sin no more, and go thy way."

## THE LORD SEES OUR INNERMOST.

A charity deed on the pinions of fame,
To heaven's high court was borne;
It savored of grace, was pretty and fair,
Came claiming a place in a casket there,
Of jewels reserved to be worn
By those whom the Savior would name.
Through the ordeal of earth it flew with *eclat*
The donor was raised to the skies;

But the external mold, tho' sparkling and bright,
Its value ne'er told to the angels of light,
   Who, looking with deep-searching eyes,
Its *innermost* particles saw.

The action apparently noble and kind
   Was tarnished by motives impure;
Though lauded by man, thro' the clear gospel glass
Where angels may ken, it never would pass;
   No rest in their kingdom so pure
Could act without goodness e'er find.

---

### THE BOY AND THE BAKER.

Once, when monopoly had made
As bad as now the eating trade,
A boy went to a baker's shop,
His gnawing appetite to stop;
A loaf for twopence there demanded,
And down a *tiny* loaf was handed.

The boy surveyed it round and round,
With many a shrug and look profound:
At length—"Why, master," said the wight,
"This loaf is very, very *light!*"

The baker, his complaint to parry,
   Replied, with look most archly dry,
    While quick conceit sat squinting in his eye—
"Light, boy? Then you've the less to carry."

The boy grinned plaudits to his joke,
   And on the counter laid down rhino,
With mien, that plainly all but spoke—
   "With you I'll soon be even, I know."
Then took his loaf, and went his way;
   But soon the baker bawl'd him back—
   "You've laid down but *three halfpence*, Jack!
And *twopence* was the loaf's amount.
How's this, you cheating rascal, eh?"
   "Sir," says the boy, "you've the *less to count!*"

CHARLES DIBDIN, JR.

# MAY-QUEEN CELEBRATION.

### SPEECH OF THE CROWNER.

Lovely, charming Queen of May,
O, may thy path through life's short day
Be strewed with flowers fresh and gay,
        To charm thee.
Still may thy face in smiles be drest,
And no rude foe thy peace molest,
Nor evil passion cross thy breast
        To harm thee.
May time mature thy buoyant mind,
And all affections good and kind
A place in thy young bosom find
        To bless thee.
May no dark cloud on thee descend,
Nor sorrows deep thy heart-strings rend,
Nor lover false, or faithless friend
        Distress thee.
May peace attend thee day and night,
And every blessing good and bright,
And angels of the realms of light,
        Surround thee.
O, may thy sun in smiles decline,
And all thy blessings be divine,
And wreaths of glory round thee shine,
        To crown thee.

[*Or.*]

When thou shalt to the tomb descend
May heaven's Sovereign be thy friend,
And guardian angels still attend
        Around thee.
And when from earth thy spirit flies,
O, may you, with the good and wise,
Immortal life find in the skies,
        To crown thee!

19

### SPEECH OF THE SCEPTER-BEARER.

O, Queen of the prettiest month in the year,
  We willingly bow to thy sway!
And crown thee, sweet fair one, triumphantly here,
  The monarch of this happy day.

We choose thee because thou art virtuous and fair,
  Nor yet for thy personal grace;
The charms which embellish thy temper and mind
  More rare than a beautiful face.

Thy subjects are happy, the breezes impart
  A fragrance through flowerets gay;
*Peace* to thy reign, and *health* to thy heart,
  Dear Queen of this pretty bright May.

The scepter then take, and, fair Queen, we will bow
  In loyalty true to thy sway;
And crown thee, sweet fair one, triumphantly here,
  The monarch of this happy day.

### SPEECH OF SPRING.

Thy faithful subject now, sweet Queen,
  An offering doth bring;
Fresh flowers, with their leaves of green,
  Low at thy feet I fling.

O, may thy life be free from care,
  And like these flowers be gay;
May sorrow ne'er shade brow so fair
  As thine appears to-day.

The gift I humbly bring to thee
  Is one of love, I ween,
Accept it, then, this day of glee,
  Our chosen beauteous Queen.

### SPEECH OF SUMMER.

I come, fair Queen, with golden wheat,
This day your royalty to greet;
And though my gift is not as gay
As that of *Spring*, to gild your way,

Still you must own that *Summer's* face
In your young bosom holds a place.
You love the warmth my sunshine yields;
You love my rich, full grain in fields;
You love my sky, so blue and fair;
You love my beauties every-where;
Then please accept, from subject true,
The simple gift I bring to you.

### SPEECH OF AUTUMN.

My sisters, Summer and young Spring,
To you their wheat and flowers bring;
But I bear ripe and luscious fruit—
Your royal taste I hope to suit.
I wear a sober mien, I own,
As now I stand before your throne;
But I have beauties, you'll agree,
That all who know me ever see.
My mellow light and hazy sky
Both have attraction for the eye;
And many love the mournful breeze
I send among the fading trees.
Then let me hope in your kind heart
That Autumn holds a loving part.

### SPEECH OF WINTER.

This simple wreath I bring to thee,
From gay and brilliant colors free;
Of lasting green this wreath is made,
So may your virtues never fade;
But bloom on *earth* while life is given,
And, *ever green*, bloom fresh in *heaven!*

### SONG OF THE FLORAS.

With faces bright
And bosoms light
    We crown the Queen of May.
Fresh flowers we bring,
Emblems of Spring,
    To strew along her way.

Let us be gay
This happy day,
    The present we'll enjoy;
We'll laugh at care,
And have no fear
    Our pleasure to alloy.

Youth is the time,
In this free clime,
    To carol forth our lay;
And as we sing,
Sweet flowers we bring,
    To crown our Queen of May.

### SPEECH OF FASHION.

My name is Fashion, and all bow
    To my imperious shrine;
I'll rule the world long as the sun
    And moon and stars doth shine.

The rich and poor all follow me
    Where'er I go or move;
No matter what my freaks impose,
    They all my power love.

'Tis Fashion rules the minds of men
    Of every clime and nation;
'Twas Fashion that invented first
    A May-queen celebration.

To you, sweet Queen, then Fashion brings
    A necklace rich and rare,
To clasp with her devotion true
    Around your neck so fair.

Accept this token of her love,
    And in this hour of glee,
O, may you reign a happy Queen,
    Is Fashion's prayer for thee.

### SPEECH OF FOLLY.

I am a merry, willful lass,
As gayly through the world I pass;

My sister, Fashion, I will own,
Has worshipers about her throne;
But, though to her they bend the knee,
As *many* turn to follow me;
For Fashion's power soon would fade
Without her sister Folly's aid;
And so together, hand in hand,
We travel over every land.
The gift I lay before thy throne
Is quite a silly one, I own:
'T is one of Fashion's modern tools
To turn the head of female fools.

### SPEECH OF CUPID.

My name is Cupid, and all know
I bear a quiver and a bow;
I travel over all the earth,
'Mid scenes of gladness and of mirth.
Tho' I am small, yet I am bold—
I strike the hearts of young and old;
I'll wait till you are seventeen,
And then, my lovely little Queen,
I'll send a sharp and pointed dart
Straight to the center of your heart.
[*Shoots an arrow at the* Queen's *feet.*]

### SPEECH OF FAITH.

I come with my sisters fair to see—
Sweet Hope and gentle Charity; ·
We three united can impart
True happiness to every heart.
This Book contains the words of truth,
To guide the wayward steps of youth;
The Cross also I bear, to show
Where we must look for strength below.
If you upon them both will lean,
A crown you'll wear in heaven, fair Queen,
A place you'll gain 'mid hosts above,
Where naught is heard but truth and love.

### SPEECH OF HOPE.

Pandora's box is one of which
   We all have heard, fair Queen;
In it was sealed up every woe
   That in this world is seen.
A woman's curiosity
   Revealed all it contained;
She raised the lid, out trouble flew,
   And Hope alone remained!

So since that day, whene'er the heart
   Is sad and sick and sore,
Hope always at the bottom stays,
   With anchor safe and sure.
This emblem then I give to thee,
   A beacon to the soul,
Still upward pointing to the land,
   The Christian's wished-for goal.

### SPEECH OF CHARITY.

O, Charity is a lovely grace,
In every heart she holds a place;
'T is long-suffering and kind,
And adds much beauty to the mind.
I come, I come with my mantle wide,
The failings of all I love to hide;
For Charity never refuses to halt
To cover a weakness or hide a fault.
Let Charity's mantle, then, fair Queen,
About thy throne be ever seen.

### SPEECH OF MUSIC.

My name is Music, with my lyre,
All hearts I often do inspire;
Music now comes to offer thee
Her plaintive notes of melody.

'T will give, I trust. a gladsome lay
To this bright festival of May;
Then let sweet Music's magic power
Be felt by all this happy hour.

### SPEECH OF THE MAY QUEEN.

My dear little subjects, the homage you bring
Falls soft on my heart like dew-drops in Spring
Upon the sweet flowers, limpid and pure,
Refreshing my heart to its innermost core.

You crown me your Queen, the Queen of sweet May,
And I for your loyalty nothing can pay
But the tribute of *love*, all ardent and true,
From a bright merry heart now tendered to you.

The trees are in verdure, the flowers are bright,
Then may our bosoms be mirthful and light
As the soft, playful zephyr which comes from afar,
Or the butterfly gay that sports through the air.

Should evils come near us to mar this blest day,
May angels attend us and chase them away ;
To children, we 're told. such guardians are given,
"Of such," said our Lord, "is the kingdom of heaven."

### ANOTHER SPEECH OF THE MAY QUEEN.

You have crowned me, kind playmates, "the Queen of the
        May,"
And my heart beats with pride and with joy;
In return I have nothing to give you all
    But a *love* that is without alloy.

To the classmate who crowns me, O, here let me say,
    You hold a dear place in my heart;
The playmate who tenders the scepter I hold
    Also in my love bears a part.

To the beautiful Spring let me now give my thanks
    For the garlands of flowers so fair;
And to Summer, for all the rich grain she has brought,
    My gratitude now I declare.

To Autumn, I thank her for fruit that I love,
    Her gift it is grateful and kind;
And to Winter, the wreath she so lovingly brings,
    Holds a very dear place in my mind.

And now, to my schoolmates around me so dear,
    My thanks to you *all* I avow;
And I never expect to enjoy while I live
    A moment more happy than now.

And when I grow old, and think of the past,
    I will often recall this glad day,
When, with hearts beating light, my playmates in glee
    Did crown me the Queen of sweet May.


### ANOTHER SPEECH OF THE MAY QUEEN.

Beloved companions of my juvenile days,
    I bring the tribute of a grateful mind;
Accept my ardent song of love and praise
    For friendship so congenial and refined.

You wish me blessings that might well attend
    Some happier being in the climes above,
Where no false lover or unfaithful friend
    Can dash with grief the cup of perfect love!

Now we are happy, but the time may come
    When fate shall sever bosoms thus entwined,
And you or I may find some distant home,
    Where friends are few and strangers seem unkind.

Then, should I go, my thoughts will linger here,
    While fancy paints this well-remembered day;
To my fond heart you ever will be dear,
    Tho' I should wander far, O, far away!

Nor can I hope, while in this clime below,
　To claim the bliss your fervent prayers would grant;
Where every flowery path thro' which we go
　Is checked with sorrow keen, or care, or want.

Then please accept my song of love and praise,
　And oft, when I recall this gladsome day,
I'll think of my companions young and fair
　With fondest love, who crowned me Queen of May.

SONG.

Air—"*Many long weary hours I've been waiting.*"

The sweet Spring is blooming,
　With flowers fresh and gay,
And we've met together blithely
　To crown our Queen of May.

　　Will we ever meet again
　　　To carol forth our lay;
　　Will we ever meet again
　　　To crown the Queen of May.

No cloud of sorrow darkens
　Our bosoms light and free,
And we hail this joyous meeting
　With hearts of youthful glee.

　　Will we ever meet again
　　　To carol forth our lay;
　　Will we ever meet again
　　　To crown the Queen of May.

O, long will we remember
　This Spring day so serene,
When merrily together
　We met to crown our Queen.

　　Will we ever meet again
　　　To carol forth our lay;
　　Will we ever meet again
　　　To crown the Queen of May

### MAY-QUEEN SONG.

*Air—"The Old Tin Horn."*

O. long we 'll remember this joyous night,
When happy together so free and so light,
We tendered bright garlands of flowers gay
To our young and fair Queen of sweet May.
O, the Queen of sweet May,
The Queen of sweet May,
Our young and fair Queen of sweet May;
O, the Queen of sweet May,
The Queen of sweet May,
Our young and fair Queen of sweet May.

Let us laugh at dull care while merrily we sing,
And happy together we welcome the Spring;
Let our voices be cheerful, our feelings be gay,
As we crown our fair Queen of sweet May.
O, the Queen of sweet May, etc.

O. long may she reign in a realm of delight,
While happily she governs her subjects aright;
With hearts of devotion our homage we pay
To our young and fair Queen of sweet May.
O, the Queen of sweet May, etc.

### SONG FOR FANNIE, QUEEN OF MAY.

*Air—"Annie of the Vale."*

The young flowers are glowing,
With beauty o'erflowing,
Their radiance crowns our fair young Queen of May;
She comes like a fairy,
So blithesome and airy,
To reign the monarch of this happy day.
Come, come, playmates, come,
Come ere the bright roses pale;
O, bring her sweet flowers,
Just fresh from the bowers,
And crown Queen Fannie of the vale.

'T is not for her beauty,
This marvel of duty,
We crown her with flowers so gay;
But for the sweet spirit
Which she doth inherit,
We crown her the Queen of sweet May.

Come, come, playmates, come,
Come ere the bright roses pale;
O, bring her sweet flowers,
Just fresh from the bowers,
And crown Queen Fannie of the vale.

NOTE.—Any name of two syllables can be substituted for Fannie.

---

## COSTUMES.

QUEEN OF MAY. Dress of white, light material, trimmed according to the taste of the teacher. A white tulle dress over a white silk petticoat; a berthe of tulle, lace, and ribbon; a broad white sash would be appropriate. The dresses of the CROWNER and SCEPTER-BEARER should be made of light material; and the effect would be prettier if they are girls of the same height, size, and complexion, dressed alike. This is not necessary. A May Queen dressed in any thing but white is in bad taste.

SPRING. Dress of white, looped over an embroidered petticoat, with bunches of small flowers; a wreath of flowers on the hair; a basket of choice flowers in one hand and a garl. nd in the other.

SUMMER. Dress of light blue over a trimmed skirt; a wreath of flowers on her head; in one hand a sheaf of grain, in the other a sickle.

AUTUMN. Dress of white, trimmed with leaves of green and brown; a wreath of green and brown leaves around her head; in one hand a basket of fruit, in the other a bunch of grapes.

WINTER. Dress of white, trimmed solely with evergreens. The effect is beautiful if the dress is of light material, and frosted with isinglass or mica. This is easily done by dampening with gum-arabic solution the *tarlatan* and sprinkling it with mica.

FASHION.   Dress in the extreme of fashion.

FOLLY.   Dress of any bright color, and trimmed in the most ridiculous manner, with ribbons of all shades, flowers, tinsel, etc.

CUPID.   All know this dress.

MUSIC.   The dress in this character can be varied to suit the taste of the young girl who acts it.   The skirt covered with sheet music would look pretty.   A guitar in the hand, or some other small musical instrument.

NOTE.—Folly presents the Queen with some article that is (at the time of the celebration) in vogue.   There is seldom a time when some ridiculous fashion is not prevalent among the ladies of this age.

# AMERICAN ORATORY.

## ANDREW JACKSON.

General Jackson imparted a high and lofty sense of honor and noble and gallant chivalry throughout his whole army. Previous to the 8th of January, whenever our artillery had silenced that of the enemy, or forced his troops to retire, loud and repeated huzzas rent the whole line. The most lively demonstrations of joy were every-where exhibited. It was a sure presage of the fate of the enemy in the general conflict. How different was the conduct of those brave and generous and gallant men after the ever-memorable battle of the 8th of January was won. The roar of artillery and musketry gave place to the most profound silence. Flushed with victory, having just repulsed an enemy who had come to scatter death in our ranks, our soldiers saw in the numerous corpses that strewed the plain only the unfortunate victims of war. *    *    *    *    * They disdained to insult them by an untimely exultation, and carefully abstained from any demonstrations of joy. *    *    *    *    *    *    * Such were General Jackson and his army! Gallant spirit! His applause should have been written across the blue arch of heaven, in the brightest rays of the most beauteous rainbow. He stands the living wonder of the age. Years have only increased his devotion to liberty. His example, like the sun, is full of light and glory. In after ages, when our children's children shall read the stories of heroes who have greatly dared in defense of their country; when their eyes shall glisten, and their young hearts throb wildly with the kindling theme, they will close the volume that speaks of their valor and renown, and proudly and fondly exclaim, "*And we too had our* ANDREW JACKSON."

DAWSON.

(229)

## ONE GREEN SPOT IN THE LIFE OF JACKSON.

Mr. Botts, the gentleman from Virginia, tells us that he has been enabled to discover but one green spot in the life of General Jackson. and that was his submission to the decision of Judge Hall, in the imposition of this fine. Sir, but one green spot in the life of Andrew Jackson! I go back to his boyhood. When he was a British prisoner during the revolutionary war, he was insolently ordered by a British officer to "black his boots." Did Andrew Jackson obey this order with the servile acquiescence common to his years and situation? No, sir! He positively refused to obey, claimed the treatment due to a prisoner of war, and although an only brother was sacrificed and fell by his side from the cruelty of his oppressor, Andrew Jackson could not be driven from his position, or forced to submit to the arrogance of his tyrant. *Was this no green spot in the life of Andrew Jackson?* I come down to the history of the last war. What was the condition of your country then? The cities upon your coast had been sacked, your country overrun, and a hostile flag waved in proud triumph from the walls of this Capitol. Go to the West. The tide of victory had spread over the upper valley of the Mississippi; your "stripes and stars" trailed in the dust; your national glory lost. The massacre of the River Raisin and the defeat of Dudley hung heavily upon every mind. Kentucky mourned the loss of her bravest sons, whose bones, denied the right of sepulture, were then whitening upon the battle-field of disaster. Andrew Jackson was appointed to the command of the American army. The effect was like magic! Hope revived, patriotism rekindled, confidence was restored. Our stars and stripes again floated in the breeze, the current of disaster was checked, the wave of victory rolled back, and battle after battle won in quick succession, until the war was ended in the blaze of glory at New Orleans. Was there no *green spot* in the life of Andrew Jackson resulting from all this? Sir, it will require no storied urn to commemorate the deeds of that illustrious man. They are recorded upon every page of his country's history. Nor will it require monumental columns to mark the spot in which his ashes will be deposited. The laurel will continue to bloom upon his grave, bedewed by the tears of a grateful nation, when the deeds and the graves of those who revile him will be forgotten and buried beneath the rubbish of oblivion.     PAYNE.

## THE DANGER OF DISCORDANT ELEMENTS OF LEGISLATION.

We are now on the very throe and travail of agitation. Omens of evil hang thick and dark along the horizon of the future! No star of hope arises! No ray of deliverance gleams out to gladden the heart of the nation! Our present is full of trouble—our future replete with doubt only less than despair. * * * * * As well might you attempt to blot out the sun and bind the solar system with cobwebs, as to waste your strength in the insane endeavor to hold the discordant elements of this confederacy in a state of adhesion while this vexing and disorganizing question is permitted to infest the halls of legislation. But if we bury this dangerous issue, and set our hearts upon the aggrandizement of the country, there may be no bound to the sacred munificence of our preservation. The coming trials and tribulations of earth may but augment our glory. Preserved amidst the "thunderings and lightnings" which appall the tribes and races of earth, we may yet be led up like the prophet to the mount, to see the face of the Eternal Lawgiver; and when the visitation has passed, the world may see us descending from the mountain and the cloud, our brow blazing, and our hands holding the Commandments of Mankind; and if, as there is great reason to suppose, the terms of metaphor employed in the Scripture to represent the destruction of the globe are only material emblems of the spiritual up-breaking and subsequent renovation of the race, then our government may stand forever. The cause of humanity bids it stand. The success of our great experiment of self-government bids it stand. "The very earth itself," as it whirls along its orbit, "carries the universal shout around *esto perpetua;*" and from the most distant realms of the coming future returns the prolonged and repeated echo, "*be thou everlasting.*"

## ENERGY THE GUARANTEE OF GREATNESS.

It is with nations as it is with individuals. The man who has energy holds the guarantee to greatness. Exile him to the wilderness and he presses milk and honey from its rocks. Launch him out on the stormy ocean and he exacts a rich revenue from its billows. Place him in a printing-office and he becomes a philosopher and a statesman. Imprison his body, and through the grated windows of his cell he sends out his soul to tread the zodiac and count the constellations of heaven. Bring out and spread in his pathway the racks and chains of Jewish persecution, and, looking forward to the results and rewards of his labors, he points to these instruments of torture, and says, with serene composure, "None of these things move me." Place him in any and all relations, whether prosperous or adverse, and still his step is firm, fearless, *forward;* and if the framery of the universe fall, its shattered ruins will strike him on his way to his object. As with individuals, so with nations—*energy is the condition and guarantee of greatness.* AKERS.

---

## IMPORTANCE OF CONSISTENCY AND EXERTION.

Experience has taught me that the strife and turmoil of political contention bring no substantial joys, and that, after all, true happiness is only to be found in the quiet and repose of domestic life. Would to God that my last words, like the song of the dying swan, could be my sweetest, and that I could be inspired with the ability and the eloquence to arouse my gallant comrades, with whom I have for years here struggled in vain, to the importance of unyielding consistency and redoubled exertion. My ambition would be fully gratified if, by one word of admonition, I could stimulate them to a more vigorous resistance to the corrupt and evil tendencies of the times. We have been defeated, but not conquered; our hearts are as proud and our spirits as unsubdued as though we were reposing on our laurels in the pride and flush of victory. Then I would appeal to them, by all the high and ennobling considerations of virtue and of patriotism, of honor and of fame, to continue to "fight the good fight" and to keep the faith. I would appeal to them, by the precepts of our fathers, to continue their efforts for the preservation of our free institutions, which were the result of their wisdom and the heritage of their gift. I would appeal to them, in the name of a mutilated constitution, which, like the blood of Abel, cries from the ground for vengeance, to "fight on, fight ever." I would appeal to them, by all the associations of our common struggles, by our bright hopes which have been blighted, and our common sufferings under defeat; by these I would appeal to them, in the language of our late glorious chieftain, "to shake off the dew-drops that glitter on their garments, and march once more to battle, to victory, and to glory."                       RAYNOR.

## REVERENCE FOR OUR NATIVE LAND.

We have no ancestral halls hung round with armorial bearings to awaken admiration of an honored ancestry, and strengthen love of country.  *  *  *  *  *  But if we have none of those monuments of antiquity peculiar to the Old World, we have our homes, ancestral homes, though not of many generations, recollections of which, if properly cherished, can never be forgotten. The sons of the rock-bound portions of New England, as well as the dwellers in the midst of the flowery plains of their own sweet sunny South, can never forget their well-regulated homes. Although the same land may not contain them, and seas divide them with "barriers of constant tempests," and though poverty and vice may overtake them, recollections of home will come back to them at times, ministering spirits wooing them back to the paths of virtue again. Should they be among the more fortunate of our race, and their lot cast in the high places of the earth, surrounded by all the allurements, the elegant luxuries, and the glittering trappings of the halls of the noble, their minds will at times break away from those enchanting scenes, and wander back with associations of the fondest recollections to the scenes of their

20

childhood and birth, as beheld from some wild turret of their native hills; for

> "There is a land, of every land the pride,
> Beloved o'er all the world beside,
> Where brighter suns dispense serener light,
> And milder moons imparadise the night;
> For in that land of Heaven's peculiar grace,
> The heritage of nature's noblest race,
> There is a spot of earth supremely blest,
> *A dearer, sweeter spot than all the rest.*"

PATERSON.

## WE STOOP TO CONQUER.

We stoop to conquer! Mr. Chairman, every word of this scroll is big with meaning and fearful admonition, and there is no man can see it without reading its full meaning, and comment is really unnecessary; but I can not forbear making a few inquiries and exposes. I begin with the word WE! Who are WE? That is an important question— who are WE? The answer will be found in the efforts of those who, at the formation of our government, were opposed to a democratic form, and who predicted its downfall in less than half a century; who boldly maintained that the common people wanted the intelligence, stability, independence, and patriotism indispensable for self-government. *The rich and better born should govern*, and it is they who set themselves up for WE. * * * Why, sir, our Declaration of Independence, Constitution, and the whole frame of our government, recognizes in their letter and their spirit the universal principles of equality. Who would have thought that, even during the life of a remnant of the revolutionary fathers, who only live to link the living with the dead, we would have an upstart aristocracy that dare to designate themselves WE? And an upstart aristocracy, too, who, presuming upon the ignorance and stupidity of those to whom they deny the qualifications of self-government, insult them by not only a name that claims for themselves superiority, but also pronouncing inferiority and contempt upon those whom they stoop to conquer. Is there

an American, proud of his country, and proud of his free
and equal institutions, who will not hold in contempt and
scorn the vile wretch who would either attempt, or tolerate
the attempt, to establish an order in this country who
should designate themselves from the great body of American citizens by the title WE, or any other title? There is
no man in whose veins courses a drop of the revolutionary
blood that purchased our emancipation, or whose heart
beats in gratitude for the services of the living and the
memory of those who broke the chains, and unriveted the
shackles that bound us to a British throne and a foreign
despotism, who will not, in the spirit of deep concern and
heartfelt emotion, inquire: Was it for this that our gallant
ancestors *lighted the beacon of rebellion that unfurled by its
blaze the triumphant banner of Liberty?* Was it for this
that they pledged their lives, their fortunes, and their
sacred honors.

    \*      \*      \*      \*      \*      \*      \*      \*

O, no! it was not. It was that there might be one spot
on the face of the earth where human equality might have
a sure and undisturbed abode for all time. It was that
there might be one spot on the face of the earth where man
might be permitted to walk erect, carry in him a responsi-
ble soul, and bear in his countenance the image of his
Maker!

But who are this rag-baron aristocracy who style themselves WE, and thus *stoop to conquer?* They are the bank-
ers, monopolists, loafers, gamblers, and blacklegs—wolves
who lap the blood of honest toil and eat the bread they
never earned (I except the honest who have been deceived);
men who, like the lily of the valley, "toil not, neither do
they spin, yet Solomon in all his glory was not arrayed like
one of these." The answer will be found in the fact that,
when all the coxcombs, all the fops, all the dandies, all the
loafers, all the drones, and all the loungers, as well as those
who live by their wits and their cunning, without honest
means, shall be assembled, ninety-nine in each hundred of
each class of the entire herd will be found to be "WE;"
and the object which governs "WE," in all their political
movements, is that system of policy which will make
"hewers of wood and drawers of water" of the many to
the few. WE stoop to conquer! O, sir, were the dead

permitted to admonish the living, the gallant spirits of all
who fell, either in our glorious revolution or have since
sunk under the afflictions of wounds or weight of years,
would marshal themselves here, and with tongues louder
than seven trumpets denounce those who would overthrow
the *free* and *equal* institutions erected by their toil, their
blood, and their lives.                    DUNCAN.

---

### TAXATION IN ENGLAND.

We can inform Jonathan what are the inevitable consequences of being too fond of glory. Taxes upon every article which enters into the mouth or covers the back, or is
placed under the foot; taxes upon every thing which it is
pleasant to see, hear, feel, smell, or taste; taxes upon
warmth, light, and locomotion; taxes on every thing in
earth and the waters under the earth; on every thing that
comes from abroad or is grown at home; taxes on the raw
material; taxes on every fresh value that is added to it by
the industry of man; taxes on the sauce which pampers
man's appetite, and the drug which restores him to health;
on the ermine which decorates the judge, and the rope
which hangs the criminal; on the poor man's salt; on the
rich man's spice; on the brass nails of the coffin, and the
ribbons of the bride—at bed or board, couchant or levant,
we must pay. The school-boy whips his taxed top; the
beardless youth manages his taxed horse, with a taxed
bridle, on a taxed road; and the dying Englishman, pouring his medicine which has paid seven per cent. into a
spoon that has paid fifteen per cent., flings himself back
upon his chintz bed, which has paid twenty-two per cent.,
makes his will on an eight-pound stamp, and expires in the
arms of an apothecary who has paid license of a hundred
pounds for the privilege of putting him to death. His
whole property is then immediately taxed from two to ten
per cent. Besides the probate, large fees are demanded for
burying him in the chancel, his virtues are handed down to
posterity on taxed marble, and he is then gathered to his
fathers to be taxed no more!

In addition to all this, the habit of dealing with large

sums will make the government avaricious and profuse; and the system itself will infallibly generate the base vermin of *spies* and *informers*, and a still more pestilent race of political tools and retainers of the meanest and most odious description, while the prodigious patronage which the collecting of this splendid revenue will throw into the hands of government, will invest it with such vast influence, and hold out such means and temptations to corruption, as all the virtue and public honesty even of republicans will be unable to resist.

Every wise Jonathan should remember this when he sees the rabble huzzaing at the heels of a naval or military hero, or inflaming the vanity of a popular leader. Such proceedings lower the character of their government with all the civilized nations of the world.          SIDNEY SMITH.

# TABLEAUX VIVANS.

## THE FOUR SEASONS.

PERFORMED BY FOUR GIRLS REPRESENTING THE FOUR SEASONS.

SPRING. Dress of light white material, trimmed tastefully with flowers; a garland of flowers in her hand.

SUMMER. Dress of blue over a petticoat of white; the upper dress looped with flowers, and a wreath of flowers on her head; a sickle in one hand and a sheaf of grain in the other.

AUTUMN. Dress of yellow looped over a petticoat of green; a basket of rich fruit in one hand and a bunch of grapes in the other; a wreath on her head of green and brown leaves intermixed.

WINTER. Dress of somber hue; a black short cloak thrown over the shoulders; a hood upon the head, of dark material. Flour must be sprinkled over the head and shoulders to represent snow. An ax in one hand and a faggot of wood in the other.

This is an appropriate tableau with which to open an exhibition, and can be performed with very little trouble and expense.

SPRING. Spring, Spring! bright blooming Spring!
What life I give to every thing!
What joy I scatter with budding flowers!
What strength I give with gentle showers!
Who does not envy my mission sweet?
Who does not with glee my coming greet?
Who does not long, after winter's embrace,
To see me come, with my smiling face?

SUMMER. My tender sister, beautiful Spring,
'T is true, to you much joy doth bring.
But Summer, with maturer grace,
Must in your hearts hold a fond place;

For beauty like mine can ne'er decay
While over the earth I hold my sway.
You love my cool, refreshing rain;
You love my hay and richer grain;
You love the mild soft summer air;
You love my flowers every-where;
You know to you a harvest I yield
Of golden hue from the teeming field.

AUTUMN.  My gay smiling sisters, Summer and Spring,
Have boasted to you of what they bring
To make the earth a gladsome place;
And tho' I come with a graver face,
Still in your eyes I have a charm,
In city large or on rustic farm.
My luscious grapes and tempting fruit
Your taste, I know, full well doth suit;
I am sure you love the mellow light
That follows fair Summer's sun so bright:
I know that you love the murmuring breeze
That I send thro' the many tinted trees.

WINTER.  My sisters three, Autumn, Summer, and Spring,
To me are never inclined to cling.
They call me cold, and say that I freeze
The balmy air, as it floats through the trees.
I know I bear a chilling mien,
And flowers about me ne'er are seen;
But still I have charms, you all must own,
That give to life great pleasure and tone.
The *children* all love me, I know full well,
As their stockings at Christmas surely tell.
I bring every year a world of mirth
To the groups that meet 'round the blazing hearth.
And tho' I am crooked, and bent, as you see,
To part from old Winter you'll never agree.

(*Curtain falls.*)

## THE COUNCIL OF BEAUTY.

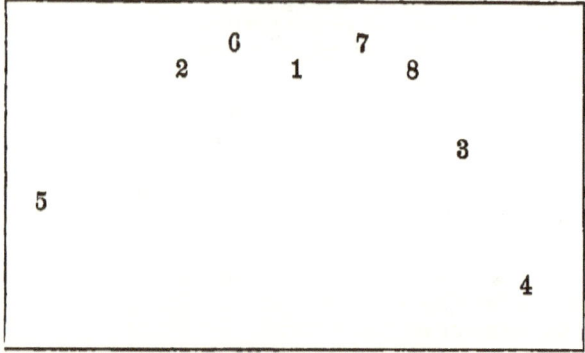

No. 1, Venus. She is described clothed with a purple mantle glittering with diamonds; by her side stands Cupid, his little hands clasping the folds of her flowing dress; around her are three graces (Nos. 6, 7, 8); one of them is holding up her train. No. 3, Flora, the Goddess of Flowers. She should be literally covered with flowers, and surrounded by cedar-trees fastened to heavy blocks of wood (the latter, of course, covered by something green). Flora is repre-sented bearing a garland of flowers in one hand and a basket of flowers in the other. A little nearer the front of the stage the Goddess of Song or Music, No. 4. She is standing with one hand resting upon a harp; a guitar, a flute, sheets of music, and elegantly bound books are thrown carelessly about her. No. 5, the Goddess of Painting. She is seated before an easel, with all the appointments of an artist. Several fine pictures should be placed negligently about her.

As this tableau represents the Council of Beauty, each one who takes part in it should be looking inquiringly at Venus.

## SCENE BETWEEN QUEEN ELIZABETH AND AMY ROBSART.

### TAKEN FROM KENILWORTH.

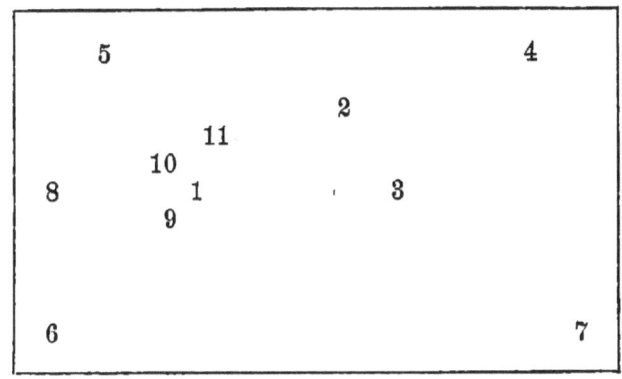

1. A Fountain.  3. Amy Robsart.  11
2. Elizabeth.  8. Earl of Leicester.
4, 5, 6, 7. Columns.

ELIZABETH.—Dress of pale blue silk, with silver lace and *aiguillettes*. The dress should be blazing with jewels.

AMY.—Dress of sea-green silk, resembling the drapery of a Grecian nymph.

LEICESTER.—Hunting suit of Lincoln green, richly embroidered with gold, and crossed by a gay baldric which sustains a bugle horn and a wood knife.

The stage must be decorated to represent an out-door scene—a grotto. 4, 5, 6, 7 are white columns. These can easily be made by fastening four poles securely (to the positions named) on the stage. Around the *top* of each pole tie a full white sheet, gathered like the skirt of a dress. After this is done the sheets can be drawn down (and tacked to the floor of the stage) in flutes, so as to resemble a fluted column. No. 1. A fountain, about which must be arranged flowers. No. 2. Elizabeth standing in an attitude of surprise. No. 3. Amy Robsart kneeling at the feet of the Queen, her hands clasped together. She is looking imploringly up in Elizabeth's face. Near her, on the ground is a casket. No. 8. Leicester: his form hidden from the view of the queen by the cedars and fountain. The expression of his face is one of painful surprise. Nos. 9, 10, 11. Cedar-trees fastened to the stage.

---

## THE FOUNTAIN OF BLISS.

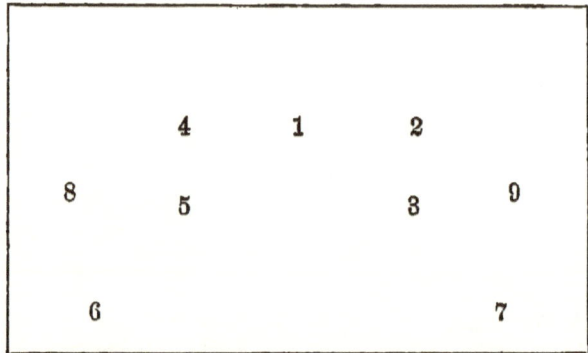

*Front of Stage.*

1. Fountain.
2. Lady.
3. Child.
4. Lady.
5. Child.
6, 7, 8, 9. Flower-pots.

This is an uncommonly pretty tableau, but requires perhaps more industry and skill than many would care about exercising; but, as I have seen it, I can safely say it will repay the trouble it takes to make it. The reservoir of the fountain is made by taking a large round wooden bowl, such as is used for kneading dough. Cover it by pasting white paper smoothly over the outside. Then take white pasteboard, cut it in oblong slips, to resemble a long leaf, narrow at the bottom, gradually widening to the top; these strips, being tacked on the inside of the bowl (at the narrow end), leaving enough surplus to roll the top (or widest part of the strips) over the edge of the bowl, form a scalloped or ornamental finish, and resemble the basin of a fountain.

Make the base on which the bowl rests to imitate the bottom and stem of a modern center-table. This must be covered with white also. Fasten the bowl firmly to the stem; then bore a hole with an auger in the center of the bowl, in which to insert a rod four or five feet long; this rod cover with white tulle (gathered full, like the top of an old-fashioned reticule), tied tightly around the top of the rod, reversely. When turned over and made to fall in the basin, it resembles falling water, if sprinkled with mica or dotted thickly with glass heads of different sizes (white). The effect is beautiful at night upon the stage, and must look natural, otherwise, a tableau, in which there was a fountain built in this way, would not have elicited the following remark from an old negro waiter, who had spent several winters in Frankfort, Ky., serving the members of the legislature: "Why, Miss Russell, dat looks jist like de fountin in de yard at de Capitol when it's froze stiff in de winter." So, tableau performers can, by the above method, have something resembling a *natural* fountain, though it may look "*froze stiff*."

The stage for this tableau should be trimmed with cedar, and the floor of the stage covered with vines, leaves, or grass, to give the scene an out-door look; the more picturesque the stage is decorated the better the effect. On the right of the fountain (No. 2) stands a lady dressed in becoming evening dress. In her hand is a silver goblet. She is in a half leaning attitude, looking down at a little girl, who is on her knees at the lady's feet, holding a silver bowl, into which the lady pours the water slowly from the goblet. The child is looking up playfully. On the left (No. 4) a lady, attired also in an evening dress, is looking, as she stands, intently at the fountain, with one hand resting on the edge of the basin, and with the other taking a bouquet from the little girl who is half kneeling at her feet. Nos. 6, 7, 8, 9 are flower-pots, filled with the most showy flowers that can be procured, placed about over the stage according to the taste of those engaged in the tableau. This tableau is intended to represent oriental life, and the dresses should be of this style.

## THE STEALING OF THE KEYS OF LOCHLEVEN CASTLE DURING THE IMPRISONMENT OF MARY, QUEEN OF SCOTS.

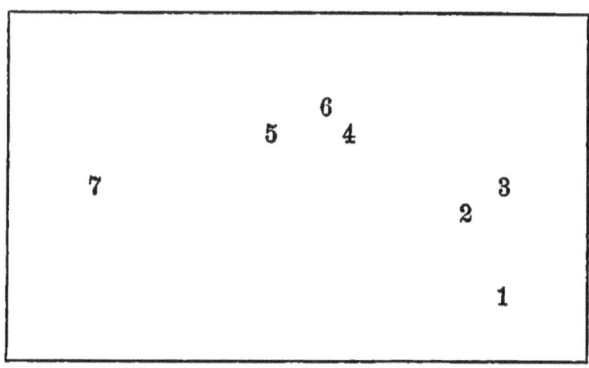

No. 1. Lady Fleming, attired in a somber-colored satin and a cap similar to Mary's, but plainer. No. 3. Catharine Seyton, dressed in plain white; no ornaments. She is standing immediately behind Mary, looking intently at Lady Lochleven. No. 2. Mary, seated. Dress of black velvet; a ruff open in front, so as to give a view of her chin and neck. On her head a small cap of lace, and a transparent white veil hanging from her shoulders over the black dress in loose folds. A cross of gold suspended from a light gold chain around her neck. A rosary of gold and ebony hanging from her girdle. No. 5. Lady Lochleven standing near the table, attired in a heavy black satin dress. A coif about her head. At her side, a little behind, stands (No. 6) the page, dressed in Highland costume, of fine cloth or velvet. A black hat and plume. No. 7. A window. No. 4. A table, on which is the Queen's supper. On the table, near the hand of Lady Lochleven (which rests on the table), is a huge bunch of "ponderous keys." The page has one hand on the keys, and is looking out of the window, to which he has called the attention of the superstitious Lady Lochleven to "lights in the church-yard." The Lady Lochleven is looking out of the window. The countenance of Lady Fleming is anxious; that of Catharine

eager and expectant. Mary's face is calm, and she is looking downward. The page looks half frightened, half quizzical.

## LOVE'S DREAM.

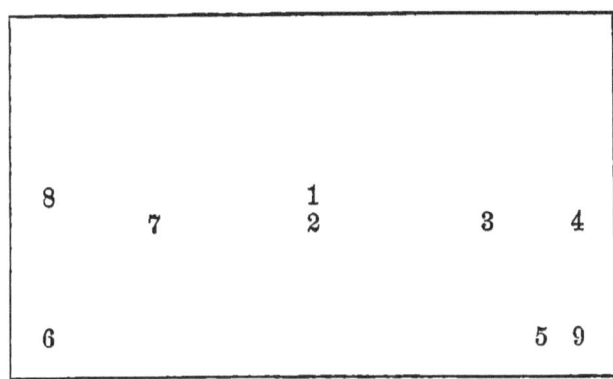

No. 1. A bower, formed by placing small cedar-trees in heavy blocks of wood; these trees decorated with flowers. Under the arbor, No. 2, a large Elizabethan chair, or a sofa lounge, on which a girl dressed in evening costume reclines asleep. By her side a guitar. Half falling from her hand a gilt-bound book. Nos. 3, 4, 5, 6, 7, 8. Flower-pots, with showy flowers. The pots must be hid by vines, leaves, or grass, so as to give the stage the appearance of a garden. No. 9. Cupid, in a half kneeling attitude, aiming an arrow at the heart of the sleeping beauty.

## BEAUTIFUL STAR.

The stage decorated as in the scene between Elizabeth and Amy Robsart. A young girl dressed becomingly, with a bandeau about her head, with a brilliant star in the center. A guitar slung across her shoulder. She sings the well-known melody,

"Star of the evening, beautiful star!"

## DEATH OF CLEOPATRA.

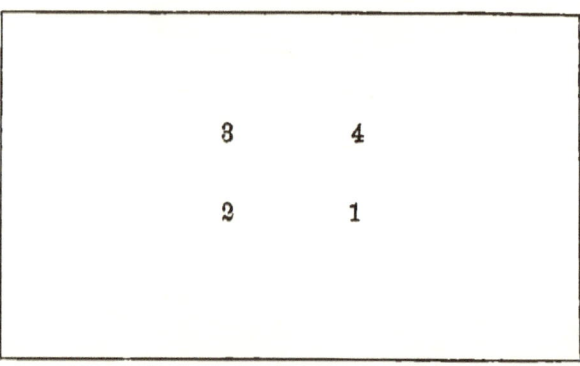

No. 1. A luxu.... us couch, upon which the queen reclines in royal dress. Her neck and arms bare. No. 2. A table. No. 3. A basket of figs, leaves, and flowers. One arm of the beauty rests near the basket, and about her wrist the asp is winding itself. A toy snake can be procured easily, or, what would be prettier, a necklace of gems in the form of a serpent. The scenery in this tableau must be strictly oriental. Much drapery makes it effective.,. No. 4. A lady attendant standing behind the couch in an attitude of surprise and horror, gazing at the queen.

## TOO LATE FOR THE CARS.

A meanly dressed man, with a carpet-sack in one hand and an umbrella in the other, which he holds in a waving attitude, as if to stop the train. Behind him is a gang of dusty, common-looking children, all with eager faces; and last in the group the mother, a faded dress, an old-fashioned bonnet, a big bundle hanging to one arm, and a baby clasped by the other. She too looks excited and angry.

## THE BEAUTIES OF ———.

```
        3        1        2

        4                 5
```

In the center of the stage a hoop (the same as the one used in Peace and Prosperity) is placed upright, and in the center of the hoop, upon the white ground, the name of the place where the tableaux are performed. This tableau can only be acted by beautiful women, dressed in beautiful and becoming costume. One stands on the right and one on the left of the hoop, with one hand resting on the hoop, and in the other a bouquet or a handsomely bound book. At the feet of No. 3, a beautiful child engaged with a beautiful doll is seated. At the feet of No. 2 is another beautiful child, scattering flowers from a basket near her. The box behind the hoop can be elevated sufficiently to place upon it a vase of fine flowers visible to the audience. The attitudes in this tableau can be varied according to the taste of the manager. It is a very pretty tableau, and has been performed with success.

Every town boasts its beautiful women. and this tableau is intended to give the citizens of a place the opportunity to take the palm in the way of beauties; and therefore it must be called the Beauties of ———, the blank filled up by the name of the place where the tableaux take place.

## PEACE AND PROSPERITY.

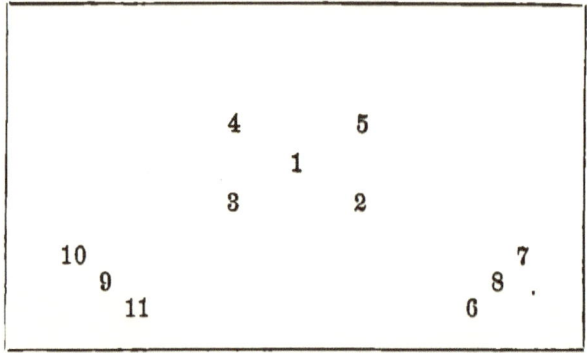

1. A large hoop.
2. Goddess of Liberty.
3. Goddess of Justice.
4. Messenger of Peace.
5. Messenger of Peace.
6. The War God.
7. The Widow.
8. The Widow's Children.
9. Agricultural Implements.
10. Plow-boy.

In the center of the stage a hoop, as large in circumference as a buggy-wheel, is placed upright. This is covered with white muslin, drawn as smooth as a drum-head. In the center of the hoop is pasted, in large gilt letters, the words Peace and Prosperity. The outer edge of the hoop must be trimmed with a wreath of flowers. No. 6. On the left hand of the stage lies the God of War, prostrate, parallel with the foot-lights; by his side the sword, shield, and helmet. No. 7. A lady in deep mourning, with a widow's cap upon her head. In her hand she holds an iron chain, one end of which is coiled about her neck, her eyes resting upon the faces of her children (No. 8), who are kneeling near her feet. No. 2. The Goddess of Liberty, with one hand resting upon the hoop; in the other hand the liberty-pole and cap. Her eyes rest upon the Messengers of Peace. No. 3. The Goddess of Justice, one hand resting on the hoop, and in the other a pair of scales. She, too, is looking at the Messengers of Peace. No. 11. Farming utensils. A sheaf of wheat and a cornucopia half emptied of its contents. No. 9. A plow. No. 10. A plow-boy in his shirt-sleeves, his collar open. One hand resting on the plow-handle, the other raising his hat in the act of welcoming peace. A large dry-goods box can be placed immediately behind the hoop, on which stands the Messengers of Peace (Nos. 4 and 5). These must be young, fair girls, dressed in pure white, their dresses of the very lightest material. Gauzy wings can easily be fastened to their shoulders. They stand upon the box (their busts only visible) with their arms outstretched, with an olive branch in the hand of each. They are looking lovingly upon the group below. As the curtain rises the widow transfers her gaze from her children to the messengers, and says in a voice clear but with deep pathos:

Hail, thou white-winged Messengers of Peace! Now the dark wing of Apollyon is withdrawn from our national sky, bid us unbind the shackles that so long have fettered our dearest liberties. Let us hurl them [*turns to the prostrate form of the* God of War] back to the dread source, and chain him to rocks of adamantine, lest he, by his expiring red-hot breath, convulse our fair country again. [*As she speaks she unwinds the chain from about her neck and hurls it upon the fallen god. Turns full to the audience.*] Now shall men beat their swords into plow-shares, their spears into pruning-hooks, and learn war no more.

(*Curtain falls slowly. Music: National air.*)

---

## THE LITTLE PEACE-MAKER.

An out-door scene. Two boys dressed in a ragged, dirty, careless manner, with their coats off and shirt bosoms torn open. They have just been engaged in a fight. Standing between them, in the act of parting them, is a third boy about the same size, dressed in the neatest manner; every thing about him must indicate order and propriety. In one hand he holds a Bible. His face must be placid, while those of the belligerents must express evil passions, but a cowed manner.

## THE THIRTEEN ORIGINAL STATES.

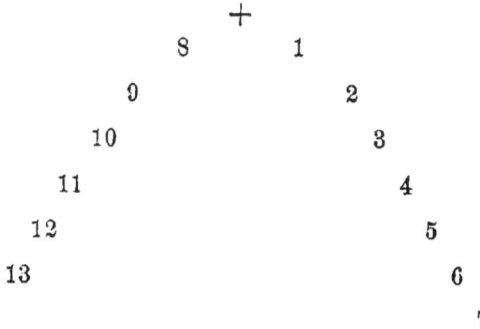

*Front of stage.*

This is a beautiful and effective tableau. The cross in the center at the back of the stage represents the Goddess of Liberty, with flowing robes and light, graceful drapery, bearing in the right hand the pole and liberty-cap. On either side of her, ranged in a semi-circle (the taller ones being placed near the Goddess), are thirteen girls, each dressed in white. In the right hand of each a small shield on which is inscribed in *distinct* letters the name of the State she represents. The shield must be held just across the waist or breast, in full view of the audience. In the left hand a bouquet of bright flowers should be held. While the tableau is exhibited the band must play a national air. The positions of the thirteen girls are indicated by the figures. The stage ought to be tastefully decorated. The shields can be made by cutting a piece of pasteboard in the shape of a shield, and pasting, four or five inches from the top, strips of red and white cambric alternately, up and down. The upper part is covered by solid blue cambric, and just where the stripes and the solid blue meet the name of the State should be pasted across. A strap on the under side, about four or five inches long, is sewed on, by which the shield is held in the desired position. I have seen this tableau performed, and it is striking.

## THE HONEYMOON.

Stage prepared as a parlor. Near the front of the stage the young wife seated. Very close to her the newly-made husband is seated, holding a bouquet near his wife's face and fanning her with the other hand. His face wears an expression of admiration and devotion combined. The wife is looking up lovingly in her husband's face. They are both dressed with precision and neatness.

## A YEAR AFTER MARRIAGE.

Stage prepared as a home scene. At one side of the stage the husband is seated with his feet propped against the wall, a cigar in his mouth, intently reading the daily paper. His face is averted from his wife, who is seated opposite, rocking a crib with her foot, in which rests the first heir to the family. Her dress is careless and tawdry, (as must be that of the husband.) There is an expression of care, ill-humor, and discontent on her face. She looks toward her husband with frowning displeasure.

## BORING FOR OIL.

The stage prepared as a business-office. An old gentleman, with white wig and broad-brimmed hat, is walking to and fro.

OLD GENTLEMAN. Petroleum stock is on the rise. Let me see! [*Studies.*] Yes, yes: with such a dividend as that I will soon be classed with the millionaires of the country. Oil, oil! There is nothing like striking oil! [*Seats himself complacently. A half-grown Boy enters unperceived by Old Man. The Boy holds a large auger in his hand; approaches behind and places the auger upon the crown of the Old Man's hat and begins to turn it round. Old Man turns and sees him.*] You young scamp. what are you doing?

BOY (*laughs*). Ha! ha! Heard you had oil on the brain, and thought I'd bore for it. [*Old Man shows fight.*]

(*Curtain falls.*)

## COMING TO GET MARRIED.

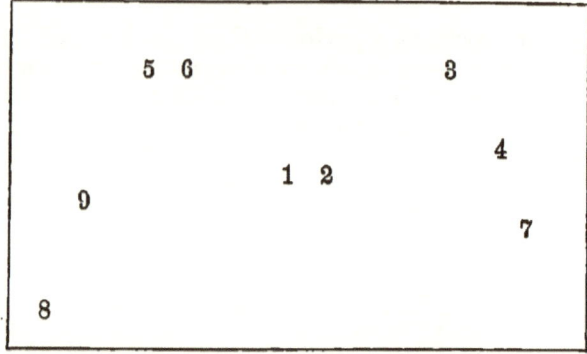

1. 'Squire.
2. Table.
3. 'Squire's wife.
7, 8, 9. Chairs.

4. 'Squire's daughter.
5. Groom.
6. Bride.

A home scene. The country 'Squire or magistrate is seated near a table filled with papers. He is just looking round at the couple who have come to get married. They are standing in the door-way. The groom, a regular country greenhorn, with a swallow-tailed coat, stove-pipe hat, pants too short, a high stock instead of a cravat, and about a half yard of shirt collar. The bride's dress is equally *outre*. There is a look of "it is us, now stand around," on the face of the groom. The bride's eyes are cast down, but she clings closely to her chosen lord. The wife and daughter of the 'Squire are in the background, peering curiously at the bridal party. The 'Squire's dress denotes his office.

THE END.